Game Change

(A Nina Bannister Mystery)

by

T' Gracie Reese and Joe Reese

This book is fiction. All characters, events, and organizations portrayed in this novel are the product of the author's imagination or are used fictitiously. Any resemblance to actual persons—living or dead—is entirely coincidental.

For information, email **Cozy Cat Press**, cozycatpress@aol.com or visit our website at: www.cozycatpress.com

ISBN: 978-1-939816-42-9
Printed in the United States of America

Cover design by Karri Klawiter
http://artbykarri.com/cover-art/e-book-print-cover-art-design/

1 2 3 4 5 6 7 8 9 10

To the Indiana University-Purdue University Fort Wayne women's basketball team: Thanks, Mastodons, for the inspiration!

"The principal is your pal."
Anonymous Spelling Tip

CHAPTER 1: THE NAME PLATE

"To understand the world, you must first understand a place like Mississippi."
—William Faulkner

On the twenty ninth day of November, a light snow began falling in Bay St. Lucy.

This was an astonishing thing, a thing which had, in the memory of even the oldest residents, never happened before. Nor were the memories of these respected and august town dwellers in error; for a check of the state records showed that snow in November in southern Mississippi had last occurred in 1871.

It was a miracle, a Thanksgiving offering, a Christmas present almost a month in advance.

The feather-fine flakes began falling around four in the afternoon, emanating like magic from a somber gray sky that blended with the ocean to eliminate the horizon line and wipe from creation all color except that of volcanic, gently scudding, ash. It was Friday. That meant there was a festive air about town anyway. But when the children stepped off the school busses and saw, felt, somehow even smelled, what was happening around them—

—well, when that happened, there was simply hell to pay.

Snow in Bay St. Lucy!

The polar tempest lasted for two hours, and, if it did not intensify, it did not actually stop, either, so that by the fall of darkness around six p.m. it had separated the town into two groups: those who were ecstatic (the children and the very old, the former having never seen snow and the latter having given up ever seeing it) and those who were panicking and driving like mad people to the nearest grocery store.

"What will the roads be like tomorrow?"

"We could be snowed in all week!"

They would not be snowed in all week, of course, but that fact did not lessen the sales in the supermarkets, or prevent filling stations from setting records for gasoline purchases, or lessen the glee of Sam Dyers, whose hardware store sold out of its entire supply of electric generators (four) within the first hour of the storm.

As for Nina Bannister, it presented her with a difficult dilemma.

She could ride her Vespa to Bay St. Lucy High School, or she could walk.

Staying home was not an option.

There was a kind of temptation about doing so, of course, because she was a lady of that kind of mentality that envisaged every tomorrow, every next week, as a potential cataclysm, demanding the continual pantry presence of emergency stores. There was hot chocolate in her seaside bungalow/shack, of course, but there was always hot chocolate, even in the middle of July.

So she did not have to go to the market to stock up on rice, milk, chili, potatoes, soups of various kinds, eggs, etc., because she already had those things.

And if she chose to bundle up a bit, sit out on her deck, and watch the dusk-roiled ocean darken and mutter, while sipping chocolate and munching popcorn—yes, she had popcorn, too—then she could certainly do that.

But not tonight.

No, tonight was basketball.

Women's basketball.

Tonight the Bay St. Lucy Lady Mariners played the Pass Christian Lady Pelicans, and Nina Bannister was going to be there.

This love of women's basketball had grown late in Nina's life, and she did not quite understand it. Of course, she and Frank had been moderate fans of high school sports during their marriage, but as much out of civic duty as anything else. They went to the Friday night football games because it was pretty much required of them. Frank, a leading attorney with offices on the town's main square, Nina, a young English teacher—they simply had to go, bringing their padded stadium seats and thermoses of hot coffee to get them through the sixty or seventy degree nights of September and October.

But they didn't really love the experience.

It was all too distant. She could not recognize the faces of the boys in her classes, and if there was some recognition of the way they hurled opponents to the ground in precisely the same way they hurled fellow classmates into the metal lockers lining the halls during the breaks between classes—it still was not the same.

She could, of course, recognize the faces of the girl students, but, as she watched them doing variations on the Can Can during halftime, with skirts no more than six inches long and legs stretching enticingly up into the Mississippi sky for all present to see, she wondered if they could have used a bit more covering, just as the boys could have used a bit less.

No, it just wasn't the Bannisters' cup of tea.

As for basketball, they went occasionally to watch the boys' team play, just to say that they had been.

No one went early to watch the girls' team, of course, except a few parents.

Girls' sports really didn't matter too much in those days.

But somehow things had changed.

The girls' team was not referred to by those terms anymore; it was now the women's team.

It did not play on the same night as the men's team.

Of course there was still a problem with nomenclature. The 'Lady Mariners' indeed. (Nina wondered how the football team would have reacted, had it been forced to be called 'The Gentlemen Mariners!').

But that was all right.

Somehow, some time—she supposed it to have been a year ago, also in late November—she had wandered over to the gym during a Saturday afternoon game, and had, for want of anything better to do, paid her five dollar entry fee to watch Bay St. Lucy's women play Portageville.

How much it had all changed since her last memories of the sport!

These women played like—

—well, no way to avoid saying it. They played like men.

They ran the entire length of the court, and not the entire length of the half-court.

No town doctors were telling them that excessive sprinting could harm their ovaries and make them unfit for motherhood (and, yes, these things had actually been told to her and to her classmates as they were growing up); no one apparently told them to avoid real pushups, which might cause in them the growth of unsightly (and definitely unsexy) muscles.

For these girls had obviously done a lot of pushups, and had very conspicuous muscles.

And yet appeared, to judge by the way the boys in the stands were watching them, very sexy indeed.

No, she had become hooked.

So tonight, she had to go.

How to get to the gym, though, remained an open question.

She loved her Vespa, and, with it, she could cover the distance of approximately two miles in short order. No problem.

But walking was healthier, even in the cold weather.

It was perhaps healthier *because* of the cold weather. Increased blood flow, that sort of thing.

She ruminated on the problem while, sitting at the kitchen table, the ocean coming and going outside her plate glass deck window, she savored a spoonful of microwaved vegetable soup.

Her boots.

They were sitting in the back of her bedroom closet.

Snow boots.

Boots that she had bought years ago during a winter vacation that she and Frank had taken in Aspen, Colorado.

How lovely it had been, he and she trudging through the streets of Aspen, snow piled high beside the sidewalks, she wearing her fur-lined silver *Star Trek* boots that made her look like Captain Kirk, all silver and spaceship-like.

The boots had not been used for at least ten years.

She could wear them!

And that decided her.

So that, a little less than one hour later, darkness having enveloped the town now, she found herself bending into a twenty-mile-per-hour wind, thinking of Jack London and various arctic expeditions, watching the scattered flakes illuminated blue by glowing street lamps, and watching, as it loomed up before her—the tall outlines of Bay St. Lucy's new high school.

Nina Bannister High School.

How bizarre it all was!

Ready by next fall.

A huge and potentially beautiful thing, more industrial park than school, and named for her.

She could never run that over in her mind without imagining how astonished Frank would be.

Little Nina, teacher of obscure poems and eliminator of comma splices, for one brief shining moment the heroine of Bay St. Lucy.

Heroine indeed.

Eve Ivory. The Robinson Mansion. That horrible slide show, and the vision of her beloved town becoming a cross between Disney World and Las Vegas.

And that one blinding moment of revelation that made her see what the rest of them were missing.

Heroine indeed.

And now it was behind her, the framework of the new school, replaced by the weathered carcass of the old school, the one she'd attended as a girl, and the one that had consumed most of her professional life as an adult. There, far to the right, the sea just visible behind it, the elementary school; and there, a bit farther on, the middle school. The high school beyond that, and then the gym, glowing as she knew it would be, its domed roof pulsing ever so slightly with the syncopations of the small but loud Bay St. Lucy pep band.

She walked on, excitement growing in her, while the gymnasium loomed ever larger and its doors simultaneously sucked in and disgorged the winter soul of the town.

There were infants in strollers, toddlers toddling, ten-year-olds with pigtails or baseball caps—depending on sex, young teenagers beginning to flirt in large physically dangerous groups, old teenagers doing something they hoped was illicit and that they were doing it correctly, young marrieds, old stand-bys, ancients, and then the whole thing starting again, life's complete circle all compacted here in the winter-radiant cavern that was THE HOME OF THE LADY MARINERS.

She felt herself transformed into a bit of flotsam or jetsam floating fast now on the compacted stream of St. Lucy humanity that surged through the battered entrance doors and into the snack bar/ticket window/trophy case/restroom entrance womb that must be passed through before one could be birthed into the court area itself.

"Hello, Ms. Bannister!"

"Hey, Nina!"

"Like your boots!"

"Keeping warm?"

"Program?"

"Sell you a ticket tonight?"

"We gonna win?"

And Nina's responses:

"Hello Jason!"

"Hey to you, Tom!"

"Just barely!"

"Love a program!"

"If you've got any tickets left!"

"Hope so!"

Thank God for small towns.

She made her way into the stands, showing her ticket to Fred Towson in his Lions Club blue vest, and then again, a few yards farther on, to Ted Llewellen in a Shriner fez, these two civic organizations working skillfully and diligently together to make sure that no terrorists infiltrated the den of the Lady Mariners, or, at least, if they did so, they had tickets for the privilege.

"Hi, Nina! Thanks for coming!"

"Meg! Good luck!"

She was walking in front of the bench now, passing within a yard or so of Meg Brennan, the coach. Meg was a perfect picture of a women's basketball coach: short blond hair, slightly aggressive posture, blue sport jacket to go with even bluer Scandinavian eyes—she did not look as though she could have donned a uniform and raced onto the court to play point guard; no, she looked like she already had on such a uniform, there pressed and ready underneath her white blouse and gray slacks.

"Go get 'em, Meg!"

"We will, Nina!"

Nina was prevented from saying more by the onslaught of the pep band, which, filling the fifteen rows immediately above the home bench, said:

"BLAAAAAAAAHHHHHH DE
BLAAAAAAAAHHH DE BLAAAAAAAHH!"

Rest rest—

"BLAAAAAAAAAAAHHH DE
BLAAAAAAAAHHH DE BLAAAAAAAHH!"

Rendering even trivial conversation impossible.

So Nina, team roster clutched in one hand, purse in the other, began to make her way up toward the higher reaches of the bleachers.

Every now and then, she turned to look at the court beneath her.

A sea of blue and white (The Bay St. Lucy Mariners) pulsated on one end, and an equally turbulent body of red and white (Pass Christian: The Lady Pelicans) formed its own intricate patterns on the other.

Layup lines.

Passing drills.

Players clapping, shouting encouragement.

"Go girl!"

"Hey babe, hey babe!"

"Looking good, Alyssha!"

"You go, Girl!"

"BLAAAAAAAAHHHHHH DE BLAAAAAAAAHHH DE BLAAAAAAAAHH!"

"BLAAAAAAAAHHHHHH DE BLAAAAAAAAHHH DE BLAAAAAAAAHH!"

Rest rest—

"BLAAAAAAAAHHHHHH DE BLAAAAAAAAHHH DE BLAAAAAAAAHH!"

"BLAAAAAAAAHHHHHH DE BLAAAAAAAAHHH DE BLAAAAAAAAHH!"

She found a seat near the top of the bleachers, spread herself out, took off several layers of winter clothing, yelled or whispered pleasant inanities to whoever was the appropriate distance away, and looked down at the scene below.

Meg caught her eye again.

Meg who, a few players gathered in a tight circle around her now, was drawing diagrams with chalk on the gym floor, pointing animatedly to them as though they were some cross between algebraic formulas and sorcerers' formulas.

Meg was a favorite in the town of Bay St. Lucy.

They completely forgave her for being gay.

In the first place, lesbianism and women's sports went hand in hand, and everybody knew that.

But more importantly, Bay St. Lucy had always prided itself as an artist community or a fishing village, or some cross between the two. Whichever one it was, it was populated by folk of a different sort, by people who, had they themselves been judged by the norms of conventional society, would have been cast into outer darkness and forced to serve penance until showing the willingness to go to work in regular jobs, and wear socks.

So they completely understood Meg's 'arrangement' with Jennifer Warren, proprietor of 'Jenny's Art Treasures,' partially because it was none of their business and, more importantly, because it made them feel liberal and free.

If such a relationship could not exist in a community of artists and beach bums, then where could it exist?

But no matter. People were standing now to hear the band's rendition of *The Star Spangled Banner.* Some had their hands over their hearts, some simply stood straight as they gazed somberly at Old Glory and the Rebel Flag (Nina had long since come to terms with the fact that Mississippi wasn't about to change its colors, and contented herself with the fact that the thing at least hung below its counterpart on the flagpole in the Northeast gym corner). Some, teenagers mostly, could not stop engaging in a bit of mild flirting, hair pulling, beneath the gym rows, kicking or wild, purposeless giggling, despite the solemnity of the occasion.

Their parents would have words for them later on.

But the end of the song always forced Nina to the brink of tears.

AND THE HOOOOOME

OF THE

BRAAAAAVE!

The last lines always made her tear up and she wished for Frank, so she could hold his hand as they resumed their seats.

But there were other things to think about, because the game had begun!

Pass Christian won the tip.

Trouble there. They had a six-foot-tall girl.

(Why did all the opposing teams always have a six-foot-tall girl?)

Still, there was hope. Bay St. Lucy stole a pass, worked the ball down the court, and began a fancy outside semicircular weave, Alyssha Bennett dribbling hard to the right, slipping it behind her back to Sarah Gray, barreling left over the top of the key, Sonia Ramirez taking it right back in the other direction, Haley Stephens right there on another switch, everyone milling inside, screening, turning, heading out, then back in, then the ball back in Haley's hands, shot clock now at ten seconds, now at eight seconds, back to Sonia and then—

Bullet pass under the basket!

Alyssha! All alone! Uncontested layup!

The crowd went wild and began singing a fight song that The University of Wisconsin had somehow in the last century stolen from Bay St. Lucy and patented under the name "On Wisconsin."

GO YOU MARE-NERS!

GO YOU MARE-NERS!

FAT FAT FAT FAT FAAAAT

(The word 'fat' being as close as southerners could come to 'fight.')

"YEEEAHHH!"

Braying like a bull (and as large as a bull), Jackson Bennett, the once quite young and naïve lawyer recruited as a partner by Frank, the now proud parent of a budding basketball star, leapt to his feet.

"YEEEAH! GO MARINERS!"

Jackson pumped his fists twice and then sat down again in a ten-foot space that he'd carved out for himself (obsessive male parents not wishing to be bothered with other human companionship while watching their offspring compete)—quickly returning to his task of filming the game on the small IPhone thrust out arms' length and gripped between two hands.

Elsewhere in the crowd, organized cheers began.

WATERMELON WATERMELON

WATERMELON RIND!

LOOK AT THE SCOREBOARD AND SEE WHO'S BEHIND!

Pass Christian inbounded

And Nina, watching the superbly confident young women representing her school and her town, each knowing exactly what to do, each with eyes fixed on her opponent—began to feel the melancholy she always felt (although she fought hard against it) while watching this team, or the volleyball team, or the softball team.

Her chance to do these things had come—and gone—almost fifty years ago.

An era before Title Nine.

Which had changed women's sports forever.

All right, she was only five feet four.

But wasn't that the perfect height for a point guard?

Look at Amanda Billingsley, hurling herself on the floor to tie the ball, and then Alyssha following, now all of them, three of our players down, two or three of theirs, a human knot contorting and writhing and fighting desperately for the ball—

—would she have been able to do that?

—and, if so, how might that willingness have changed her life?

In 1963, her year of graduation, what choices did she have?

She could have gotten married, of course, as she did, to her eternal happiness.

But what if Frank had not—well, happened to her—what then?

What if there had not been that junior prom (Frank was a senior), and the kiss in the vacant lot behind the Presbyterian Church, wisteria all abloom on the May night and a thunderstorm rumbling in the distance out over the twinkling coastal oil rigs—

—what if there had been no Frank (because there certainly was no other, nor could she have ever conceived another)?

She would have gone on to teachers college, as she did.

She would have become a teacher, as she did.

And as for other choices?

A secretary.

A nurse.

And that was about the limit of it.

She would not have joined the Air Force to become a fighter pilot, a choice which lay before Haley. She would not have become a firefighter, which Alyssha could do if she so chose. She could not have become a police officer, nor would she probably have considered attending The University of Mississippi Law School (nor The Yale Law School, for that matter).

No, these young women inhabited a different world.

One which began for them with stolen passes at center court, and fierce rebounding battles, and pressure three point shots in the last seconds of the ball game, the entire town standing as one and bellowing like a sea beast come aground in this glowing, pulsating, huge hall of a gymnasium.

What was the call?

Bay St. Lucy ball!

Long pass—

Haley open from the three point line, then a long, arching shot, soft, soft—

SWISH!

THREE POINTS!

Bay St. Lucy five, Pass Christian nothing!

The quarter wore on, and all players, even the opposing ones, assumed identities, became heroes or villains as the action developed.

Haley off to Alyssha over to—nope, ball stolen by the tall red-haired girl from Pass Christian down court to the slender girl with glowing ebony skin over to the feisty blonde who was built like a fire plug and who hurtled over everything in her path then her pass re-stolen by Sarah across to Sonia and then—OH NO BAD PASS knocked away by tall Hispanic girl with ponytail taken by fireplug girl—my god, she's everywhere—down court to red head over to frizz hair number thirty-two—who'd just checked into the ball game—and bounce pass to ponytail back to frizz over to taller-than-anybody-on-our-team, then back to fireplug—

—and two points.

And so it went.

Halftime score, 28 to 28.

The entrance hall into the gym had been transformed into a winter version of the county fair. The choices of food were somewhat more limited, of course: hot dogs or popcorn or pizza or nachos (with cheese sauce) or huge pickles.

But Nina was satisfied with her hot dog, and her big orange drink, and the ability to filter through the crowd and overhear shreds of conversation.

"You think we got enough height this year?"

"I don't know. We got that Bennett girl, but she's a little on the slender side."

"Just a freshman, too."

"We have speed, I will say that."

"It's not gonna be enough when they go up against Hattiesburg."

These comments from farmers from inland, fishermen from seaward, drillers, shopkeepers, housewives, loafers, drunks, no-accounts, and, at the bottom end of the social spectrum, artists of various kinds.

All drawn like moths, flies, and mosquitoes to the luminescent Bay St. Lucy Gymnasium where Basketball Evening Services were being celebrated and First Communion of Hot Dog and Pickle was divided among the populace.

It was all quite wonderful.

It was made more wonderful by the fact that Bay St. Lucy won the game, pulling away gradually through the third quarter, and building a double digit lead in the end, so that even the bench players were able to play a minute or so.

It seemed an inevitable thing, this outcome. Perhaps because all of the diagrams on the gym floor—which would have been complete gibberish to Nina—were not gibberish at all.

Meg was a superb coach. She simply saw what the other team was doing, and had an answer for it.

The crowd filtered out in a festive mood.

Nina, one of the last people to clamber down from the stands, placed a hand on the shoulder of Meg, who was standing by herself, and staring down the bench at a group of her celebrating players.

"Great game, Meg. You guys were wonderful."

"We got lucky."

"No. Your players are just good. And so is their coach."

"Thank you, Nina. That means a lot. And—well, there's something I wanted to tell you."

"Oh?"

"It's just, well—something that's going to happen."

"To you?"

"To Jennifer and me. We're getting married."

For a time Nina knew nothing to say.

There was nothing to say.

The only appropriate thing was an embrace.

And so she and Meg embraced.

Finally she said:

"When, Meg?"

"Towards the end of January. The State of New Mexico has just legalized gay marriage. We're going to drive over there and do it. Finally. After so many years of being together."

"It's wonderful news."

"You've always been one of our favorite people in Bay St. Lucy, so I wanted you to know."

"I'm honored. I truly am. Of course, you have to have a wedding shower."

"You know that's not necessary."

"Of course, it's necessary. We'll have it at Margot's shop."

Another embrace. Finally Meg said:

"I guess I need to go down and tell the players congratulations. Donaldsville next week; then Logansport, then the big one with Hattiesburg."

"Give them all a high five for me."

"I will, Nina. I definitely will."

"And the real congratulations go to you and Jennifer; the whole town will be excited for both of you!"

"Thanks, Nina!"

And, feeling the warm glow of certainty that the whole town—*this* whole town at least, this Bay St. Lucy if not every other town in the south—actually would be excited for Meg and Jennifer's happiness, Nina left the court.

She let herself be carried along with the flow of the crowd as it made its way through the entry hall and out into the somber night, noticing that, to her and everyone else's delight, the snow was still continuing to fall.

The film of powder on the streets had collected, at some points, to almost an inch thick.

An inch of snow!

She was just crossing the high school parking lot when she felt an arm slither snake-like between her elbow and ribcage.

Almost simultaneously, another arm did the same thing on the left side of her body.

She was pancaked. A Nina sandwich between two human buns, one of which could talk.

"Keep walking," it whispered.

"I was going to keep walking," she answered, wondering what condiments were to follow.

"You're our prisoner," came mustard from the left.

"You must go," (mayonnaise from the right) "where we take you."

After hearing this, she decided that she'd gone as far as she could with the food analogy and might as well address her kidnappers as Paul and Macy Cox, since that was who they in fact were.

All right; but where are the two of you taking me?"

"Into the high school building," answered Macy, who, Nina could see from the corner of her eye, was still emanating the slightly green/gold glow of happiness that had been radiating from her body since her marriage five months earlier.

"The high school," Nina said, "is closed."

"I'm the principal," Paul responded. "I have a key."

"What are we going to do in the high school at ten o'clock on a Friday night?"

"Vandalism."

"Well. That sounds like fun."

"I would be willing to bet," said Macy, tightening her grip on Nina's bicep, "that you've never committed an act of vandalism in your life."

"Not true. I have a dark side that the two of you know nothing about. I broke an ashtray once. And that's only the tip of the iceberg."

"Don't go any further," said Paul, reaching into his pocket as the building loomed before them, "or we'll have to turn you in."

"I don't mind. Prison doesn't scare me. So what's going on, really?"

"We have," whispered Macy, "something to tell you, and something to give you."

"And you have to do these things in a deserted high school building? You can't tell me something and give me something at, say, Sergio's or McGee's Landing or any other place where they have martinis?"

The whispering continued:

"It wouldn't be as appropriate."

"I've never known an inappropriate martini."

"Your dark side speaking again?"

"Don't toy with me, I'm warning you."

"We wouldn't think of it," said Paul, slipping his key into the lock and swinging open the ponderous door.

"Voila."

"Well, this is certainly exciting. Bay St. Lucy High, only two short hours before the witching hour."

"Come on. Let's go inside."

"If the police see us—"

"The police are directing traffic."

"You've got it all figured out, don't you?"

"You have to trust us."

"The last time I heard that, Paul, someone was murdered."

"That was months ago. Surely you don't still remember it."

"Only because I solved it."

"That's true, but still—you need to think happy thoughts."

"There's no place for happy thoughts here; this is a school."

And, she mused upon entering the great glass and tile mausoleum, it certainly was. The main hall loomed before them, fluorescent ceiling lights darkened now, the glass on the trophy cases illuminated only by emergency red generator lights glowing and hissing quietly in ceiling panels.

She could see in her mind's eye the ghostly images of students stampeding like drunken cattle down the corridor before them, letter jackets in place of brands and pony tails for horns.

"Come on. Into my office."

He produced yet another key and opened the door to the main office.

Nina entered just behind him, Macy coming third to cover their getaway.

She wondered where the spray paint was.

"Now. A little light."

He flipped the switch and gestured toward chairs.

In a matter of seconds, they were all seated—Paul behind his mahogany desk, Nina and Macy in the places reserved for truant teenagers.

She fought back an urge to say, 'I didn't do it!' realizing, somewhat to her shame, that she had in fact never done it, whatever the 'it' might have been, and that she'd been disgustingly good all of her life, and that she had no dark side whatsoever.

If one thought about it, she had no sides at all.

She was just Nina, plain and true.

How boring.

"So," she said, wistfully, "what crime are we plotting?"

Macy smiled:

"Give it to her, Paul."

"Give it to me?" she responded. "Am I being assassinated?"

Paul was smiling too now, as he handed her a small package, wrapped in gold paper, that he'd taken from his desk drawer.

"Maybe worse. You should open it."

She took it from him. It was a foot or so long, and heavy, as though made of metal.

"What is this? Three sticks of dynamite?"

"Worse. This is the thing we have to give you. There's the other thing first, though—the thing we have to tell you."

"What is it?"

Macy stood, took two steps, and wound up behind Paul.

"There's a good chance," she said, her fingers massaging his shoulders, "that we'll be leaving Bay St. Lucy."

Nina sat forward in her chair, looking for further smiles, then realizing the joke was over.

"You're what?"

"Leaving Bay St. Lucy," Paul said, quietly.

"Oh, no! But this is awful! You can't go!"

"Well, it's not certain. It depends on you."

"On me? How? What's going on, Coxes? Paul, you're the best principal we've ever had, and, Macy, you're unquestionably the best English teacher. We can't lose you!"

"I don't know about the English teacher thing," said Macy. "But as for the principal—well, we can deal with that part."

"How? And—and—why are you leaving."

"I've had a job offer," said Paul.

"What kind of a job offer?"

Macy stepped forward, her smile infectious.

"They want him to go to Jackson, Nina. He's been offered a job as special educational assistant to the Governor of Mississippi."

"Oh, my God."

"The pay is obscenely high. But Paul wants to do it because of the reforms he'll be able to make. There's an obsession with standardized testing, for example; he's going to fight that. As well as a lot of other things."

Nina nodded, simultaneously thrilled for the two of them and depressed that they would be going.

"But how does this—how does this depend on me?"

"It depends," said Paul, "on whether or not you accept your present."

"I don't understand."

"Open it."

She did so, the paper rustling as she tore it back.

"Here," said Paul, turning the desk lamp toward her.

The light glowed yellow on a metal plate that had been affixed to a walnut, triangular box.

It was name plate.

On it were inscribed the words:

NINA BANNISTER: PRINCIPAL

CHAPTER 2: ADVICE FROM A FRIEND

"If a story is in you, it has got to come out."
—William Faulkner

What a night.

She had gotten home around midnight with a thousand contradictory thoughts buzzing around in her brain like a nest of psychedelic bumble bees.

Going back.

And not just going back to teaching, which was her first love. No, going back into administration.

Principal Nina Bannister.

She'd only spent four years as a principal—the last four in her thirty year career in the schools—and they had, by all accounts, been good ones. She'd been thought of by the town, and by the students, and by the parents, and by the state authorities, as being competent.

No horrible disasters, budgetary crises, student riots, or money laundering scams, had taken place on her watch.

But, oh, the innumerable headaches!

Hamlet: "And who would fardels bear, to grunt and sweat under a weary life…"

And what was a 'fardel,' anyway?

(She'd always meant to look that up.)

Who would go back?

She'd spent half the night asking herself the question.

The other half of the night had been spent feeding Furl, and petting him, until finally he'd grown disgusted with her unwanted attention and hidden in the clothes hamper. She'd made cocoa, and drunk it; she'd read the fourth chapter of an Agatha Christie novel (not quite remembering which one. A Poirot? A Miss Marple? Who knew?). She'd toasted and eaten an Eggo.

And she'd paced, wondering whether to go down to the beach and pace there and deciding ultimately against it, for fear of disturbing teenagers who might have wanted to neck.

Real sleep never came. There was a period of dozing that must have taken place between three and five a.m. by her best reckoning, but that was worst of all. "For in that endless sleep of re-principalization what dreams may come?"

Why was she always associating going back into the schools with *Hamlet*? That was not a good sign, not a good sign at all.

So she'd tossed and turned for a time on her little bed, visualizing all of the fights she'd have to break up, and preferring even the most savage of them to one parent conference dealing with the fact that Susan or Johnny had been found stashing condoms in a locker, or had been suspected of smoking marijuana behind the ag building.

There was no hope. She would simply have to get up and face the day.

So she did, resolving how best to confront this "To be or not to be a principal"—

Shoo Hamlet! Shoo, shoo!

—crisis.

She would, as soon as sufficient light had spread over the isthmus of Mississippiland, wander into town and do some pastry shopping at Bagatelli's bakery.

There she'd meet Margot Gavin, who always bought croissants at precisely seven a.m.

Margot was always curious about anything going on in Nina's life—despite the fact that nothing very interesting ever was going on in Nina's life, except when she was solving murders, which had happened twice in the past year, go figure—and would pump her for information, would grill her about this decision she now had to make, would carefully, in great detail, go over the pros and cons of the matter (were there any pros, really?), and would, by midmorning, have presented her with a concise summary of what she should or should not do.

That was the ticket.

Bagatelli's, then back to Elementals: Treasures of the Earth and Sea (Margot's gift shop, where Nina spent most of her mornings these days anyway) and then home by lunch, having soaked in the careful counsel of a dear friend, and what did dear friends exist for anyway if not to give such counsel?

At six fifty, she wrapped herself in a scarf, donned her heavy winter coat, pulled on a woolen hat, slipped into her winter, fur-lined gloves, and, secure in long underwear and two sweaters as well as thermal socks, lurched out into the frigid air of Bay St. Lucy, air which, overnight, had been chilled to a temperature as low as (at least rumor had it) thirty-eight degrees.

The snow, she noted, was all gone.

Darn.

But the crisp air actually felt good as she walked, and the sight of lights going on in various coffee shops and boutiques heartened her.

She'd have to give up her morning walks if she became a principal again.

Ridiculous!

She turned the corner of L Street and Archie Manning Boulevard and rejoiced to see the little frame house that was Bagatelli's Bakery a hundred or so yards in front of her, its brick chimneys emanating gray smoke and succulent aromas.

She entered the shop to find the Bagatellis shouting at each other.

They were always the same, always in their bakery, he always covered in flour, she always bustling around with the same absolutely perfect blue-striped apron, both of them yelling at each other at the top of their lungs: 'ADEPENTO! ADEPENTO, DECCOLATERI, SOPALIUSCIA!' or some such gibberish, that nobody in town could ever understand—

—and it was so strange, because they were the most amiable, the most outgoing, the most loving and giving and caring and caressing and smiling and hugging and 'We love life and everybody in it-ing' couple in the world, except when they happened to be addressing each other, which they did only in terms of seemingly bitter hostility and with words of Italianate hatred.

'MOSCOTARI! NON-CIALENTO QUATORCE! NON SPOSE SENTURURARI COME NUNCIO ADUE!

'ANDENTO CONMIUS NON SCENTE!"

Who knew what it all meant?

But after a few moments of it, Senora Bagatelli would appear at the counter with sacks of wonderful things, beaming that star-white smile that seemed to explode out of her every time she opened her mouth and scream deliriously:

"Questo!"

HERE IT IS!

Nina stood for a time and marveled at the effect of flour floating in the air, mixing with both sunbeams streaming through the great windows in the back of the shop and baking aromas hanging so densely about the ovens that they could almost be seen as well as smelled—and ordered, expertly, as she always did:

"I'll take one of that, and three of those things, and give me maybe a half of that thing—no, no, the whole thing—and then—oh, I don't know, a dozen of those doohickeys over there."

Which would send the Bagatellis rolling into action.

"ADEPENTO!"

"NON SCOLARSI PARMIENTO!"

And while this chaos was going on, Margot Gavin walked in—as Nina knew she would—and asked: "Want to go on a trip?"

"What?"

"A trip. I've got to go on a trip, be gone a little over a week, and I'm wondering if you want to go with me."

"I can't go on a trip right now, Margot. I've got a big decision to make. Last night—"

"Oh, you can make decisions any time. You need to come with me. It'll get you out of the house."

"I don't want to get out of the house. I like being *in* the house. It's just that—"

"It's just that I need to do some shopping and get my morning croissants. Then we'll go back to 'Elementals' and I'll tell you about this trip."

"Okay, but I need some advice. This is kind of a big thing, Margot. You're always so good at taking things apart and putting things together so that they make sense. You're analytical."

"Am not."

"Are too."

"Well, all right, if you say so. But we'll do the analyzing back at the shop over some hot coffee and cinnamon croissants."

"Good."

And so they made their purchases and returned to Elementals: Treasures etc. etc.

They had seated themselves comfortably in the garden area and were chowing down, butter melting evilly and fatteningly before them in two croissants that lay like prehistoric pastry-monsters, when Nina said: "Okay. So last night Paul and Macy Cox asked me…"

And Margot, not hearing at all and letting her eyes play across a new series of Ramoula Peters seascapes that hung on the south wall and, improbably, not lighting a cigarette for Margot was attempting, if not to give up smoking, at least to keep her consumption levels under thirteen or fourteen packs a day said: "I have to go check out a plantation house and I want you to go with me."

Margot not smoking. What a bizarre thing!

What was happening?

Nina's brain, out of sheer mental muscle memory, began to supply the smoking gestures usually made by SMOKINGMARGOT—and it was fine, because she was now able to enjoy the elegance of Margot Gavin Smoking with none of the smells.

"Where is the plantation house?"

Margot did not lift a cigarette to her lips, did not inhale deeply upon it nor let the thick gray smoke escape from her mouth and rise swirling toward the ceiling. But she *did* say: "Mississippi."

"We're already in Mississippi."

"Different part."

Then she did not lay her cigarette on an ashtray that sat on the table between her and Nina, since none existed there. But she did continue: "I have a kind of—well, a kind of commission to do."

"What does that mean?"

"I'm to look into buying a plantation house."

"A whole plantation house?"

"Yes."

"For whom?"

"I've been asked to look at it by a group of colleagues from Chicago. People I used to know from my days in fundraising."

"All right; and why does this group want to buy a plantation house?"

"They've conceived a plan to offer singers, painters, writers, etc., a kind of retreat."

"Retreat?"

"Yes. Artists spend their lives charging. Administrators such as myself and the group I'll be meeting at the plantation spend our lives retreating. It's what *we* do. We're always looking over our shoulder to see if someone is coming up behind us to hit us over the head with the fact that we have no actual talent."

"You retreat."

"Constantly. And so this group has conceived a place where artists from the North can come to the South and be anesthetized."

"They can rest."

Margot shook her head.

"Artists never rest. But they can come here and be warm, and stroll across the grounds, and suffer in a more comfortable climate than might otherwise be possible. Also, they can perhaps meet some people from Mississippi, which will give them something to make fun of when they return home."

"Do you have to put any money into this venture?"

"No. It's all from other sources. Mostly places where there is money and nothing to do with it."

"Well, that doesn't sound too difficult. It should be an easy thing for you to do."

"It wouldn't be difficult, except for one thing."

"What thing?"

"The place is haunted."

"It's what?"

"It's haunted."

"Who haunts it?"

"Ghosts haunt it. Or at least ghosts are going to be haunting it, when I will be there."

"Ghosts are not real, Margot."

"They're as real as paintings. And if it weren't for paintings, I wouldn't have had a career."

"I suppose there's a kind of twisted logic there, somewhere."

"The logic is not twisted. It's perfectly reasonable, and in line with common sense. Also—there will be other ghosts. The group of people that is going to be there. Several of them will be ghosts."

"How is that possible?"

"It's possible because these people were alive to me once, in another life, quite another life entirely—and then they were dead to me, to my existence. And now I'm sure I don't know which they will be when I see them: dead or alive. So do you want to go?"

"And why do you want me to go?"

"Because of the ghosts. They're real, and I need protection from them. I'm going to a haunted house, Nina. It's HAUNTED HAUNTED HAUNTED AND THERE ARE GHOSTS GHOSTS GHOSTS EVERYWHERE AND THEY TERRIFY ME!"

"I can't go."

"Why not?"

"Last night Paul and Macy Cox asked me to come back to the high school and be the new principal."

"They asked you what?"

"To be the new principal."

Margot stood up.

"That is absolutely the most ridiculous, fantastic, utterly unbelievable thing I've ever heard."

And, not stubbing out her cigarette, Margot walked out of the garden.

So the plan to discuss, at length, the entire matter with Margot, did not exactly work out.

There was, of course, another option, for Nina had at least one more friend she could confide in.

It thus happened that the following conversation took place along a stretch of beach some half mile distant from her shack, in the early afternoon, with the wintry disc of a washed out sun playing ragtag with the shreds of clouds, and the mournful bray of an oil tanker serving as bass backdrop for the screeching of what seemed an abnormally large number of seagulls.

"I'm not sure what to do about this."

"So what's your initial thought?"

"That it's crazy."

"Then turn it down."

"I don't know. Maybe it's not that crazy."

"Why isn't it?"

"Because I miss it; I miss school."

"Why?"

"It's what I do. Who I am."

"Do you need the money?"

"Not really. I don't have much. But I have enough. Retirement pays me enough."

"Are you miserable in your life, the way it's going now?"

"Of course not. I like hanging out with Margot, helping at the shop. I go and come as I wish. It's nice not having to be here or there at a certain time. And all the grading. The hassles with whatever kid is mad or whatever parent has screwed up."

"You really miss all those things?"

"For a while I tell myself that I don't; but somehow—somehow, I guess I do."

"Couldn't they get somebody else?"

"I'm sure they could. But they asked me. Paul and Macy asked me. And that means a lot. I don't want to let them down."

"Are you in good enough health for this? I mean, you're in your late sixties, you know. Most people your age are retiring."

"Well, if we want to look at it that way, a lot of people my age are dead. Doesn't mean I have to be dead. And as for health, I feel better than I used to when I was teaching."

"That's because you're not teaching."

"Good point."

"Nina, you've been away from the whole thing for almost ten years now. Surely a lot of things have changed."

"I guess so."

"There's testing. From what you can read about in the papers, all the students do these days is take standardized tests. If they don't do well enough, the teachers get laid off. As principal, you'd be right in the middle of that."

"I know. But maybe I can make it easier on everybody."

"How?"

"I'll figure out a way to cheat."

"Oh, right, I can see you doing that."

"If the students like what they're studying, if it's genuinely interesting in class—then the test scores will take care of themselves."

"How many students like what they're studying?"

"None of them."

"So that kinds of leaves us where we were, doesn't it?"

"You're just being difficult."

"I'm being a realist. And I'm telling you, Nina: you killed yourself in the educational salt mines for thirty years. You deserve a break now."

"I know. You're right."

"Paul will find somebody else. Somebody younger."

"I know. You're right."

"The school will survive. And you'll live a lot longer. And a lot happier."

"I know. You're right."

"So you're going to turn it down, right? You're going to call Paul Cox this afternoon, after you get back to your shack, and apologize to him, and tell him how gratified you are for the offer, and how you thought about it a long time, but how, after all is said and done, it would be better if you said 'no.'"

"I know. You're right."

Pause pause pause pause—

The waves breaking, the tanker honking, the fish white and jumping in the afternoon tide—

"But then, of course, Nina, there is that thing that you're always saying. You know the thing I mean."

"Yes. I know it."

"How does it go?"

"It goes, 'If human ignorance is the raw material upon which educators do their work, then no true teacher has any excuse ever—*ever*—to be unemployed."

"Yeah. That."

Pause pause pause pause—

"You're going to take the job aren't you? You're going to go back into the schools, and be a principal again."

"Yes."

"And you always were. You had your mind made up the minute Paul made the offer. We've been talking for no reason at all."

"I wouldn't say that."

"You wouldn't?"

"No, of course not. We always have a reason to talk. And we always will."

"Good to hear you say that, Nina. Now—why don't you go back home, and accept your new job?"

"All right, Frank. And thanks."

So saying, she turned and went back to her shack.

CHAPTER 3: ONCE MORE INTO THE BREACH, DEAR FRIENDS!

Thus it came to be that, slightly more than one month later—she had spent a number of days following Paul around and re-learning the ropes, and a certain amount of time had been needed for contract signing, re-licensure, etc.—she found herself sitting in her shack, preparing to eat dinner, savoring her last night as a civilian.

It was a microwave dinner, but there was nothing wrong with that. There were going to be evenings spent in her office at school, and time for cooking would be less than before.

She walked into her bedroom and opened the closet door.

Three new suits, four pair of new shoes, a new purse.

Had she chosen to open the vanity drawers, she would have found new underwear and new stockings.

Christmas gifts to herself.

No, she was ready to look like a principal again.

So she took the lasagna out of the microwave, set its black plastic tray on the dining room table, stared at Furl, who was staring back at her, and said quietly:

"All right cat. This is it. After this, life changes."

Then she poured herself a glass of milk—the old Nina would have had a glass of wine, but no more of that in the new life—and gave a toast to her reflection in the glass of the sliding deck door.

"Here's to tomorrow!"

She had just sipped the first drops when she heard a knock at the front door.

Strange.

Sunday night.

Funny time for visitors.

She rose, apologized to Furl, who hated visitors on any night, and walked across the living room.

She opened the door to reveal Jackson Bennett.

"Nina. Sorry to bother you."

His huge frame darkened the doorway and blocked the quietly glowing blue porch light.

He glowered down at her.

Few people had the capability to glower.

Nina certainly did not.

She could squint but not glower, and she'd never been tall enough look down at anyone.

"Jackson—come in."

"I can't, Nina."

"Why? What's up?"

"Nina, I—"

He seemed uncertain, which was strange for Jackson, who was always certain about everything.

"What is it, Jackson?"

"Well, there's—"

"Come on. Tell me."

"Something's come up. Something pretty serious."

"Is anybody hurt? Has there been an accident?"

"Oh, no. Nothing like that."

"Then what is it?"

"I think you need to come with me."

"Come with you? Where, Jackson?"

"Downtown. We need to go downtown."

"Well, all right. But what's this about?"

"Why don't you get a jacket on. It's chilly. I'll tell you about it in the car."

And so she did.

But he did not.

Actually he was silent as a stone during the two mile ride into the center of Bay St. Lucy, nor did he speak while parking the big black limousine he now drove regularly.

Lights in the town hall glowed.

"Can't you tell me what's going on?"

"In a minute, Nina."

"Is this city business?"

"In a way."

"You know I'm not on the town council anymore."

"Yes. I know that."

"Surely I haven't done anything wrong as a principal. I haven't started yet."

"It's not that."

"Is there some last minute objection about my taking the job? I thought we'd gone over all the paperwork, checked my certificate, gotten everything up to date, crossed all the 't's, dotted the—"

"Let's just go inside."

He opened the door for her.

The main chamber of the town hall glowed before her like a Christmas tree.

There must have been fifty people inside, all smiling at her, most holding glasses of champagne in their hands, which were stretched upward toward the door.

A huge banner, hanging from the chandeliers, read:

WELCOME BACK, NINA!

She was speechless.

Alanna Delafosse stood beneath one of the great windows, a street light shining through the half-closed blinds and making her face a caramel glow. John Giusti stood beside her, his wife Helen, late of the Broadway stage, standing only a few feet away. Even Tom Broussard was there, standing in a far corner. And there, bringing him a cup of something, ostensibly coffee, more probably bourbon or some unknown brew even stronger, was his wife of not quite a year, Penelope Royale.

Penelope had recognized that, as the town's most obscene speaker—she spoke only in obscenities—she shared kinship with Tom, the town's most successful dirty novelist, and the two had married.

Before the marriage, each had lived the most disreputable lifestyle imaginable. Penelope had a small living space down by the boat docks, and apparently, as far as anyone could tell, survived by eating bait. Tom's place was worse, and no one knew how he survived.

After the marriage, nothing apparently changed for either of them.

They each lived precisely as they had before.

Penelope kept her shack; Tom kept his.

And now they were here like everyone else.

Honoring her.

Penelope stepped forward and announced:

“Nina, we———but———if we don’t———and you———deserve it!”

Laughter, applause—

And then they were upon her.

The party lasted until well after midnight and involved the consumption on Nina’s part of at least two glasses of champagne.

Perhaps three.

At any rate, too many for a hard working woman on the eve of a scary day.

It did end, though, as all deliciously evil things must, and slightly before one a.m., she found herself in yet another car, being taken home, not by Jackson Bennett, who had been forced to leave early, but by Paul Cox.

His car meandered through the deserted streets, and his aquiline, almost birdlike, face reflected in the glow of the dashboard.

“Well, this is it.”

“This was wonderful, Paul. I can’t tell you how thrilled it made me feel. Thank you for organizing it.”

“I didn’t organize it. Your friends did. And you have a lot of them.”

“I know. I’m lucky.”

He nodded and slowed the car, as they turned onto Breakers Boulevard, which would lead down to the sea and her shack.

“We’re the ones who are lucky. The whole town.”

“I hope I’ll do okay.”

“You’ll do fine.”

“There are so many things to remember, so many things that come up every day.”

"Just trust the people working around you. And trust your judgment."

He was silent for a time.

The orange-lighted square windows of her shack loomed up before them.

The car stopped. Even though the windows of Paul's van were tightly closed, she could still hear the roar of the surf.

And there was Furl, outlined in the window, looking down.

"Nina…"

"Yes, Paul?"

"There is one more thing I need to tell you."

She stared at him across the seat.

"What is it?"

"Something I just learned today. We all just learned it today."

"All right. Go on."

"Well—"

"Let me have it. Get it over with."

"I'd heard that something like this might happen. Politics being the way politics always are. And of course, it's all politics."

"What's happened?"

"Nina, there's been a new appointee."

"What kind of an appointee?"

He shook his head.

"You know that the world in Jackson—like pretty much the whole country—is divided in its way of looking at things."

"Yes. Go on."

"Well, my appointment as educational consultant to the governor reflects one of those ways of seeing the world. I'm viewed as a reformer."

"Who is the appointee?"

"A woman I don't really know, and haven't met. She's to be the new 'Commissioner of Educational Excellence for Southwest Mississippi,' based in Hattiesburg. She has broad ranging powers."

"Over me?"

"Over pretty much everybody. She answers to people who oppose the governor. But those people have a lot of power—and so does she."

"Power to achieve what goal?"

"Get the test scores up."

"Oh God."

"Yes. And keep the schools running like—well, like these people want the schools to run."

"Oh God."

"There's still time to quit."

She felt herself laughing softly as she thought of the party tonight, and of the huge banner, and of Penelope's obscene and wonderful speech.

She looked up at bedroom window. Furl was laughing too.

"No. No, Paul, it's a little too late for that. So. What's this woman's name?"

"Dr. April van Osdale."

"What?"

"I said her name is Dr. April van Osdale. Apparently she's from…"

"I know where she's from."

"You do?"

"Yes. I know her from The University of Mississippi. About fifteen years ago, I'm sure you know, I went back there one summer to do the course work I needed to become principal. April and I had several education classes together, and we worked on group projects. She was in her early twenties and I in my mid-forties. I haven't seen her in years. But, yes, I know her."

"Well. I had no idea. That's good then. You have a history together. Maybe that will make it easier for you to work together."

"Maybe."

She opened her car door and stepped outside.

A light rain had begun to fall.

"I'm going up now. Thanks for telling me about this. And thanks for everything else."

"Sure thing. By ten o'clock tomorrow morning Macy and I and the moving van will be half way to Jackson. But you've got my phone number, and you know that, well, if there's anything I can do—"

"Sure, Paul."

"All right. Good luck then!"

And, so saying, he pulled away.

She stood for a time in the cool rain.

Then she walked up her stairway, pausing to take the key out of her purse.

"April van Osdale," she whispered to the doorknob.

It did not answer.

Yes, she knew April van Osdale.

She knew her quite well.

She had never, in her entire life, detested another human being so completely.

CHAPTER 4: FIRST DAY BACK

"...I give you the mausoleum of all hope and desire."
—William Faulkner, *The Sound and the Fury*

"I don't think anybody can teach anybody anything."
—William Faulkner

Ten years retired, ten years retired…

So much had changed. Not the students, for students are always the same. They behaved and misbehaved just as they always had in class, and they rampaged down the hallways between periods in precisely the same breakneck manner, the football players hurling themselves against the rattling locker doors, their coaches joining in the horseplay, the young girls gibbering and gossiping, somehow immune to being pinned against the lockers themselves, and always pretending to be oblivious to the mayhem.

Not the building, for it was just as it had always been.

Mid-sixties style, low and sprawling, wall of windows, lockers along the corridors, hospital lighting—

—no, the building certainly had not changed.

But many other things had.

Everything was done by email now. People could no longer talk to each other. When the server was down—and what in heaven's name was a 'server,' anyway?—well, whatever it was, when it was down, the entire chain of communications broke down with it, and people simply wandered around the hallways, unable to fix meeting times or plan luncheons or even gripe with each other about whatever latest outrage had taken place in class.

Cell phones.

Although there were large signs posted along the corridors saying "Do not Bring Your Cell Phones to Class!", the strange glowing things always appeared anyway, held furtively beneath desk tops, making their faint music at inopportune times, saving the students from the horrors of even momentary isolation, and allowing every boy and girl the reassuring knowledge that another human voice was whispering, at all times, if not into their ears, then at least into their palms.

And, of course, there were the tests now.

The Mississippi Academic Certification Evaluation.

The M.A.C.E.

Everything now depended on these examinations, and how well the students fared on them.

Reputation.

Prestige.

And above all, funding.

One good thing: Paul Cox had always hated standardized testing. "We do not," he had insisted, "teach standardized students." So he had protected teachers from the need to give continual "practice" tests.

One bad thing: as a result, Bay St. Lucy's test scores were usually among the lowest in the state.

One other bad thing: April van Osdale was coming to town to change all that.

Well. Worry about one thing at time.

For example, the budget.

Budgetary matters were now handled by computer, of course, there being one website for this document and another for that document. It was and had always been stunning to her that in every educational establishment in the country (and probably the world) there was never enough money to get things done and always too much money to keep up with properly.

So that finances and the proper dealing with them were going to take up, she knew, a majority of her time, making her yearn for the chance simply to pop into one of the classrooms opening onto the central hall and teach, if only for a moment, one of Shakespeare's sonnets or Jane Austen's novels.

That, of course, remained the province of Macy and her fellow English teachers.

There was to be one more English teacher in Bay St. Lucy High School. Word had filtered down the prior week that Macy's replacement (at least for the remainder of the school year) had been personally hired by Jackson Bennett, head of the school board, and would begin the following day, on Tuesday.

Max Lirpa.

No one seemed to know much about Max Lirpa, but if he'd seemed impressive to Jackson, then he was surely suitable.

Except that he was a man.

Nina made a mental note to herself: She would have to remember to warn Ms. Eunice Duncan, now head of the department, not to start each weekly meeting of the English teachers with the greeting "Good afternoon, Ladies!"

All of these things, then, were different.

But the main things, the basics, never changed.

Despite everything, it was just as she remembered it.

There remained, and always would remain, the golden, eternal rule of being a principal: that being 'there is no golden rule.'

There is no book.

There is no syllabus.

There is simply arriving every day at precisely seven o'clock, realizing that whatever was to come in the next ten or twelve or fourteen or sixteen or whatever hours would be completely unexpected, and arrive neatly packaged on her desk in shining gold paper, labeled with the word "Crisis."

And realizing also that there was an invisible sign outside her door from the time she walked into the building every morning, this sign reading:

I'M HERE. BRING IT ON.

And, of course, people did.

Monday morning, first official day back for Nina Bannister, 7:50 a.m.

Her office door opened, and Thelma Blankenship, her administrative assistant, said:

"A school bus, Nina, has just slid off the road."

"Oh, my God. Where?"

"Somewhere between Lee's Landing and Portageville (these being villages adjacent to Bay St. Lucy, but in the St. Lucy School District.)"

"Anybody hurt?"

"Apparently not. But they're just stuck out there."

The phone rang; Nina answered it.

"Yes? Yes, I've just been told about it. I'm taking care of it now. No. No, there's no injury. No, I'm not sure how it happened. No. No, it's certain that he wasn't drinking. No. No, I just know. That's Cal Taylor's bus. He's one of our best and most veteran drivers. Yes. Yes. No. No Yes No. I'm trying to get him on the phone now. No. No, we're sending an auxiliary bus out to pick them up. No No. Yes, definitely. Not at all. No there's no chance of that. Drugs were definitely not involved. I know it's cold, but the bus is heated. No. No, Cal knows to guard against carbon monoxide poisoning. He'll keep the heater on, but the children won't be asphyxiated. I'm sure of it. No, I did read something about that, and, yes, they did freeze to death, but that was in northern Alaska. No. No, definitely not. Yes. Yes, they will all be given excuses and not be counted late. I've just informed their teachers. Yes, I know who they are, and I'm calling their teachers. Yes, of course, you can call me any time."

Which they would.

And did, but that mattered little, because other crises came up, and still others.

They were all unimportant, though.

Only one truly important thing was scheduled for the first day back.

One essential thing.

That was, of course, the decoration of her office.

Until that happened, she was in limbo.

It did happen, though, shortly after lunch when the school van arrived carrying several boxes which she had stacked neatly, at six o'clock that morning, on her bottom step.

The boxes were brought in, and opened.

So that by one-thirty, the office looked as she wanted it.

A picture of Frank, a picture of her and Frank just married, a picture of her parents, a picture of her grandparents, a picture of Furl, a picture of her and Margot, a picture of Elementals: Treasures from the Earth and Sea, a picture of her and John Giusti and Helen Giusti just married, two ivy plants, a picture of her beach shack with the sun going down behind it, a stuffed dog, a copy of her Bachelor's Degree, two blue pennants with the word 'Mariner' on them, a stuffed rabbit, a stuffed bear, fifteen books of various kinds, a pillow, a big spherical glass that had snow falling in it when you shook it, a calendar, several ball point pens, a stapler, two reams of copy paper, a mouse pad for the computer—

—and the nameplate that said NINA BANNISTER: PRINCIPAL.

After that, it was all something one did by instinct.

And she had the instinct.

She didn't know when or how she had developed it.

Some people never did, or never would.

And she could not have explained how she knew what was going to happen after school at the end of her first day.

She just did.

Perhaps word of it had filtered down through the ventilation system.

Perhaps she had overheard it talked of in another language, the language of students.

How did she know?

No matter; she just did.

So that she was standing in a particular place in the hall when fifth period bell rang. Normal hall chaos ensued. Bodies flew by here and there and someone ran into the blue and white Mariner mascot, knocking its paper Mache sword loose and separating the gold ring from its ear.

No matter. That could be cleaned up later.

Somehow, though, she singled out a student who was hurtling by in the flood of youthful humanity, much as a wrangler might cut out an unbranded calf, and, by means of an assortment of judo holds and subtle jabs and uppercuts disguised as gestures of affection, mangled him into a space beside the water fountain, where relative calm reigned.

"Hey Jeremy."

"Hello, Ms. Bannister."

"What's going on, Jeremy?"

"Not much."

"Really?"

"Not much at all, Ma'am."

"Nothing at all?"

"No, Ma'am."

"That's not what I'm hearing, Jeremy."

"Well…"

"So what's going on?"

"I guess, maybe, I'm not sure, but, just guessing, some kids might be getting together."

"That so?"

"Just what I'm hearing. Don't know who told me."

"Sure."

"Just, you know, just getting together."

"This afternoon?"

"I guess."

"Where?"

"I wouldn't know about that. Not exactly."

"Where?"

"That lot behind the old Dairy Queen that's closed."

"When?"

"I don't know for sure."

"When?"

"Right after school."

"You going to be there?"

"Not sure."

"You going to be there?"

"No, Ma'am."

"Good. Well. You have a nice rest of the day, Jeremy."

"Yes, Ma'am."

And Jeremy disappeared.

An hour and a half later, she was in the school's mini-van, approaching Bay St. Lucy's most disreputable neighborhood. It was not really a 'neighborhood' at all, though it had at one time been so. But it had fallen into disrepair and neglect, as certain areas do, for no discernable reason. It had been home to prosperous middle class families (though never to wealthy ones). These had been replaced by a certain economic level of off-shore oil workers who lived in the homes only sporadically and thus allowed them to decay; these had been replaced by painters, curio makers, and postcard writers, who lived as artists do and there needed nothing more to be said about that; and these last had been replaced by nothing at all except the novelist and drunkard Tom Broussard, who inhabited a shack that was safe to live in merely because the area had become feared by the town's criminals and was inhabited only by stray dogs that had gotten poisoned somewhere else and had come there to die.

Somehow, improbably, in the mix of all this, was the shell of an ancient Dairy Queen, its red neon sign crumbling, the pavement of its parking lot cracked and weed infested.

The sun hung low in the winter sky, a dusky plate covered by the volcanic ash that passed for cloud cover over southern Mississippi in this somehow simultaneously benign and threatening off-time of year.

She got out of the minivan.

A rabble of students stood before her looking like zombies, but staring at her as though she was the zombie.

In many schools this was something coaches would have taken care of.

Big coaches, their heads shaven bald, whistles dangling around their meaty necks.

But Nina was—well, not the kind of principal to leave things to other people.

"Afternoon, everybody."

Silence.

Faces looking down.

A few nervous giggles.

The zombies getting together at the dead Dairy Queen to bury onion rings and disembowel hot dogs.

"What's going on?"

No answer of course.

Small conversations.

Snide remarks.

An indeterminate and chirpy voice from somewhere in the crowd:

"Good afternoon to you, Ma'am!"

Laughter.

She stepped forward.

She was now in the middle of a circle of students.

Chuckles, animal noises, more giggles, and the imitation of various body parts.

"Who's fighting?"

Silence.

Even the giggles stopped.

"Who's fighting?"

Finally one gawky red-headed boy appeared, having taken one step into the center of the circle of onlookers. He'd taken off his shirt.

"Tom Baxter," she said.

She knew him, of course, from church, and from the fact that she'd taught both his parents.

"Yes, Ma'am."

"Who are you fighting today, Tom?"

Nina sensed movement behind her and turned.

Another boy, a bigger one, a swarthier one, a more menacing one, a living boy who would have been less menacing had he in fact been a zombie and thus to some degree decayed—stepped forward and said nothing.

She stared at him for a second or so, then said:

"Tony Zerrapini."

Tony Zerrapini nodded.

The center of a hurricane hung over them. Air pressure dropped by fifty points or so and Nina asked herself the question that had often formed in her mind, namely, which was more terrible despite its romantic and completely deceptive veneer: violence itself, or the moments preceding it?

"Tony, your father is working on an oil rig right now. Fifteen miles offshore. Your mother's cleaning fish down at the wharf. Tom, I've taught both of your parents. Years ago. I've known all of you for more years than I remember."

Then:

"This is Bay St. Lucy. We're a community here. We work together: always have."

Dead silence for a few seconds.

Ten seconds.

An eternity.

"We're not in school now," came a voice from the back of the crowd.

To which Nina, in something like a split second, replied:

"Yes you are."

More silence.

She repeated:

"Yes you are."

From somewhere in the distance came the wail of a siren.

It grew louder, then faded away.

"Shit," said somebody.

The crowd began to disperse.

Somehow the two antagonists had disappeared.

Within two minutes she was standing by herself.

CHAPTER 5: THE OXFORD MAN

On Tuesday morning she arrived at 6:55 a.m., opened the door to the high school, walked inside, opened the door to the central office, and found the lights on.

A pot of coffee was percolating.

"Hi there!"

Flitting about in the ante-room that adjoined her office was a man of indeterminate age, about five feet ten in height, shaggy of hair, a pendant of some kind (was that a silver werewolf hanging from it? Surely not.), wire-rimmed glasses, sandals, and a greenish sport jacket that seemed to have been plucked from one of the large bins in the city center labeled "For the Less Fortunate."

"I hope you don't mind that I've brought my own coffee; one does get used to certain pleasure, don't you know."

British.

Long-haired, disheveled, and British.

"I thought I should get a good start on the day. You, too, or so it seems. Are you in maintenance?"

"I'm—"

"Because I'm afraid I have to tell you, one of the loos is stopped up."

"One of the what?"

"The loos. Stopped up, you know. Not working. Or—oh, that's right, you call them 'WCs' over here, don't you?"

"We call them toilets."

"Well, at any rate, one of them isn't working right. Popped in there half an hour ago to, you know, eliminate last night's ingestives, that sort of thing, and—well, it looks a total mess. Thought you might want to know."

"I do."

"Yes, well, not the kind of thing one loves talking about, but there it is. Will you have some coffee?"

"Thank you."

"This is a special blend. Some mates sent it to me from Leicester. It's somewhat like gin, isn't it? Gin and tea and beer, none of them even extant in this country in any consumable form. Of course, the gin can be disposed of for a day or so but not the coffee and certainly not the tea. Oh! Are there strictures about smoking?"

"You can't."

"What?"

"You can't."

"I'm not talking about pot, you know. I simply mean…"

"You can't."

"Why in God's name not?"

"Cancer."

"But isn't that my own concern?"

"No."

"Blast. Do you mean to tell me there is no place at all where one might smoke a fag?"

"The docks."

"You're joking. It can't be true!"

"Well, now that I think about it, it may not be true. I think they've made that a no smoking zone too."

"My God, what a country! How can you live here?"

"It's tough."

"Of course, it is! Well, there it is then. Nothing to be done about it. So. I must tell you though—despite your infantile Puritanism—I love your town. Absolutely love it."

"Glad to hear that."

"You know, it's very much like Cornwall. Have you seen Cornwall?"

"No, I haven't."

"You must go."

"All right."

"You would be struck by the similarities. Of course, there's a kind of, I dunno, a kind of 'craggy grandeur' about Cornwall that you don't get here."

"No, we miss that."

"But that quality of earth and sky, and roar of the ocean sort of, I don't know, sort of—imploding against man and yet bringing him back to his sources. It's all very Masefield for want of a better term. I'm not keeping you from your duties, am I?"

"No, no."

"Do you like the coffee?"

"I do. It's wonderful. Who are you?"

"What?"

"Who are you?"

"In what sense?"

"Identity sense."

"Oh you want my—"

"Name. Like—who you are. What you're called."

"Oh that!"

"Yes!"

"Lirpa. Max Lirpa. The name is Italian, but I was conceived in Oxford and grew up there. I'm here to teach English. Just hired some days ago, actually."

"Oh, my God."

"Pardon?"

"Nothing."

"I suppose I'll be meeting the students shortly."

"Yes. Yes, you will."

"And you're in maintenance, you say?"

"Actually I'm the principal."

"The what?"

"The principal."

"You mean the Headmistress?"

"You could put it that way."

"Oh! Then I'm honored!"

"Me too."

"So what are the students like? I'm dreadfully curious."

"The students are curious too, Max, and some of them are pretty dreadful."

"Are they versed in Byron?"

"No."

"Chaucer then?"

"No."

"My word. What are they versed in?"

"Justin Bieber."

"Well, that's a start. Are they somewhat mature intellectually? Can they handle scatological or phallic imagery?"

"They don't know what those things are."

"Well, then, we shall have to teach them, shan't we?"

"No."

People began arriving. A few students, a few teachers—there was the rattle of lockers, the click-clacking of doors being unlocked—

—there was Eunice Duncan, head of the English department, who, being a woman of some heft and little height, had allowed her immensely thick winter jacket to turn her into a spherical object, which appeared to be rolling down the hall followed by a box-like object, which was a computer cart that rolled behind her.

"Eunice, this is Max Lirpa."

Oh, my God, Eunice could be seen thinking.

Oh my God Oh my God—

"—it's nice to meet you, Max."

"And you too, I'm sure."

"Eunice, as you know, this is Max's first day. He comes to us from the British Isles."

"So I've heard, so I've heard!"

"And I wonder if you might show him his classroom, and, well, kind of get him started."

"I'll be happy to!"

"Good, then! I've got a few things to do, so I'll see both of you a little later. Goodbye, Max!"

"Cheerio, Headmistress!"

"Just—just *principal*."

"All right then! Ta-ta!"

"Ta-ta!"

Nina turned away.

She walked back into her office, saying good morning to Ms. Johnson who taught history, and to Pearl Emory, an administrative assistant who was just then taking the cover off her computer.

She closed the door and locked it.

This was a disaster.

How could Jackson Bennett have been so stupid?

He must have heard the words ‘Oxford’ and simply lost his mind.

This man was an *impossible* fit for any public high school in Mississippi, even a rather liberal one like Bay St. Lucy!

Phallic imagery?

Are you crazy, Jackson?

She thought about this the entire day.

At two-fifty—end of fifth period—she forced herself to be close to Werewolf Man’s classroom when students came emptying out of it.

She buttonholed a group of three girls.

“Hello, young ladies. I’m Ms. Bannister.”

“We know! How are you, ma’am?”

“I’m fine. Did you just come from English?”

“Yes, ma’am!”

“Learn a lot?”

“I’m not sure,” said one of them. “We talked about a poem called ‘Naming of Parts.’ It’s supposed to be about the parts of a gun, but when you read it closer, it’s about…”

“I know what it’s about,” she said.

She spent the rest of the afternoon hidden in her office.

That night at the basketball game, a group of mothers spotted her, seated on the highest row of the gym.

It was halftime; she was eating a hot dog.

“Ms. Bannister?”

“Yes?”

“We’re parents of students at the high school.”

“Oh. Good.”

They all looked like the mothers of high school students: pinched, arch, worried, the joy of youth having left them, the mindless pleasantries of dementia still too far off to be hoped for.

“What may I do for you?”

"Well, hope this isn't the wrong time to talk to you."

"No. Not at all."

"It's just that—well, we know you're a new principal. And we thought you should know what's happening in the school."

"I would like to know."

The group closing tighter about her.

"Our kids have a new English teacher."

"Mr. Lirpa?"

"That's his name. Did you know anything about him?"

"Some. Just a bit."

"Were you involved in hiring him?"

"Actually I wasn't."

"Well, we just wanted to let you know."

"Please do."

"Today they studied poetry."

"Yes."

"And my son said it was the best class he'd ever had in his life."

"Mine too."

"Mine too."

"So did my daughter."

"Well. That's good to hear!"

"We just wanted you to know."

"I'm glad you told me."

"Enjoy the game."

"I'm sure I will. I'm sure I will."

She went home and drank half a bottle of wine.

CHAPTER 6: THE UNCERTAIN GLORY OF AN APRIL DAY

"Now she hates me. I have taught her that, at least."
—William Faulkner, *Light in August*

Several things happened on Friday morning, the last school day before Christmas break.

First, it rained.

It rained hard, as though the weather was exacting payment from Bay St. Lucy for the penurious little snifter of snow it had rationed out some days before. You want some snow to let your kids slide around in and to inspire you to sing Bing Crosby songs? Okay, but it's going to cost you! Here, take six and a half inches of rain!

Cold rain.

Rain that came down horizontally in a thirty mile an hour north wind; that rattled and spattered on Nina's window, that made Furl want to put his cold little nose up against the plate glass and stare through it, waving his tail slowly and thinking:

"I'm one of the chosen cats. The indoor cats. The hell with all the rest of them."

It also made Nina realize that most high ranking school officials—or low ranking school officials, for that matter—

—or anybody at all, for that matter—

—had a car.

Most people did not sputter around on Vespas, saving money on gas mileage and waving merrily to shop owners and pedestrians, but foregoing advantages such as speeds above ten MPH or sounds from radios or protection from driving rain.

Such as this.

How was she going to get to school?

The Nina of the last months, the last years, would simply have brewed herself a pot of tea, texted Margo that she would not be coming in, fed Furl, watered Furl, unlittered and littered Furl, forgotten about Furl, and then curled like a sow bug beneath her down comforter to read about English people murdering each other in villages with several names (Eaton Vale on the Donnybrook, or whatever), until some human necessity or other made her get up and pad about.

But not now.

Now she had to eat a quick bite of breakfast, poke around in her closet, lug out the heavy yellow slicker, find and extract the galoshes (the snow boots were so much more fun! They looked like Captain Kirk; these looked like Tugboat Annie). Put them on.

Take several deep breaths.

And wade out into the storm.

It roared and pattered and howled and saturated around her, obscuring the trees on Ocean View Boulevard, which now offered no ocean view and had been transformed into Ocean Obscured Panamacanal way.

She somehow managed to ignore the four-inch pool of water that the galoshes were failing at keeping out of her wool socks while she unchained the Vespa, straddled it, turned it on, and backed up.

An angel assigned specifically to her hovered just inches above her yellow vinyl rain hood and poured an even and steady stream of water on the visor, so that it trickled down onto her glasses and kept them barely transparent enough to see through.

Heading up the oyster shell lane, chug chug chug, pothole here SPLASH pothole there SPLASH and the wind driving at her as she drove into it, always lashing away at her face, as though it changed direction every time she did, never mind which damned direction anyway, just as long as it could be blowing straight into her.

Chug chug SPLASH—chug chug SPLASH.

Had a good time with your precious snow, eh? Well this is for YOU, Nina! And your little dog, too!

Or cat, whatever.

HOW ABOUT A LITTLE *RAIN*, SCARECROW!?

So that, then, was the first thing that happened on Friday morning.

The second thing that happened was an 8:15 conference with Sonia Ramirez, her mother, her history teacher (Ms. Douglas), her math teacher (Coach Burris), her science teacher (Coach Jorganson) and her English teacher (Ms. Forbes).

Sonia had been having problems.

She was a very nice girl, everyone agreed, and she was an excellent outside shooter and ball handler (eleven points last night and five assists against Portageville, very nice job, Sonia, very nice job). She also seemed to have a good mind. She was not doing that badly in math, which seemed her best subject. But the other subjects—no, the others were not going so well. She'd fallen behind in science, and far behind in English (several failing grades on essays, *Wuthering Heights* remaining unread)—and had a very poor understanding of Herodotus' *Commentaries on The Peloponnesian War*, which was, and had been for some time now, required reading for any Mississippi sophomore.

What was the problem?

Several theories were discussed, each teacher making a contribution in turn, both Sonia and her mother nodding in consternation and agreement.

Diet.

Be certain Sonia had a good breakfast each day.

Routine.

Be certain she had time each evening to do her homework.

Help.

Be sure she had a mentor to help her after every assignment.

Eyesight.

Have her eyes checked. Perhaps she needed glasses.

(Although the fact that she'd nailed two three-pointers from well beyond the arch the night before seemed somewhat to belie this theory.)

And this theory and that theory and this theory and that theory for twenty minutes or so, all of it coming to an end by 8:30 thirty when everybody had to be back in class, and the meeting breaking up with the mutual assurance of all concerned that these things would continue to be tried until a solution was found and Sonia had begun to perform up to the level everyone knew she was capable of reaching.

The fact that Sonia did not speak English was not mentioned.

Because there was not a helluva lot anybody could do about that.

So why worry about it?

And the meeting was adjourned.

That was the second thing that happened on Friday morning.

The third thing was, she heard from the ghost-hunting Margot Gavin.

It was early afternoon. Her cell phone rang, and she opened it.

"Nina Bannister..."

"Hey Nina!"

"Margot! You're back!"

"I am."

"What kept you? I thought you were only going to stay a week; it's almost two weeks now."

"Well…it's complicated."

"I want to hear all about it."

"And so you shall, my dear"

"Great. By the way, did you hear already? Meg Brennan and Jennifer Warren are getting married!"

"Wonderful!"

"Isn't it? There's a wedding shower planned for them tomorrow night."

"Excellent. What time?"

"Seven."

"Where is it to be?"

"Your shop."

"Ah. Well, good. I was worried that I wouldn't be able to find it."

"No such worries now."

"No indeed. Have I been planning it for long?"

"About a week. You've sent out all the invitations."

"Good for me. I'm very proud of myself. By the way though, what was going to happen if I hadn't made it back to Bay St. Lucy on time?"

"I would have opened the shop—I have a key, you know—and ordered a lot of liquor in your name. Nobody would have missed you."

"Did you order the liquor anyway?"

"Of course I did."

"Splendid."

"By the way, Margot…"

"Yes?"

"Did you find a ghost?"

Pause.

Did Margot's voice soften slightly?

"Yes," she said. "Yes I did."

It may have softened, or it may not have.

But whatever had happened to it, the humor had disappeared.

She meant it.

"I did meet several ghosts, Nina. But one of them—well. I'll tell you about it tomorrow night, at the shower."

For a moment, Nina knew nothing to say.

She finally settled on:

"Good to have you back, Margot."

"It's good to be back. I'll see you tomorrow."

"Sure. See you then."

And, so saying, she flipped her cell phone shut.

There followed two hours of chaotic bliss, since this was Friday, and the last Friday, before a long holiday.

"One o'clock! Not much time to go!"

"What are you going to do tomorrow?"

"I'm going to sleep late!"

"Ha ha ha! Ha ha ha! Give me some of that egg nog!"

The students were in a festive mood too, of course, but they were locked in classrooms. The teachers and staff members, at liberty to roam the halls and pop in and out of various offices, felt no restraints and gave vent to the POTENTIAL HOLIDAY FRENZY that arises inevitably from the fact that no one hates school as much as the people who have to run it.

Two o'clock.

Two forty-five.

What could go wrong?

NOTHING COULD GO WRONG, THE DAY WAS ALMOST OVER—

And something did go wrong.

At precisely three o'clock, a man wearing a uniform—not an athletic uniform but a uniform like those worn by hotel bellmen or butlers in old movies—walked into the school, asked to see Ms. Bannister, the principal, and said to her:

"Your car is waiting, Ma'am."

This pretty much stopped things in the office.

Ms. Peterson, Ms. Forbes, Ms. Janekosky, Tommy Lawrence, Lakeesha Roosevelt, and Coach Suggs (the offensive line coach in fall and the drivers' training teacher the rest of the time), all froze.

The man, who was standing, framed in Nina's doorway, his blue captain's hat held under his arm, repeated:

"Ma'am, your car is waiting."

Nina, who'd been sitting at her desk wondering whether to go over attendance reports or attempt the *New York Times* Friday crossword puzzle (which she had never succeeded in doing) rose, looked at everybody in the outer office, each of whom was looking back at her, and asked, firmly:

"What car?"

"For the yacht, Ma'am."

"The yacht."

"Yes, Ma'am."

Don't ask what yacht, don't ask what yacht, don't ask what yacht—

"What yacht?"

"*The Sea Beagle*."

"*The Sea Beagle*."

"Yes, Ma'am."

"Well, I hate to tell you, young man, but I—"

At which point, Pearl Johnson, not the main administrative assistant (secretary), but the associate administrative assistant (secretary), stepped out into the middle of the anteroom, slapped both of her palms against her cheeks, so that her face began to resemble Edward Munch's great and frightening painting "The Scream," and uttered the scream:

"Oh, my God."

Silence.

The rain had become harder; it now sounded as though a stream of gravel was being poured upon the roof of the building.

"Oh, my God. I'm sorry."

The conversation did not seem, Nina thought, to be giving her many options.

"For what?" she said, which, like 'what yacht' a minute ago, was obviously the only thing she could say.

"I forgot to tell you."

Nina nodded:

"You forgot to tell me something about a yacht?"

"Yes, Ma'am."

"Well, that begins to clarify things a little bit."

"You're supposed to go to a yacht after school today."

"I see."

"Now, actually."

"And the reason?"

"The press conference."

"What press conference?"

"A Doctor van Tinsdale or van Mothdale or…"

'Van Osdale? April van Osdale?"

"I forgot the name exactly. It sounded something like that. They called early this morning to invite you but you were in with Ms. Ramirez and we were trying to find a substitute for Mr. Thompson and somebody found a condom in—"

Nina interrupted, not wishing to hear more details concerning the condom, or its location, or its owner, or its destination.

"It's all right. I'd heard there was going to be a press conference, but I thought it was going to be after Christmas."

"No, ma'am. It's today."

"I also assumed it was going to take place downtown somewhere."

"No, ma'am. It's on the yacht."

"And I really didn't know I was invited."

"Yes, ma'am. You are."

"Well, then—"

Nina looked back at the young man who had initially brought this news, and who was, she now realized, a chauffeur.

Whose chauffeur?

Probably the chauffeur of the man whose yacht it was.

And so, every day has its little surprises.

She walked around her desk, assembled her rain gear, smiled at the man standing in the doorway, and said:

"Let's go to the yacht."

And that (her going to a yacht) became the fourth thing to happen on Friday afternoon.

"And when I say women I don't mean you."
—William Faulkner, *Soldiers' Pay*

The limousine was the color of the rain, which was the color of the mud running in dark rivulets across the school parking lot, which was the color of the sky, which was the color of the ocean.

All of these elements ran together, so that all she really remembered was being tugged or pushed gently from one place to another—the school road, the beach drive, the wharf, the motor launch, the boat ramp—until, someone's sensitive hands peeling her rain gear off her, she was ushered below decks into a stateroom the size and splendor of the Robinson Mansion.

She looked around her.

It did remind her of the Robinson Mansion!

And if that opulent palace, as rebuilt by old mob money and Eve Ivory's taste, had resembled the sunken Titanic inverted and put right, this yacht's interior—had she ever been in a yacht before? Maybe, but not this kind of yacht—reversed the process, taking a mansion, and making it a seagoing thing.

All glass and brass, all shining mahogany hand rails and thick colorless carpeting, hutches smiling with dishware and cutlery, paintings of ships and enlarged group pictures with various United States presidents grinning and shaking hands.

A waiter, his shirt starched and white, skin starched and white, approached her and smiled:

"Welcome to *The Sea Beagle*, ma'am."

"Thank you."

"Can I get you something to drink?"

"Cup of coffee?"

"Of course. Would you care for a pastry?"

"Just the coffee will be fine."

She looked around her at the milling crowd. There was a familiar face here or there, but for the most part, these were people she did not know well, because they were the truly wealthy set of Bay St. Lucy.

Among them were people in BIG OIL.

The owner of *The Sea Beagle*, she remembered having heard, was a highly placed executive in Mississippi Oil and Petroleum, the corporation that ran one of the huge drilling platforms forty miles or more offshore.

These were people who played golf in foursomes. They wore suits to work and were proud of their ties.

She filtered through the crowd, and several people, a few men, a few women, felt sorry for her and introduced themselves.

"Tom Harkness. I'm in digital sales."

"Hi, I'm Jill. My husband and I do financial analysis."

"I'm Morgan Carpenter. I'm a systems engineer."

Her mind went back to Sonia Ramirez, who was struggling to learn how to conjugate the verb "the."

"Good luck, Sonia," she whispered to herself.

And then there were lights flashing in the front of the room—

—or 'fore,' she probably should have said—

—and there, scurrying around like mice attempting to flee the ship, were two reporters she recognized from *The Bay St. Lucy Gazette*.

They were not alone.

More reporters now.

And TV cameras.

Which produced, conjured up as though from celestial education dust—

April van Osdale.

There she was.

After at least fifteen years.

April van Osdale. Who must now have been in her late thirties, but who seemed ageless.

April van Osdale was a cake. With a long, tangled, glowing, blonde wig.

She looked like something that had been baked and decorated.

She also wore not make-up, but frosting.

Everything about her was artificial—including the massive, curled, flowing, upswept blonde, blonde, blonde wig—and always had been, dating back to that afternoon years earlier when she had walked into the study room and extended a vanilla greeting and a marzipan hand, saying:

"I'm April. You must be Nina."

No one had ever said anything more damning to her.

The study sessions—there had been three of them during the semester—had turned into nightmares. Each had involved four women: Nina, April, and two others. The task had been to prepare oral reports on Thomas Dewey or some educator or theoretician or another. April had never been satisfied with the work of her co-reporters.

"We don't want an 'A' on this project, ladies. We want an 'A+.' Or at least I do."

It was during the second session that she had stood and screamed:

"I WILL NOT BE ASSOCIATED WITH—WITH SECOND RATE PEOPLE!"

The second rate people, Nina remembered, had sat in stunned silence.

April had gone to the teacher, requesting not a new group, but the chance to be her own group.

To do the report by herself.

The teacher had refused, of course, citing some gibberish about it being a good thing to learn to work with other people—gibberish, because April herself, though certainly 'other,' was hardly a person and April had returned for a third attempt, during which Nina had sprung to her feet and would have leveled at her a stream of obscenities had she known any obscenities other than "Shame on you!"

They received a "B-" on the report.

April never spoke to any of them again.

And now she was at the speaker's stand, waiting for the hubbub surrounding her to diminish.

Her suit was perfectly pressed, perfectly white, and expertly trimmed in cherry-flavored ice cream.

Nina was perhaps thirty feet away from her, and could not stop staring at her face, upon which there were neither age lines nor wrinkles. Had they been removed by medical procedures or had they never come into existence in the first place? Did April van Osdale have finger prints?

No, the woman had sprung fully-formed from a seed pod, like the creatures from some science fiction movie that had postulated the overthrow of earth by spores floating through space.

Perhaps that was it: perhaps she was not a cake at all but a flower, or a greenhouse orchid.

What had it been about her that had so disturbed, so frightened Nina, even from the first moments?

Not her unbridled, stupendous, unceasing, and measureless ambition, for many people had been ambitious.

No, it was simply the fact that she was not real.

What seemed to be there was not really there.

And what was there in place of what should have been?

"Thank you! Thank you all! I want you all to know how grateful I and the senator—and all of the senator's supporters at the capitol—are for your support. You make us feel very special!"

Applause.

"As you all know, I've recently been appointed to work with school officials here in this part of our state. I see my job as extremely important, blah de blah de blah…

More applause.

Nodding of heads.

Mutter mutter mutter—

"Our children, as you know, are our most important blah de blah de blah—"

And after what seemed another fourteen or fifteen hours of 'the test scores must rise,' and such not, but was really only two minutes of real time—

—the speech was over.

April van Osdale stepped down from the podium.

There was a mild hubbub surrounding the podium for a time, and Nina, almost against her will, found herself drifting forward, magnetized toward the polar ice cap that was this woman.

She was going to have to greet her.

And how would that go?

If she had never in her life met and tried to work with a woman she so completely despised, did the same not hold true for April? Did she not continue to despise Nina?

Probably.

Of course, it would be masked.

Nina was a principal now and April was surrounded by the press. There would be a frothy and sugar-laden show of surprise and joy.

"Oh, how good it is to see you Nina! How long has it been? It's going to be so good working together again!"

But would there be a momentary glint of iron gray in those flinty eyes peering out of the confection that was masquerading as a face?

Would there be just hint of the old animosity?

Well, no more time to speculate, one way or another.

Nina was near the podium now, three golfers in front of her, now two data consultants, now one off-shore exporter—

—and now April van Osdale.

Standing there, in the yeast, if not in the flesh, before her.

She extended her hand.

"Hello, April. It's been a long time."

April van Osdale stared back into her face, blinked once, stared a bit longer, and finally asked:

"Do I know you?"

There was a pause.

After a time, Nina shook her head, said:

"No."

Then she turned around and left.

"When I have one martini, I feel bigger, wiser, taller. When I have a second, I feel superlative. When I have more, there's no holding me."

—William Faulkner

Saturday morning was spent running back and forth to Margot's, answering the shop door to accept presents, arranging presents, telling Margot all about her adventures as principal, waiting for Margot to tell her all about the ghost she'd encountered at this haunted plantation/artists' retreat, mixing punch bowls, and making sure all was in readiness. All this joy Nina might have shared, of course, had it not been for her rage at being snubbed—forgotten actually—by April van Osdale.

How could this woman have the gall, the unmitigated gall, not to hate back as much as she was hated?

"Do I know you?"

PULEEEZE!

True, Nina had not thought much about April van Osdale during the last fifteen years. But there was a special little niche in her brain reserved for bitter enemies, and that niche was sacrosanct. It was an important place. What kind of a lifetime was it that might be spent wholly devoid of just the smallest piece of utter detestation?

Why, no life at all, obviously!

And April van Osdale, as horrid a human being as she was, must have an especially large niche.

But Nina wasn't even worthy of being in it!

The woman had dismissed her exactly as Lysander had dismissed Hermia in *A Midsummer Night's Dream*:

"Get you gone, you dwarf; you minimus of hindring knot glass made, you bead, you acorn!"

April van Snobbery, surrounded and adored by all those reporters, while Nina stood invisible in the back of the crowd.

Nina should have screamed back at her:

"Are you grown so high in their esteem because I am so dwarfish and so low? How low am I thou painted maypole?"

That's what you are, April van Osdale! You're a painted maypole!

Damn her!

But, by and large, her rage subsided.

So that the afternoon could be spent in her shack, taking a nap.

And then, as dusk settled and the street lamps of Bay St. Lucy began emitting their soft blue glow and God's fingernail of a new moon hovered over the hills to the west of town, the guests began arriving and the shower of Meg and Jennifer came into being.

It was a perfect shower, just the way Nina had planned it.

The gifts were beautiful.

Meg and Jennifer were radiant.

There were many laughs about Margot chasing ghosts, and thus almost missing the shower.

Nina thought of her favorite banquet toast:

"I shall dine late, but the room will be well lighted, and the guests few and select."

You have dined late, Meg and Jenny, she found herself thinking.

A lot of years.

But the lights were right in this room, and the guests were few and select.

And the punch was viciously spiked.

It must have been eight o'clock or so when, holding a glass of it up high, and spying Meg and Jennifer holding hands on the far side of the room, Nina shouted out her toast:

"To those who are about to wed!"

All eyes, smiling, stayed fixed on the couple for an instant.

But only for an instant.

Then they turned.

Nina was aware of movement behind her, and she turned, too.

Margot Gavin was standing up.

CHAPTER 7: A CHRISTMAS IDYLL

"You don't want your hands froze on Christmas, do you?"

—William Faulkner, *The Sound and the Fury*

Christmas Eve had, for some time following Frank's passing, been a difficult time for Nina. The two of them had always exchanged gifts at precisely nine p.m. (There was no particular reason for that time, but ritual had somehow taken root, and could not be changed). Then they had watched a film version of *A Child's Christmas in Wales*, the beautiful Dylan Thomas narrative.

For years, they'd lived in the old house on Magnolia Avenue which had a fireplace. There were only a few nights of the year cold enough to warrant a fire, but Frank insisted on building one every Christmas Eve, and so it was always there, crackling and glowing, while they drank a glass of mulled wine and sang "All Through the Night" at the film's closing.

The first years without him were hard every night, but that one night—that one was particularly difficult.

It was better now though.

She had her own place and had grown in time to enjoy making it cozy and habitable.

The mournful growling of the sea comforted rather than depressed her; and the small artificial tree in the corner of the shack's main room; the photographs of loved ones hanging on the walls; the various decorations that had been sent to her over the years by relatives; the Christmas cards that had come during the previous week—all of these things made her feel snug and secure in the little Nina-Cave that she had hollowed out here on this remote stretch of

Mississippi sand and water, and if the new moon sparkled clear and high in the sky, as it was doing tonight, why, so much the better.

There was a bit more of a melancholy touch than usual this particular Christmas Eve, of course, because she was now faced with the prospect of losing Margot, her best friend.

'Losing?' That was putting it a bit harshly, was it not?

Margot was not dying.

But she was getting married.

She was selling Elementals: Treasures from the Earth and Sea, the shop that had become almost a second home to Nina.

And she was, almost certainly, moving away from Bay St. Lucy to join her new husband—a psychologist of all things—in running The Candles, the dilapidated plantation that Chicago money was to transform into a retreat for writers, actors, and painters.

The shock of hearing all this news the night of Meg and Jenny's shower still pained her.

That was, of course, what Margot had meant about encountering a ghost.

An old acquaintance.

One she knew would be looking over the plantation along with her.

A man she had always gotten along well with, but had never…

…well, never thought about in precisely that way.

"And I don't think he had ever thought of me in that way. But we were glad to see each other. It was fun to stroll about on the grounds, and laugh about how dreadfully boring the other people were, and speculate about how much it would cost to fix up this or bring in a new one of that…"

"…and then, somehow, we both realized it was changing."

"So strange. I could have sworn I was—well, past all of that."

"I suppose one never is."

No.

Nina knew, of course, that she was past all of that. There would never be another Frank.

But Margot had never had a Frank. Not that one irreplaceable person.

Well, now perhaps, she would have.

Good for her.

A bit of sadness for Nina though and another hole in her life that would have to be filled in somehow.

But she could do it. She had filled in one hole and could find ways to fill another.

So she was not that sad as she sat in her main room, the reading light glowing above her left shoulder, a paperback book open on her lap, and the blue cell phone sitting motionless on the small table beside her.

Nine o'clock.

She took pleasure in knowing that the phone would ring soon, and it would ring several times in the following hour. Frank's sister would call from Shreveport. It was always good to hear from her. Tom and Phyllis, a couple she and Frank had enjoyed many good times with, would call from Little Rock.

And there were two or three others, old friends, even a few acquaintances from here in Bay St. Lucy.

Alanna Delafosse would undoubtedly call.

Always a pleasure to hear from Alanna, who seemed in a state of perpetual ecstasy, whether the occasion was Christmas Eve or some dreary Monday morning in late February.

It was a game she enjoyed playing as she sat and watched the little phone.

Nine fifteen now.

Who would call first?

What news would she be told?

What cheery bit of business would further add to the quiet sanctity of the evening?

A minute later the phone did ring.

She flipped it open and said, excitedly:

"This is Nina! Merry Christmas! Who is it?"

"Moon Rivard down at the sheriff's office. Some guy named Max Lirpa is here drunk. You need to post bail for him."

"I…"

"He's here with Tom Broussard. Broussard's drunk too. Better get here quick before I kill one of them."

"All right."

Moon hung up.

And there it was: Nina's Christmas present!

"No man can write who is not first a humanitarian"
—William Faulkner

Bay St. Lucy's jail was not a nice place. It could not have been labeled 'convivial.' It exuded no sense of intimacy and it lacked the warmth that Nina had felt while sitting comfortably in her arm chair.

No, rather it was dank, rusted, murky, dirty, cheerless, cold, cramped, and stinking of urine. Its walls would have been completely covered by the vilest known graffiti, had it not been for the fact that the bile green paint upon which this graffiti had been scrawled was constantly peeling off and disintegrating in small pools of some kind of acid which continually collected on the concrete floor.

She did not like it.

She did not like having to visit it.

Especially on Christmas Eve.

And so she was in no better mood than Moon Rivard was when he let her into the sheriff's office, offered her a cup of coffee (she did not accept), sat her down at a desk, gave her several papers to sign, and asked for a check for two hundred dollars.

She wondered if there was that much in her account.

Oh, well, what could they do to her if the check bounced?

Put her in jail?

My God, they could, couldn't they?

"What were they doing?"

Moon scratched his iron gray hair and shook his iron gray head.

"Fighting. Drunk as skunks and fighting. This Lirpa guy gave me your name, said you'd come down and get him out. Apparently he doesn't know anybody else in town. How do you know him?"

"He's a teacher."

"A what?"

"A teacher."

"The hell he is!"

"I know, I know, it seems strange, but there it is."

"What does the damned fool teach?"

"English."

"Is that what he's speaking?"

"It is when he's sober; I don't know what he's speaking now. What about Tom, how is he getting out?"

"I called Penelope down at the docks. She's on her way over here now."

"Mad?"

Moon rolled his eyes.

"That woman knows words…"

"I know. Maybe it would have been better to keep Tom in jail. He would have been safe, anyway."

"Yeah, maybe. Except I ain't about to stay here all night with those two tomcats. I got a family to get home to. It's Christmas Eve."

"Yes," she sighed. "Yes, it is."

"Well. Let's go down and get the English professor out of the can."

He led the way across the room, then opened a door which led down to the cells.

The winding stairway was narrow, and pools of water glistened as her sneakers plopped and splashed upon them.

Finally, the stairs opened into a small musky cave, illuminated only by light bulbs hanging bare and glowing dimly.

There, on a bench in the first cell, sat Max Lirpa.

There was a cut on his forehead.

He wore no shirt.

Tom Broussard lay on the bench beside him, passed out.

Max leapt to his feet upon seeing Nina.

He grasped the bars, then half turned and pointed to the motionless figure lying on the bench.

"This man," he shouted, "is a bleeding literary genius!"

"Oh, my God," said Nina, disgustedly.

"I was in the supermarket, see? The damned supermarket, of all places!"

"Max…"

"And I find this novel called *Delectably Disemboweled.* Nice title, what? Well anyway, it struck me as being so. So I buy the damn thing and take it back to the flat, and two hours later I finish it. 'You've got to talk to this writer!' I tell myself. Then, on the back page, I read his bio. Turns out he lives right here in Bay St. Lucy! Can you believe that?"

"No. No, I can never quite bring myself to believe that."

"So I ask around and find out where he lives. I go to see him. Great place he's got! Just where a writer should live."

"I suppose that's true," she said, quietly.

"You're bleedin' right it is! So anyway, we have a couple of beers together, then a couple more, then we think, why not go out and paint the damned town a little…"

"And then you wind up here."

"Not immediately. There were a couple of places we were in first."

She turned to Moon, whose shirt was two buttons opened as always, and who seemed to be trying to pull out his massive tangle of chest hairs one by one.

"Where did you find them?"

"Boozers by the Bay."

"They were fighting?"

"Some riggers."

"Any damage?"

"Not really. Owner had the good sense to get them outside. There were a couple of broken doors, couple of broken mirrors, a glass or two shattered, something about a pool cue, a busted out window, and somehow a dog got its lip cut."

"A dog."

"Yes, ma'am. We're still trying to piece it together."

"Those bloody off shore blokes!" Max screamed, balling up his fist and banging on the bars.

"They think they're so almighty tough! Not one of them, though, not one of them, is a match for a real literary man!"

Upon hearing the words 'literary man,' Tom Broussard grunted, swore inaudibly, and turned over on his stomach, where he passed out again.

"My God that man can write!" whispered Max Lirpa.

It was at this time that Penelope Royale arrived, hurtling down the stairs with the mincing delicacy of a rhinoceros.

She barged into the cell area, stared at Moon, then bellowed at him:

"YOU ----!! IF YOU-------I'LL-------AND---

"Yes, ma'am," Moon replied.

Then Penelope turned on Max:

"---!!"

She stopped to catch her breath.

He'd taken a step back, then another step as the fusillade continued.

Now he was standing pressed against the wall, staring at Penelope, his mouth open.

As for her, she was now glaring at Moon.

"Open the ---------------------- door!" she bellowed.

Nina had never heard a door described in such a way.

She stared at it; it seemed to shrink and cower.

Moon took from his pocket a key made for The Tower of London.

He turned it in the lock, yanked once, and pulled the door open.

Penelope, ignoring Max, somehow got her arms around her husband, and with massive strength, got him upright.

This action brought him into a semi-conscious state, so that he could look down at her as she was supporting him.

"Honey?"

She stroked his cheek with one of her massive palms and said, quietly:

"Are you all right, Baby?"

He nodded, a bit of brown drool seeping from his mouth as he did so.

"I think so."

"Let's go home, Darling. I'll take you to the boat. You'll be okay."

He nodded, dazedly:

"All right."

Somehow the tangle of muscle and hair and vomit and flesh that was now both of them lurched and staggered its way up the stairwell.

Penelope turned and said to Moon:

"-----!"

Then she said to Max:

"-----!"

Then she disappeared up the stairwell.

Max Lirpa continued to stare at the now empty stairs for a time.

Finally, he walked to the now open cell door, looked at Nina, and said:

"What a magnificent woman."

Nina turned and left.

CHAPTER 8: FIRST MEETING

"And I reckon them that are good must suffer for it the same as them that are bad."

—William Faulkner, *Light in August*

On Monday, January 5th, school resumed in Bay St. Lucy.

On Wednesday, January 7th, April van Osdale made her first appearance.

Nina had been apprised of it and was waiting in the doorway when a large black van, dispatched from city hall, pulled to the front curb and stopped.

April van Osdale, a briefcase clutched in her right hand, got out of the car and waved:

"Ms. Bannister!"

Nina waved back.

The woman walking up to her had inverted her outfit, and was now wearing not a white angel food cake with strawberry trim but a strawberry cake with white angel food trim.

Red red red…

…and a little white white white.

She extended a hand, which Nina took, thinking as she did so that the handshake was firmer than one would have expected from a pastry.

"I'm so sorry we didn't get to talk more at the press conference!"

"I am, too."

"So many people, you know."

"There was a crowd. Have you gotten moved in at city hall?"

"Yes. Everything's been done. They've created a nice office for me. You'll get to see it, I'm sure. We'll be spending a lot of time together in the next months."

"I'm looking forward to it," said Nina.

Gag a maggot.

"And so—what does our schedule look like today?"

"English faculty first, then, history, then math. That should give you a pretty full morning."

"Wonderful. And by the way, Nina—I can call you Nina, can't I?"

"Of course."

"By the way, I've been hearing some wonderful things about you. You've just come out of retirement?"

"Yes. Paul Cox asked me to."

"So I hear. Well, Mr. Cox has some interesting ideas. I'm sure he'll be a major help to the governor."

"I hope so."

"At any rate, everyone in town remembers you as a teacher. Wherever I go, it's 'Nina taught us this' and 'Nina taught us that.' And then, you spent your last years as principal?"

"Yes. The last four."

"You must be somewhat overwhelmed. So much has changed."

They were inside now, walking along the main corridor toward room 102, where Eunice Duncan and the five other English teachers were awaiting them.

Except for Max Lirpa, who had called in sick this morning.

Thank God.

Some time April van Osdale would have to find out about Max.

But not today. Not today.

"And Nina, this is somewhat embarrassing, but—"

"Yes?"

"I do feel as though, thinking about it, we may have met somewhere."

"Strange. I have that feeling too."

"Were you at the state conference on Innovative Teaching Strategies last March?"

"No. No, didn't make that one."

"Well, that's not it, then. Sometime though, and somewhere, our paths have crossed. It will come to me."

Not from me, thought Nina.

If you don't remember, then to hell with you.

She did not say this.

"I'll try to figure it out too," is what she did say.

And they were at the door of the meeting room.

Most faculty meetings were held in the library, which could seat seventy people comfortably. The room they were now entering was known simply as a conference room. It held a round table, several chairs, and audio visual equipment that allowed Power Point presentations to be flashed on a screen in the front of the space.

"Good morning, Ladies!" said Nina, in a voice that was much cheerier than her mood.

Group response:

"GOOD MORNING!"

Everyone standing.

"Take a seat," she said, "Take a seat."

Everyone did so.

Now she and the vegetative growth beside her stood before the group.

"I want to introduce to you Dr. April van Osdale. Dr. van Osdale, as I'm sure you know by now, has been named Educational Liaison Officer by the office of our state senator and will, in the following months, be helping us to improve the performance of our students. And so, I give you Dr. van Osdale!"

Some faint applause.

Then April van Osdale:

"I want to begin by telling you how much I look forward to working with you, and how much I appreciate the toil and effort you put in, each and every day. I've spent more than my share of years in the classroom, and I realize just how arduous the job can be."

Pause.

"Still...."

Uh oh, Nina found herself thinking.

Something ominous about that 'still.'

"Still, ladies, we've got a lot of work to do. Bay St. Lucy's combined scores for the November tests are extremely low in comparison to similar institutions elsewhere in the state. This is not satisfactory to anyone. Not to the people who represent us in Jackson; not to the parents of our children, who represent, as I'm certain you all know, our most precious asset; and not to me. In short, it's going to change."

No answering that.

The five 'ladies' addressed; Eunice, Cyntha Barnhart, Candice Wilkins, Terry Starr, and Ronda Wilkinson, all sat quietly and continued to nod.

A bell went off, uselessly.

Two coaches sauntered down the hall, uselessly.

"First, Ms. Duncan, I must ask you: how often are you MOCK MACEING?"

The Mock Mace was an approximation of the actual MACE. It was a practice test.

"We try to do one MOCK MACE per month."

"That's all?"

"Well, there are other activities that..."

"What activities?"

Silence.

"Do you not understand that this test takes precedence over everything else?"

"Yes, we know that, Dr. van Osdale. It's just that..."

"Just that what?"

No answer.

"Ms. Bannister?"

"Yes, Dr. van Osdale?"

"Do you have an explanation for this?"

"I'm not sure what you're referring to."

"I'm referring to the fact that not nearly enough MOCK MACEs are being administrated. Do you know if this is true in other departments as well?"

"I have to say, I'm not sure."

"Nina," piped up Eunice, bravely, "has only been with us a few weeks."

"I see. That does explain a few things."

"And Paul—"

April van Osdale cut her off.

"—that doesn't matter now. What Mr. Cox's policies—or lack of policies—might have been, is irrelevant."

She glared at everyone evenly and said:

"Our policy is now going to be weekly MOCK MACEing. Let me be very clear: if the test scores go up, good things will happen to this faculty. If not..."

Silence in the room.

A few drops of dust filtered down from air ducts in the ceiling and could be heard making a crashing noise on the carpet.

Otherwise, there was complete, utter, unbroken, endless, interminable, and unendurable, silence.

"Are there questions?"

There were no questions.

"Good. Well. So far as I'm concerned, the meeting is over."

And it was.

Of course, everything else was only beginning. The history meeting took place, and the math meeting took place, and each went like the other, and the women teachers sat with smiles frozen on their faces and the men teachers who were not coaches (there were five of them in the school) sat with no expressions at all, and the coaches found excuses to be absent.

April van Osdale, not wanting to be subjected to fish sticks and tater tots, left shortly before lunch.

During lunch, and for most of the afternoon, Nina sat in her office and tried to console various teachers or groups of teachers who entered in panic mode:

"Who *is* she, anyway?"

"Does she really have the power to do all of these things?"

"We can't prepare for a MOCK MACE every week!"

"We won't have time to do anything else!"

"Can she fire me?"

"I've been here twenty years: can she fire me?"

Nina, knowing the answers to none of these questions, decided it would be boring simply to answer "I don't know" to every query, and so she decided to spice up her life a bit by choosing three answers out of an answer hat and alternating them.

"Yes."

"No."

"I don't know."

"No."

"Yes."

"I don't know."

"I don't know."

"No."

"Yes."

And so on and so on.

Finally, there was a lull in the storm, and she had time to call Jackson Bennett.

"Jackson?"

"Nina? What's going on? Oh, by the way, I heard about Lirpa and the fight. I think we're going to be able to keep it quiet."

"Good. But I've got to see you."

"Can't. Got to be at the court."

"You have a case?"

Silence for a time. Then:

"Not in court, Nina. At court."

"What are you talking about?"

"The girls have an afternoon game at Hatteras. Aren't you keeping up with the schedule?"

"You're going to a basketball game?"

"The Hattiesburg game won't mean anything if we don't win this one. I'm leaving the office to drive over now."

"When will you be back?"

"Around dinner. But I'm buying dinner for the team at Dee Tee's."

"Can I meet you there?"

"Sure, if you want to. Be warned though; they get a little rowdy."

"Rowdy? You should have been here this morning."

"What's going on?"

"April van Osdale is going on."

"Oh."

"Yeah, oh. Jackson, can she…"

He cut her off:

"Let's talk about it tonight."

Then he hung up.

Every real town—even an artistic community such as Bay St. Lucy—has a restaurant like Dee Tee's. It was not a trendy restaurant. It did not serve gourmet food or trendy food or healthy food or food that was to be eaten while sitting on a veranda and looking out over the sea.

It served hamburgers for lunch and breaded veal cutlets for dinner.

These things were lugged to tables by big strong waitresses dressed in sky white uniforms, who called the men 'honey' or 'sugar,' and who carried six platters of breaded fish on one upturned palm and a continual, always full, pot of coffee, in the other.

Nina arrived at 5:30, a few minutes before the team did.

There were two big tables at the back of the restaurant that sat, empty, waiting for them.

"What are you going to have tonight, honey?"

Damn. She must look like a man. The waitress called her honey.

"Just a salad."

The waitress looked as though Nina had stuck a fork into her stomach. Crestfallen to the point of tears, she said, in a tone reminiscent of a minister whose congregation was refusing en masse to take communion:

"No meat?"

Nina shook her head.

"I'm sorry."

"None at all?"

"No."

"Just a salad?"

She answered as though she were answering the question, "Is your sister really dead?"

She said:

"Yes."

The waitress, heartbroken, turned and left.

A short time afterward, the huge yellow cockroach that was the school bus crawled to a stop outside the south window, and the team poured out.

One second. Two seconds.

Then they all came hurtling into the restaurant.

Meg was not with them.

For Meg, immediately following the game, had headed out to New Mexico.

By this time two days from now, she and Jennifer would be married.

The girls had been chaperoned home by Jackson Bennett, who drove just behind them.

They did not act like one expected giggling girls to act. They were athletes and they comported themselves as such. They brayed, horse played, shoved, pushed, broke into delirious laughter (the team had obviously won) and threw each other into tables, some of which were empty, others were occupied by smiling people who recognized their status as jocks and, being people from The South, forgave them.

Once having seated themselves at the tables reserved for them, they engaged in the time-honored ritual of unscrewing the tops of the sugar bottles and the salt shakers, then pouring one of the ingredients into the other's bottle, and vice versa.

No one at Dee Tee's seemed to mind.

Dee Tee's was the kind of restaurant that had seen much worse, and sucked this kind of behavior into its cream gravy bowls much as a midway swallows rubes and yokels.

It was ready for whatever the girls could throw at them.

Two of the players spotted Nina.

"Hey, Ms. Bannister!"

"Hello, Ms. Bannister!"

She nodded primly and answered:

"Hello, girls. How did it go?"

"We won! Fifty to thirty five!"

"Congratulations!"

"Now bring on Logansport and Hattiesburg!"

Upon hearing the hated name, the remainder of the team slammed down onto their tables the bottles of sugar and salt—the contents of which had now been thoroughly switched—and made animal noises.

Nina was so proud of them.

A few minutes later food began to arrive.

The young women did not order salads.

They did not order as though thinking first and foremost of their slender figures.

They ordered MEAT! MEAT! MEAT! as though they were Odysseus' men slaughtering the cattle of the sun, and soon their tables were covered with steaming bowls of mashed potatoes, grease-filled platters of French fries, rolls, biscuits, tureens of thick cream gravy, and great thick slabs of steak, chicken, ham, fish, pork, mullet, hen, squab, and, perhaps if one researched too thoroughly, horse and dog.

GO YOU, MARINERS! GO YOU, MARINERS! GO YOU, MARINERS!"

Nina was forced to rethink her literary analogy.

Odysseus' men could not have been this loud.

They had finished their second chant and begun asking for seconds (But were there any animals left alive in the city?) when Jackson Bennett walked through the door.

"YAAAAY, MR. BENNETT!"

"YAAAAY, MR. BENNETT!"

He beamed, and opened his arms to embrace Alyssha, who'd hurtled across the room and thrown herself against him, shattering as she did so two chairs which seemed to have been made of balsa wood.

"Good game!" he crowed, looking down at her as she beamed up at him.

She accepted the praise and nodded, her face glowing only slightly more intensely than the fluorescent lights in the ceiling above.

Then she returned to her teammates while Jackson shouted:

"Good game, ladies!"

"YAAAAY, Mr. Bennett!"

"YAAAAY, Mr. Bennett!"

All of the standing girls sat down again and renewed their carnage. The people brave enough to still be in the restaurant nodded approval, whispering to themselves things like:

"Aren't they cute?"

...and not:

"Let's get the hell out of here."

...like non-Mississippians might have said.

"Nina! May I join you?"

"Sure. Sit down, Jackson."

He did so, the table rocking as he leaned forward on it, the chair creaking as his weight began the process of intimidating it.

"What are you having?"

"Salad."

He shook his head, perusing the menu:

"You've got to do better than that. This meal is my treat, you know."

"You're buying dinner for the whole team?"

He looked at the girls, who, having finished off fifty pounds or so of main course, were now contemplating dessert.

"The law firm did pretty well last year. We can use the profits to put down a deposit. So, come on, chow down."

"No, a salad's fine."

"Wimp," he growled, peering at the wall behind the players.

It was covered with a gigantic rebel flag and pictures of Jeb Stuart, Robert E Lee, and Stonewall Jackson.

"Great restaurant," he said quietly, "for a Black man to be frequenting."

"So why do you come here? Why did you bring the team here?"

"I like," he said, gesturing to the waitress, "the breaded veal cutlet."

"Well. So much for principles."

"The only principal I'm really concerned about is you. How's the job going?"

She said nothing while Jackson ordered, his two-minute litany of desires obviously pleasing the woman who stood beside him, scribbling earnestly, her weekly salary apparently depending on the poundage of meat and potatoes she was able to dole out and see consumed.

She left.

The Confederate heroes on the far wall continued to stare out over the room, stern-faced, wishing apparently to have no more truck with Jackson Bennett that he wanted with them.

"We're all a little concerned, Jackson."

He took a deep breath and nodded.

"Van Osdale?"

"Yes. She spent the morning at school."

"How did that go?"

"How did the Civil War go?"

"Pretty good for my side."

"But for the other side?"

He smiled.

"I heard they had some difficulties."

"Yes, they did."

"And you feel like…"

"Atlanta. And she's Sherman."

"Is it that bad, Nina?"

"I'm not sure how bad it is. That's why we need to talk."

"All right. Talk."

"Jackson, how much power does this woman really have?"

'I'm not sure."

"How can you not be sure? You're one of the best attorneys in town. You know people in the state capital. You've got contacts. You're also head of the school board."

"Sherman, from what I've been able to read, didn't talk to those folks either."

"So, you don't know how much power she really has? This woman basically threatened every teacher in the building this morning. The test scores must go up, or people will be fired."

"Which people?"

"All people. Any people. How can she do that? Isn't it the school board's place to hire and fire people?"

"Technically, yes."

"I hate that word 'technically.' What it really means is, 'the thing that I just said is true isn't true at all."

He took a deep breath and began to do what Nina had learned years before, in watching Frank deal with clients, lawyers always did when they either had bad news or had to admit they didn't know something:

...he whispered.

This just gets worse and worse, she found herself thinking.

"Years ago, Nina, it was probably true that the school board of a little town like Bay St. Lucy could decide pretty much everything that was going to happen. Curriculum, textbooks, hiring, firing—the school superintendent or the principal, depending on the size of the district, made recommendations, and the board rubber-stamped them. Hell, what did the local feed store owner or grocer care about what math book the kids had to buy?"

"That's changed, I guess."

A dozen or so people brought Jackson's order. It surrounded Nina's minute and pitiful little salad much as the Confederate gunboats and infantry batteries must have surrounded Vicksburg.

It was time to stop, she told herself, *these Civil War analogies.*

They were making her uneasy.

"Yes."

A smooth sea of white cream gravy lay shimmering before him, the hypothetical veal cutlet, like the Loch Ness Monster, lying hidden below it.

His whisper, coming up from the East, caused a gravy tsunami to begin making its way to the West, where, in some seconds, it would threaten to overwhelm a village of turnip greens.

"Yes, it's changed. Public education has become completely political."

"Somehow, I seem to have missed all of that in the last ten years."

"I know. And I was hoping you could come back for a few months and just be a good principal, without having to be in the center of a hurricane."

"Didn't work out that way, I guess."

"No. No, I guess it didn't."

"But, Jackson, these tests…"

He shook his head disgustedly.

"There's nothing we can do about them. I can't tell you how much I'd love, as president of the school board, to make an edict saying, 'For two months, no tests at all. Let's let our teachers teach. Let creative people *be* creative. Maybe then we could lure back into the classroom a few more Nina Bannisters."

He found the cutlet, impaled it, watched it die on the fork in front of him, and swallowed it whole while the rest of the food on the table, knowing now what lay before it, shuddered in sauces of despair.

"Nina," he then said quietly (any utterance at all an amazing feat since his throat was filled with fifty ounces of chicken pretending to be veal), "the tests are a fact of life. If we don't administer them—just the way the state mandates that we administer them—we lose our funding. And then, talk about people getting fired–"

"I understand. So we're prisoners."

"I'm not sure that's the term I'd use."

"What term would you use?"

He thought for a time and finally said:

"Prisoners."

"Oh. Well, you put it a little better."

"It's my legal training."

"What else can she do, Jackson?"

He shook his head.

"She is one major faction of an entire state government; Paul is in Jackson representing the other faction. But…"

"She came here because of Paul, didn't she?"

"It's very possible. Nobody put it into writing, but…"

"We send our champion into battle, they send a champion back into his home town to…well, to make an example of us."

"I wish I could tell you that you're wrong."

"So Bay St. Lucy High School—and Middle School and Elementary School—are going to be "what if" schools. April van Osdale is here to show the state what can be done if everybody just does exactly what the powers that be say must be done."

"That's about it."

There was silence for a time.

Then it became clear that the girls at the far two tables, having finished off their peach cobbler or chocolate cake or cheese cake or vanilla sundaes or cherries melba—were getting hungry again and thinking about breakfast.

"Ma'am?" said Jackson, lifting an arm and gesturing to the waitress. "Bring the check to me, please."

The players cheered. The waitress appeared with the check, Jackson put four fifty dollar bills on the table to cover it, and then said:

"All that I can advise you to do, Nina, is what you always do. Use your common sense."

"If I used my common sense," she said, "I'd leave Atlanta and go back to Tara."

He shook his head:

"If I remember right, that burned too."

Then he set about finishing his turnip greens.

". . . in August in Mississippi there's a few days somewhere about the middle of the month when suddenly there's a foretaste of fall, it's cool, there's an ambiance, a soft, a luminous quality to the light, as though it came not from just today but from back in the old classic times. It might have fauns and satyrs and the gods and—from Greece, from Olympus in it somewhere. It lasts just for a day or two, then

it's gone. . . the title reminded me of that time, of a luminosity older than our Christian civilization."

—William Faulkner, *Light in August*

It was 8:00 when Nina got home.

A beautiful evening. The snow was gone, the rain had not returned in some days, and the South was showing its inhabitants how lucky they were to be a part of it. Ice storms in the Northeast, snow in North Dakota, blizzards in Denver—

—but here in Bay St. Lucy there were only a few puffy gulf clouds out over the off shore oil rigs, while the three-star belt and sword of Orion shone in readiness for its eternally-upcoming battle with Taurus the Bull, a battle which probably would not happen tonight, since Taurus was still grazing peacefully in the sky of the southern hemisphere.

Nina gazed down the beach before making her way up the rickety stairs that led to her shack.

Some fifty yards distant, a family had found enough driftwood in the nearby dunes to make a fire. They were sitting beside it, roasting marshmallows, while the waves combed in before them leaving white tracery a foot or so from their beach blanket.

"April van Osdale," she found herself whispering.

"Tests, tests, tests."

She began climbing the stairs.

A shooting star began writing a piece of cursive overhead, then forgot what it was going to say, gave up, and disappeared.

The ponderous ocean ignored it.

Nina reached into her purse for her key, then noticed that, a foot or so above the door handle, a note had been stuck between the screen and the door facing.

This, she thought to herself, *could be good news*.

She could have won something.

A lottery or something.

Or it could be an invitation to a party frequented by several friends, all of whom had a sense of humor and drank a lot.

Or it could be a notice announcing, with deep regret, the untimely passing of one Dr. April van Osdale, who had, been captured by a sea monster, torn to pieces, and eaten.

She pulled the note out and began unfolding it.

"It's going to be good news," she whispered down at the fine quality caramel-color paper. "Yeah, right."

A dust-covered bulb burned over the door. There was just enough light to read in the small sphere of illumination where the three of them—Nina, the note, and her sense of reality—found themselves.

NINA DARLING:

SOMETHING VERY TROUBLING HAS HAPPENED, AND I AM DEEPLY UPSET. I DO HATE TO BOTHER YOU, BUT I WONDER IF YOU COULD COME OVER TO THE AUBERGE AS SOON AS POSSIBLE.

THANK YOU SO MUCH FOR YOUR TROUBLE.

ADMIRINGLY, AS EVER,

ALANNA DELAFOSSE.

"I would say that music is the easiest means in which to express, but since words are my talent, I must try to express clumsily in words what the pure music would have done better."

—William Faulkner

The Auberge des Arts was the Robinson Mansion and always would be to Nina. It emanated darkness, even despite the numerous yard lights that had been installed in its extensive, magnolia-dotted lawns, and its Gothic windows would always hide secrets behind the curtains that hung, silent and diaphanous, as though held by invisible hands.

She approached it carefully, revving down the Vespa's little motor even more than normal. The paths seemed to encircle her. There were lights in some of the windows. She began to ask herself the question she'd always asked while approaching this vast and bat-filled building, even as a girl, even before its restoration and artistic transformation:

Was she more frightened of people who might be inhabiting these rooms, or of the rooms themselves, silent and empty, growing dark, growing light, day after day after day?

It was a question she did not want answered.

She parked the Vespa, hearing as she did so, the sounds of several guitars which seemed to be playing in one of the front rooms.

She climbed two steps that led up to the wide wooden porch, and she could see now that, through a window to her left, several people were sitting in a tight circle, guitars before them, their hands active as spiders weaving nests among the strings.

She rang the bell. A soft and sonorous moan seemed to grow beneath the arabesques of the *Malaguena*, then soften and finally disappear.

The door opened. Alanna Delafosse stood before her.

That was about like saying 'The Grandeur of the East,' 'The Mystery of the Orient,' and 'The Splendor of the Old South' stood before her.

Or perhaps that was an exaggeration.

It was not much of an exaggeration though, for Alanna never tired of attempting to portray humanity as it was depicted in museums, and not how it was lived in school buildings and feed stores.

She was a Creole woman, not as dark as the sky had become in the last ten minutes, but somewhat deeper in texture and a good deal more mysterious. She was wearing a brightly-colored tent with the signs of the zodiac burned celestially upon it; a garment which could, Nina found herself thinking, have come straight from the closet of Margot Gavin.

"Nina! Thank you so much for coming!"

"No problem. I just got home and found your note, Alanna. What's happening?"

"I'm grief stricken. You cannot imagine."

"Tell me."

"It's a letter I received today. It must have been written several days ago. I'm still in shock. It concerns our 'Arts in the Schools' program. We have, as you know, been bringing groups of high school students weekly to the Auberge, so that they could meet writers, painters, actors, from various towns and cities throughout the state. We pay these artists a stipend, of course, with part of the funds coming from the school's budget. It was Paul who suggested it, after all. But now, this letter…"

"Can you show it to me?"

"Of course. I have it inside. Come, come. The guitar ensemble is practicing in what used to be a front parlor, and which we now use as a practice room for any groups of musicians that care to come."

Nina walked in and Alanna closed the door behind her. The ponderous chandelier that hung in the entrance hallway examined her and, showing a sign of its good will, did not come crashing to the floor.

"So many people are using the Auberge these days, Alanna."

"Yes. Theater groups, painting classes, music students—it's functioning exactly as we had hoped. That's precisely why this news is so disheartening. It's simply—well, I can't imagine why such a decision could have been made."

"What decision?"

"You'll have to read for yourself, my dear. I can't seem to talk about it. I begin to stammer. Then there is a temptation to fall into profanity, which, as you know, is never warranted."

Nina knew no such thing, but she had learned dirty words so late in life, and their use so ill-suited her saccharine personality, that she avoided using them for fear of making people break into laughter.

"Come. This way, down the hall. The letter is in the original music room of the mansion. Actually, it's my favorite room. I've left the old instruments, and the pictures, just as they were; but I've transformed what space is left into my own special study."

"You like living here?"

"Very much."

"Isn't it a little spooky?"

"Not at all. To me, bungalows and house trailers are spooky."

"Well. I suppose you may have a point there."

"Of course, I do, darling."

"It's just that this place is based on money made by criminals."

"I believe that can be said about all art."

Why did she ever try to converse with Alanna?

She would give it up in the future, and confine her utterances to grunts of slight pain and yowls of delight.

"Here we are. Come in, Nina."

Nina could see the yellow glow emanating from inside before she could see the room itself.

"Oh my!"

"Yes. Isn't it wonderful?"

And it was.

The first thing to catch one's eye was a harp, golden, shaped like angels' wings, standing exactly in the center of the room, forming the sun around which various planets—grand piano, smaller spinet piano, violins mounted on walls, pictures of opera houses and composers—had been frozen in their rotation and now stood ready for some final concert which would probably never come.

The two women entered and padded like cats, their shoes scuffing on a worn hardwood floor, their hands not daring to touch the instruments, their mouths turned respectfully away, for fear of careless breaths clouding enamel and gold finishes.

"The original music room of The Robinson Mansion."

"It's incredible."

"Yes. Yes, it is. But here is the most wonderful part. Over here, on this stand. Come, come this way."

Nina followed and found herself led to a phonograph, its great curved bell yawning out over the rest of the room like some giant sea shell out of which one might hear the roar of breakers, the comings and goings of the tide. It sat regally on a square oaken box, which, like a desk upended, seemed to have been made specifically to support it.

"When I was a young girl," she whispered to the center of the record, where a dog was listening to a replica of the phonograph that now sat staring down at them—"A wealthy friend took me from New Iberia to New Orleans to hear my first opera. Oh, how I remember it!—I could only gawk at the massive balconies, the people in their evening clothes, the quiet talk between acts mixed with the clinking of champagne glasses—all such things.

"Just last week, Emil Reittinger, Director of the Mississippi State Opera Ensemble—they're based in Vicksburg—came here to talk to six of our music students. He was marvelous. He played several recordings on this old, wonderful Victrola, then talked about the lives of Caruso, Gobi, and others. The students were enchanted."

"I remember," Nina said, quietly, "when the bus brought them back to the high school. They were almost in tears."

"So was I, darling. It was unforgettable. We paid Emil Reittinger—the great Emil Reittinger—one hundred dollars. One hundred. Now. Look at this letter."

She pulled a sheet of paper out of a cavernous pocket.

Nina took it.

It was carefully embossed, official in its appearance, dirty to the touch, and evil in intent.

"Dear Ms. Delafosse," it began.

"It has come to my attention that several sums of money have been dispersed, over the past three months, to both you and to an institution known as Auberge des Arts. While I am quite certain that your intent in utilizing these sums has been constructive, you must realize that they have been made available without prior authorization and are, consequently, to be viewed as in no way other than illicit, and highly objectionable. It is the intent of the school system of Bay St. Lucy to provide for its students a broad range of cultural and scientific opportunities, and, toward this end, we seek to identify and utilize all resources within our purview; still, in light of ever shrinking budgetary parameters and ever growing demands for precious classroom time, I cannot allow the continuance of activities which are simultaneously unsanctioned, unscrutinized by official channels, and irrelevant to clearly-stated classroom goals and objectives."

"In short, these dispersals of funding shall cease and desist immediately, and all future projects potentially involving them are to be summarily cancelled."

"Again, I appreciate your efforts to be a part of our ongoing mandate of community excellence; I cannot though refrain from adding my astonishment that such activities have been allowed to escape proper administrative supervision."

My Regards,

Dr. April van Osdale

"The bitch," said Nina, quietly.

Alanna did not laugh.

Perhaps Nina was learning to use profanity after all.

CHAPTER 9: SECOND MEETING

"It's better to build a tight chicken coop than a shoddy courthouse."

—William Faulkner, *As I Lay Dying*

The following morning—Friday—Nina arrived early at school only to be told she was expected later on at city hall.

She had been summoned by April van Osdale.

Oh God.

But there was nothing for it. She had to go.

She delegated a few duties, then took the school van downtown.

At 9:30, she parked and walked up to the building.

A receptionist met her at the door.

"Ma'am?"

"I'm Nina Bannister. I believe Dr. van Osdale wants to see me?"

"If you'll wait, I'll see if she's available."

"Thank you."

The receptionist left and disappeared into the bowels of the building, while, behind various desks, people came and went and whispered and laughed and took things out of printers and stared at computer screens.

Two minutes passed.

"Ms. Bannister?"

"Yes?"

"Dr. van Osdale can see you now."

"Thank you."

She followed the woman, who, every few steps, looked around to be sure that she had not gotten lost.

April van Osdale's office was situated in the back of a massive room, and had been cordoned off by several massive green curtains.

She appeared through a crack in these curtains, much as though she were taking a bow after a theatrical performance.

"Nina!"

"Dr. van Osdale."

"April! You must call me April. Thank you so much for coming! I know you have millions of things to do!"

"It was no problem."

"Come in, come in. Everything is a shambles. We've got packets of mock tests coming in from Jackson. Over there on that desk are the math tests. There, on the one beyond it, English exams. They're exactly the same in format as the real ones will be. We're taking the real examinations on February 16, you know."

"Yes. All the teachers have that date circled on their calendars."

"Here. Sit down."

Nina did so.

April van Osdale said:

"I wanted you to know how much I enjoyed my time at the high school yesterday."

"That's good. We enjoyed having you."

"Do you think the meetings went well?"

"Oh, yes. The faculty were very impressed."

"I'm so glad! I want them to be inspired and not overwhelmed. There's so much that can be done to help get these scores up; we just have to focus, focus, focus."

"I understand."

"Simply to disseminate the information we've already gleaned about test taking will be a major help. It's been shown, for example, that students who have no idea what a correct answer to a particular question is, will have a better chance of getting it right by choosing "C" over any of the other choices."

"You're joking."

"No. It's been proven. Not just on the MACE exam but on various others that have been given around the country."

"That's astonishing. You mean, no matter what the subject matter might be?"

"No matter. Math, English, History—always choose "C" when in doubt. Have our teachers been letting the kiddoes know that?"

"I don't think so. I wasn't aware of it."

"Well, you've been 'out of the loop,' for a while, so to speak."

"I have. I truly have."

"Don't worry about it; we're going to get you current as soon as possible. Now, though, as I told you, I'm very glad you were able to free some time to come by this morning."

Did I have a choice? wondered Nina.

No.

But don't let yourself be intimidated, Nina.

Go on the offensive.

"April, I got a call last evening from Alanna Delafosse."

April's expression withered.

The uncertain glory, Nina found herself thinking, *of an April day.*

"Alanna had received your letter. She's…well, she's upset."

"I see."

The wind had changed.

The words 'I see' drifted across the desk in temperatures significantly cooler than the previous half-minute had seen.

Nina bent forward, shivered slightly, and proceeded.

"A number of artists had come to the Auberge. The program seemed a success."

"Nina, did you know about these visits?"

"Not originally. I wasn't a part of the planning process. But I did learn about them last week."

"Why didn't you say anything?"

"They seemed a good idea."

"To send students off-campus, halfway across town—during class time?"

"They were meeting professional artists. Painters, writers…"

"And these people were being paid by public school funds?"

"Yes, from what I understand."

"From what I understand, too. Nina, such a thing is simply intolerable."

"The sums were quite small."

"It doesn't matter. Small, large—money is money, and the school doesn't have an infinite amount of it."

"No. That's true, of course."

"The point is, we have no time for artsy-fartsy."

"For what?"

"For artsy-fartsy. We have serious work to do and we can't be bussing our students halfway across the state to subject them to Greek opera."

Nina said nothing.

"But I also made it clear that in the future all dispersals of funds, as well as all decisions on curricular matters and the use of time meant to be spent in classrooms, would be made by proper authorities."

You, thought Nina.

"I understand," said Nina.

April continued:

"I'm glad we're clear on this, then. Now. There was another matter. The actual reason that I asked you to come. I wanted to make a—well, a 'social suggestion,' if I may call it that. I hope you won't take it amiss."

"I'm sure I won't."

"I've been able to make several good friends in the short time I've been in Bay St. Lucy."

"I'm glad to hear that. We're a friendly town."

"Yes, you are. Do you know Bill Kreisler?"

"I know of him. He's involved in real estate."

'Yes, he is. He's made a lovely home available for me. It's over in the Berkshire section of town, on Fairway Drive."

"Yes, I know that area. It's very nice."

"Oh, I love it. Nice sidewalks, tree-lined driveways."

"And a golf course."

"Yes. In fact, my home overlooks one of the greens. It's very pleasant. But at any rate…"

What's coming here?

Was April van Osdale inviting Nina over to play golf?

Probably not.

Then what?

“Well, the long and short of it is that Bill has a couple of nice condos—also overlooking the golf course, I might add—that are currently available. The question is, would you consider moving into one of them?”

“Would I what?”

“Like to live in a new condo. I haven’t seen them, but they’re supposed to be fantastic.”

“I have a place, April.”

April sighed.

“I know, Nina, but…”

April sighed again.

“It isn’t really appropriate, is it?”

“It isn’t what?”

“Appropriate. For the position you find yourself in at the present.”

“What do you mean?”

“You are a principal, Nina.”

“So?”

“You’re living in a shack. This would be fine for a beach bum…”

“It’s been fine for me. And for Furl.”

‘Oh, is Furl your cat?”

“Yes.”

“What an adorable name!”

“Thank you. Furl and I like it.”

“I’m sure you do, but, back to the main issue…your husband died some years ago, I hear.”

“Seven years ago.”

“I’m not sure what your financial situation is.”

“I have a little money. Not much. The firm didn’t do too well in Frank’s last years. He was ill for a while. That cost money.”

“Of course, it did. And now you’ve been living only on teacher retirement.”

“Yes.”

“So you’ve not been able to afford anything much better than where you are now. That’s understandable But your salary is going to increase, Nina. And, as I told the teachers at the high school yesterday, I'm going to have some discretionary funding available to dispose of as I see fit."

"Bonuses."

"Yes, bonuses. The bottom line is, we can afford to upgrade your—well, your living standard."

"My living standard."

"I suppose that's the best way to put it. You're going to want to entertain, Nina. That's what people in your position do."

"You mean parties and such."

"Of course. There are various people in town who—well, who don't really know you very well."

They don't hang out, Nina found herself thinking, *with curio shop owners. Or beach bums.*

They hang out on golf courses.

"I guess I have been rather limited in my social contacts."

"And that's completely understandable! It really is!"

It's really understandable because I hate those people.

"I'm very sorry, April, if my living situation embarrasses the school."

"Oh, that's putting it much too strongly. You are, as I told you earlier, clearly one of the most respected people in Bay St. Lucy. But it's for precisely that reason that, if I or Bill or any of a number of contacts that I've been able to make recently—well, if we can help you out a bit—we'd all be happy to do so."

"That's very good to hear."

"So you'll consider it?"

"I certainly will."

"Good! Well, if there's nothing more…perhaps you'll allow me to walk you out?"

"It's fine, April. I can make it by myself."

"You'll be going back to school now?"

"Yes. Have to eat lunch with the kids. Fish sticks today."

"It's such a shame. I'd ask you to have lunch with me at Gambrelli's but some of the senator's staff are flying in from Jackson…"

"I understand."

"In the meantime, do you want to take these mock tests over to the school and distribute them to the various teachers?"

"Sure."

"I had meant to have a courier bring them over later in the afternoon, but…"

"…but as long as I'm here. We can't get started too soon!"

"That's the spirit, Nina!"

"Well, then. Bye-bye, April."

So saying, she took the cumbersome manila envelopes in her arms and walked from the building.

"A condo," she whispered to herself as she made her way through the parking lot.

"I could have a whole new set of friends. I wouldn't have to live like a bum anymore."

She opened the door of the school van and put the MOCK MACEs carefully into the back seat.

"Furl's life would change too. I could get him a collar. Maybe even a diamond collar. And a little red vest that he could wear while we were out walking."

She went round to the front of the van, pulled the sliding door open, and got in.

"I wouldn't be an embarrassment to the school any more. And I could entertain."

She started the engine and backed out of the parking lot.

Have to be careful. Not on your Vespa any more.

She threaded her way along Avenue E and turned onto Breakers Boulevard.

"And, then, there are these tests. Probably should give them out this afternoon. April will be over in a day or so to be sure we're practicing with them. She'll probably want to actually *see* the students practicing with them."

A mile on Breakers Boulevard, then left onto Pelican Drive.

Finally, she had arrived at the wharf area.

First along the main quay, where nicer craft were kept.

Then farther down, where more modest craft were kept.

Then to the end, where Penelope Royale's flat bottom fishing boat lay gently rocking in the waves.

"Penn!"

She got out of the car and waved to Penelope, who was stashing canned goods of some kind in the bow of the boat.

"Hey, Penn!"

Penelope saw her and waved back, then shouted a convivial and amiable curse.

"Nina! Y---! How ---?"

"I'm fine, Penn! I'm fine!"

She walked around the van, slid back the door, and gathered the manila folders up in her arms.

Then she walked to the side of the wharf, high fiving Penn, who scowled and said:

"The other ---night, that ---Max Lirpa and that---of a--- Moon Rivard, if I ever---!"

"I know, Penn. How is Tom?"

"He's fine, poor guy, but those two---almost---and if I hadn't---it would have been their---!"

"Well, I'm glad he's okay."

"----."

"Look, I've got a favor to ask."

"----."

"Do you have a charter this afternoon?"

"Yeah, I've got---and---."

"How far are you going out?"

"Oh, at least about---if we don't---."

"Good. Do you have a sack of some kind and a weight that you could put in it?"

"---!"

"Wonderful. Would you mind to take these manila envelopes, put them in the sack, put the weights in the sack, tie up the sack, and dump it in the ocean?"

Penelope stared at her:

"Course I ---wouldn't---mind."

Then:

"What's in the envelopes?"

"A bunch of ---," answered Nina.

"Who gave them to you?"

"A ---!"

Penn, amazed, shook her head and said:

"I've never heard you use that kind of language."

"Well," said Nina, handing over the mock tests, "Maybe I'm ---learning."

"Maybe you---are."

The two women high fived, and Nina walked back to the van.

Once back at the high school, she parked the van, entered the building, and opened her cell phone.

She dialed City Hall.

"Dr. van Osdale, please."

Pause.

"This is April van Osdale."

"April, it's Nina."

"Nina? You barely caught me; I was just going out to my luncheon."

"Something's happened."

"Happened? What is it?"

"We had a theft."

"Oh, my God. At the school?"

"Well. In the parking lot."

"A car was stolen?"

"No. But someone apparently got into my van. I have to tell you, April. I may have forgotten to lock it."

"So what actually *was* taken?"

"The mock tests."

"Oh, no."

"I'm so sorry, April. I know they were valuable."

"Extremely valuable. And it's going to take some time to get replacements here."

"That's the worst of it, isn't it?"

"Yes, it is. We were all ready to start Mocking by—tomorrow actually. Now it's going to take at least another week."

"Everyone here will be devastated."

"Of course the question is, Nina, where are those tests now? Where will they be by, say, this afternoon?"

"That's anybody's guess, isn't it?"

"It certainly is; but I can promise you, by five o'clock today someone will be poring over those mocks."

"Flounder," Nina whispered, despite herself.

"What?"

"Found her. School cat went missing and we—we found her."

"Oh. Well, that's something, I suppose."

"Yes, it is. Yes, it is. Once again, April, I'm so sorry for my negligence. And you have a good lunch at Gambrelli's."

"I'll try to. You enjoy your meal also."

"I will. Good bye."

She flipped shut the phone.

"And an entire school of fish," she said, quietly, "will soon be moving from 'good' to 'exemplary.'"

She smiled to herself, left the office, walked to the lunch room, and chowed down on fish sticks.

CHAPTER 10: A FEW MOMENTS WITH TIMOTHIES

"The sun, an hour above the horizon, is poised like a bloody egg upon a crest of thunderheads; the light has turned copper: in the eye portentous, in the nose sulphurous, smelling of lightning."

—William Faulkner, *As I Lay Dying*

On Saturday morning, Aurora, Goddess of the Dawn, came sweeping across the cove and into Bay St. Lucy.

She appeared first as a slight lightening in an octopus-ink black sky that had blanketed the town. Then she slipped an aquamarine-clad arm through the crack of the doorway that leads from earth to heaven. Then, opening the door, she stepped through it.

The eastern sky exploded into all the colors—saffron, red, gold, purple—that were her robes, and Nina, who had been sitting on her deck watching since five a.m., felt the urge to fall on her knees and worship.

She thought of Timothies, the mortal who had loved the goddess of the dawn so deeply that he'd been granted a wish by her.

Any wish.

"Eternal life, so that I might rise each morning throughout eternity and sing your praises."

Wrong wish, of course.

Should have included eternal *youth*, Timothies.

What were you thinking?

Things had gone all right, of course, for fifty years or so.

Then age began to have its effect.

And Timothies had begun to shrink, and shrivel, and harden, and blacken.

"Let me die! Let me die!"

But the gods cannot take back the wishes they have granted.

And so Timothies remains until this day, haunting the basements and the curbsides and the wet cold grasslands, his tiny blackened body screeching out in piteous miniature cries:

"Let me die! Let me die!"

Incomprehensible to all that are not aware of his presence, of his story.

Audible only as:

"Creeech! Creech!"

The chirp of the cricket.

Which is what Timothies had become.

A dangerous thing, making deals with the gods.

But one could always watch them!

She continued to do so, beginning to sip another cup of coffee as the sun itself, a flaming orange peel appearing as if by magic—which is, of course, what the whole spectacle was—over the perfectly flat line that was the sea.

Then she spotted the porpoises.

They greeted her every morning, of course, and why should this morning be unlike any other? Black, glistening, and perfectly synchronized, they came bounding into her field of vision as far to the left as she could see—then they made their way before her, continuing to leap and submerge, leap and submerge, first one and then the other, one and then the other, until they finally faded from sight and let sea air and distance extinguish them.

Now the sun was all the way up.

It was absolutely perfectly exquisitely circular. It was globular and fruitlike. It was—was—

Oh, just look at the damn sun, Nina, and stop trying to be a poet.

Or look at—look at that, look at that! Two, now three pelicans sweeping low over the surf, one dives, another dives, whap into the water then out again and look at the fish, look at the fish just squirming half in and half out of the beak and now jerk with the pelican head and SLURP down goes the fish!

But there are more fish! Look at the fish!

The waves are full of them!

Whitefish, their foot-long bodies glistening in the arch of the green waves.

Fish jumping, now twisting and turning their black glistening backs over and over, white black, white black.

Here come the gulls!

"Hey everybody! It's what all of us gulls have been waiting for! A billion fish! Let's fly low and circle and screech and caw like crows and bark like dogs and drop excrement all over the beachcombers and get ourselves some SEAFOOD!

Which they were now doing.

This was not a chance, Nina decided, to miss.

She set her coffee cup aside on the small deck table.

She looked reassuringly at Furl, who, not moving at all in his corner of the deck, saw no reason why she should do so.

Then she made her way into the kitchen, opened the refrigerator, and took from a carefully taped white package four shrimp that she had bought two days earlier from one of the bait shops in town. She crossed the living room, shuffled out to the stairs, and made her way down to the dew-wet concrete slab that spread out fifteen feet below the shack's floor.

Leaning against one of the fifteen-foot tall support poles was her rod and reel.

She baited the hook with one of the fat curved shrimp, then walked down to the ocean.

The morning air bathed her.

Sixty-five degrees, she would have seen the circular thermometer on the wall behind her deck indicating, had she been standing on the deck looking not out at the sea but back toward her shack.

But she was not standing there. She was walking across the hard-packed sand, enjoying the sixty-five degrees rather than reading about it—

—and now she was slipping out of her sandals, letting them lie dormant and secure behind her like two black sea anemone, while the tan beach sucked and squiggled beneath the soles of her feet.

The surf pounded in front of her.

Tide coming in.

Waves, waves—

BRASH! CRABBLE! ROOOOAAAAR!

An air full of fish, a wave full of fish, fish everywhere!

She was in the ocean now, exquisitely cold water washing around her ankles, almost reaching up to the cuffs of her cutoff jeans.

"Okay, you whitefish! Come and get it!"

She flipped the reel's bale, held her finger on the line, arched, leaned back, took one breath, now two…

Then HURLED with all her might, letting her finger up at just the right moment and sending the shrimphooksinker apparatus flying out over the sea.

PLOP

Which it all now fell into.

There it was: the miniature half-red, half-white, two-inch buoy-bobber bobbering before her, waiting to be pulled down into the drink.

One second, two seconds.

The bobber disappeared.

There then followed an instant of nothing at all.

Then came the tenth most sensual and exciting, at least according to Nina, physical feeling in the world.

The first nine had to do with the act of reproduction and did not need to be dwelt upon.

The tenth though was—

—NOW! NOW THIS FEELING!

FISH ON THE LINE FISH ON THE LINE!

The reel whirred and buzzed in her hand; she saw the tiny spot where the fishing line entered the water as it circled and darted away from her.

Flip.

She closed the bale, fixed her legs firmly in the twisting water beneath her, and closed her fingers hard on the reel crank.

Then she began to pull the fish toward her.

One revolution. Two revolutions.

CREECH CREECH CREECH!

Gulls circling above her, diving all around her, flapping and honking and diving and screaming.

CRASH CRASH CRASH AND

ROOOOOOAAAR!

The waves broke around her, drenching her sweatshirt and jeans, filming and obscuring the lenses of her glasses.

Pull again.

Pull hard again.

The fish fighting back.

BIG FISH!

STRONG FISH!

This went on for perhaps a minute.

But finally she won, and, with a last tug, pulled the whitefish up out of the water, so that it now hung wriggling and lurching before her.

It was a foot out of the water, scales silver and flashing in the sunlight.

She addressed the fish.

"Hello, dinner."

It replied by flapping, jerking, inflating and deflating its gills.

She turned and waded out of the surf.

Frank had taught her how to clean a fish, and she felt that, during the last years, she had become even more adept at the process than he had ever been.

The area beneath her shack was her treasure trove. A charcoal grill ready to use in one corner; a freezer buzzed quietly in another; and, in a third, the one closest to the surf, there stood her work table, its thick wooden surface pockmarked, knife scarred, and redolent of oozings and slime from past cleaning.

The knife stood ready for her, and beside it the whetstone.

"Never try to do this," she could remember Frank saying, "with a dull knife."

Whish whish whish.

Then plop, fish on the cutting board.

One careful slit, no more than an inch deep, under the fish, from the pectoral fin to the tail.

Now, turn the fish—

—trickiest of all, cut off the head, but don't go too deep.

Pull.

The head comes off, and all the digestive apparatus out with it.

Bread bag ready for purpose, all entrails dumped inside.

Bag into the garbage can.

Now filet the fish, quick cut, another quick cut.

Two filets.

Wash the board.

Stand the rod and reel up, leaning on its pole.

And upstairs.

Two filets into the refrigerator.

Dinner dinner dinner.

A little lemon sprinkled on the fish.

Charcoal grill it down below, or just let it simmer in the frying pan up here in the kitchen?

She would decide later on.

After her afternoon nap.

But that was dinner.

—this was breakfast, which she had decidedly earned.

She carefully made herself one egg, over easy, and toasted a slice of garlic bread.

Another cup of coffee—

—outside, at the foot of the stairs, the rolled-up copy of *The Bay St. Lucy Gazette*.

Within minutes she was breakfasting on her deck.

What was in the paper this morning? Let's see, Republicans disagreeing with Democrats, tension in The Middle East, meth lab raided north of town—

And enough of that.

She threw the newspaper away and looked up.

The sea before her was magnificent, the sun now high enough in the sky to be whitening, the oil rigs having turned off their lights.

To the South, a tanker, huge and ponderous, chugging its way across the horizon so slowly as to seem almost motionless.

"Unsuitable," she whispered. "Unsuitable for a principal."

"You could move to a new condo."

"You could live on a golf course."

She rose, walked inside, found paper and pen, and returned to her deck.

TO WHOM IT MAY CONCERN…

She wrote.

Then:

IT IS WITH DEEP REGRET THAT I MUST RESIGN AS PRINCIPAL OF BAY ST. LUCY HIGH SCHOOL.

I WISH YOU ALL THE LUCK IN THE FUTURE.

She signed the letter:

NINA BANNISTER

Then she put it in an envelope, sealed the envelope, addressed it to Jackson Bennett, and went back down for her walk along the beach.

CHAPTER 11: BEING RESIGNED TO BEING RESIGNED

"As long as I live under the capitalistic system I expect to have my life influenced by the demands of moneyed people. But I will be damned if I propose to be at the beck and call of every itinerant scoundrel who has two cents to invest in a postage stamp. This, sir, is my resignation."

—William Faulkner

She had her Monday morning planned.

She would arrive early at school, call into her office a small circle of teachers and staff, and tell them personally of her resignation. There would be some shock about the matter, and perhaps a few tears—some from her—but she had only been back a few weeks and her presence had not grown into a comfortable habit. The school would run itself without her, at least until someone new could be found.

Then she would seek out Jackson Bennett, either in his office or at the courthouse, and hand deliver to him the letter of resignation.

Her reasons?

Multitudinous.

It was all just too much for her. Her health was not up to it. Too many changes had taken place. She missed her old lifestyle too much.

And these reasons were in fact true. Every one of them.

The real reason for her resignation though was April van Osdale, her intense passion for TESTING TESTING TESTING, and her refusal to let professional educators run their own institution without pressure from political forces.

The job of principal as she had once known it no longer existed.

The job of teacher as she had known it no longer existed.

And so she parked and locked her Vespa with a calm sense of having done the best she could, and the eager anticipation of being able to put her new clothes in a trunk which would live forever in the back of her closet.

She walked into the building.

Chaos reigned.

Teachers were running everywhere, secretaries (forget using 'administrative assistants' now, when they were this upset they could go back to being secretaries) scurried about shaking their heads, and parents roamed the halls looking for someone to yell at.

'I want you all to come into my office, because I have something to tell you' is what she'd planned to say to a select group of calm women, all of whom were having their first cup of morning coffee and going about their "let's begin the school day" duties.'

"What' going on?" is what she did say.

Ms. Fitzwalder (tenth grade civics) stared at her, and finally said:

"The letters!"

"What letters?"

Ms. Blankenship (eleventh grade social studies) stared at her, and said, without quite the long pause that Ms. Fitzwalder had taken:

"A whole bunch of letters must have gone out on Friday."

"From whom?"

Then, before anyone could answer, she took note again at the small knots of weeping mothers, and the veins standing out red and dark blue in the sunburned necks of several pre-fisticatory fathers, and she caught herself:

"I know from whom," she said, quietly.

Then, unlocking the door to her office, she said to whoever happened to be closest behind her:

"Come in."

She put up her coat, put her things away, and sat down.

A line of people had already formed in the doorway.

It snaked out into the main hallway.

Sonia Ramirez' mother was first, her daughter gripped fast beside her.

"Ms. Ramirez, what can I do for you?"

"It's Sonia, Ms. Bannister. They have done this to her."

"What have they done to her?"

The woman shook her head; she looked exactly like Sonia, coal black hair and deep-night eyes. Her hair was cut shorter than her daughter's, and she'd gained a few pounds since the days when she, too, could probably have nailed the outside three that won the game.

"The two of you," said Nina, gesturing at two chairs that stood ready for emergencies in not only this but every good principal's office.

They did so.

Nina glanced at her brown leather purse, which lay like a good dog on the carpet beside the desk.

Her resignation letter, imprisoned within the purse, cried out:

"Let me out! Let me out! Use me! Use me now!"

She ignored it.

"On Saturday," Ms. Ramirez choked, "we receive this letter. My husband and I. It is about Sonia we think. But we do not understand it!"

Nina took the sheet of paper that was handed to her, opened it, and read:

DEAR MR. AND MRS. RAMIREZ:

AFTER A CAREFUL ANALYSIS OF YOUR DAUGHTER'S ACADEMIC PERFORMANCE DURING THE PAST FALL SEMESTER, WE HAVE BEEN FORCED AS EDUCATORS TO INFORM YOU THAT SHE IS UNABLE AT THIS TIME TO PROCEED AT THE PACE SET BY HER OTHER CLASSMATES. THIS DOES NOT AUTOMATICALLY MEAN THAT SHE IS 'SLOW' OR MENTALLY INCAPABLE; IT DOES INDICATE TO US, HOWEVER, THAT A DIFFERENT CLASSROOM ENVIRONMENT MIGHT BE MORE APPROPRIATE FOR HER SPECIAL NEEDS. WE HAVE THEREFORE DETERMINED THAT SHE BE LABELED 'LD' (OR LEARNING DISABLED) AND THAT A GROUP OF TEACHERS SPECIALLY TRAINED IN THIS AREA (THE AREA OF SPECIAL EDUCATION) CREATE FOR

HER A PERSONALIZED SYLLABUS WHICH MAY MORE ADEQUATELY FIT HER ABILITIES.

WE THANK YOU FOR YOUR UNDERSTANDING IN THIS MATTER,

EDUCATIONAL STAFF,

BAY ST. LUCY HIGH SCHOOL

“What does this mean, Ms. Bannister?”

“I don’t know. I’m not sure.”

She of course was sure.

Just as sure as she now was about what was going on down the halls, and in the parking lots, and in the classrooms.

“Would you excuse me a moment, Ms. Ramirez?”

“Yes! Yes! But…”

“I’ll just be a moment.”

“Does this mean that our Sonia is—what is the word? ‘Retarded?’”

“No, of course not.”

But, Nina told herself on the way out, *somebody damn sure is.*

She looked at the group of men and women standing beside the coffee table, gesturing, shouting, and crying.

There was a parent: no. There was a teacher: no. There was another parent: no. There was a coach: definitely no.

There was a woman who was none of these things, meaning she was ‘staff,’ meaning she might know what was going on

She buttonholed the woman and manipulated her into a corner.

“How many of these letters went out?”

“We don’t know, Ms. Bannister.”

“Who sent them?”

“We don’t know that, either.”

“What do we know?”

The woman gestured:

“We know that all this is happening.”

“Yes. Yes, it certainly is happening.”

She went back into the office, where the two Ramirez women were crying in each other's arms.

"Will Sonia have to go to another school?"

"No, of course not."

"But—another classroom? Because, all of her friends are with her now. Will she have to leave them?"

Yes, of course, she'll have to leave them. She's been SPEK-EDDED.

"I don't know. I just…"

"Have *you* sent this letter, Ms. Bannister?"

"No, Ms. Ramirez. This is the first I've heard of it."

"But…you are principal!"

"I know. Listen: I'm going to do everything I can to find out about this."

And she did.

Of course, she pretty much knew everything there was to know about it before she began to see people, to seek out teachers, and to read Hector Martinez' letter, Fasal Aban's letter, Chin Chi Choo's letter—the letters, in short, that had been sent to parents of children unfamiliar with the English language—and there were an inordinately high number of such children in Bay St. Lucy, due to the offshore drilling industry, the motel industry, the fishing industry, etc.—and the letters sent to other students, those who simply had for one reason or another made failing grades.

She knew exactly what was happening.

At 9:30 she called City Hall.

"Is Dr. van Osdale in?"

"No. She's breakfasting out in Larchmont with a group from the capitol."

I just bet she is.

"Pardon?"

"Nothing. Ah…this is Ms. Bannister."

"Yes, Ms. Bannister?"

"Is there a space in Dr. van Osdale's schedule today?"

"I'll check."

Pause.

"Her luncheon hour is free."

"That's from…"

"Twelve to one."

"Good. Could you tell her that I would like to buy her lunch today?"

"Certainly. And where would that be?"

Several of the more elegant restaurants in town flashed through Nina's mind:

Sergio's by the Sea; Fabrizzi's Fine Dining; Gabriellia's; Les Fruits de Mer…

"Could you tell her I'll meet her at Dee Tee's?"

"Ah…"

"Dee Tee's. It's on Third and Packer Streets. She'll love it."

"All right. I'll tell her."

"Good," said Nina, and hung up.

"What sets a man writhing sleepless in bed at night is not having injured his fellow so much as having been wrong; the mere injury he can efface by destroying the victim and the witness but the mistake is his and that is one of his cats which he always prefers to choke to death with butter."

—William Faulkner, *Intruder in the Dust*

She arrived at Dee Tee's at 11:50.

She wanted to be early, in order to see April van Osdale's expression upon entering the restaurant.

This event happened precisely at noon. (Nina was not surprised at April's punctuality.)

The expression did not disappoint her at all.

It was the expression almost certainly worn by rescue workers upon entering a village in The Philippines that had, a week earlier, been wiped out by a tsunami.

Now bodies were lying everywhere, beneath rubble, atop rotting and rusted cars.

The workers were forced to wear masks, and so a great deal of their individual expressions were covered.

April van Osdale had no mask—unless one wanted to make the point that her entire face was a mask—and so her individual expression was out there for the whole restaurant—truckers, riggers, drunks, farmers, and fishermen—to study and enjoy.

Which Nina did, from a corner table.

The woman stood frozen in the doorway, her silver pumps tightly glued to the floor, her beige jacket—good grief, she was wearing something not as bright as a celestial event—hanging limply upon her, as though the muscles and veins beneath it had instantly atrophied.

No. No doubt about it.

April van Osdale was just not a Dee Tee's kinda gal.

"April! Over here!"

The head turned mechanically, eyes still glazed in shock, the small, turquoise purse that had been gripped tightly before her shifting subtly to her back, so that it would not be stolen, or at least not without a fight.

"Nina."

Nina feared for her own name, which she'd never heard pronounced in such a way, and which had come out sounding like 'Help me.'"

"Over here!"

April thought about the matter.

Between herself and Nina's table lay the Andersonville Prison Camp.

But she was a trooper, if nothing else.

And so, with mincing, gingerly, deeply-repentant footsteps, she made her way through the close-packed tables, as though they were the corpses of rotting Confederate soldiers, who'd starved rather than partake of the mustard and ketchup bottles sitting upon them.

"Thank you so much for coming, April. I do appreciate it."

"Unnnggggg," answered April.

At least that's what it sounded like.

"I know you have a busy schedule."

"Rrrgggttttm."

Finally April arrived, as did the waitress.

This was the same waitress who had waited on Nina and Jackson, some nights earlier.

"What can I bring y'all?"

"Just...just a salad," said April.

"No meat?"

"No. Just a salad."

"Ranch dressing?"

"A little vinegar and oil."

"What?"

"No dressing."

"None at all? We've got Thousand Island."

"No, just the salad."

"All right. And for you, honey?"

"I'll have a breaded veal cutlet," said Nina. "And an extra portion of cream gravy. Oh, and do you have calf fries?"

"We sure do!"

"I'll have a side of those, too."

"All right. I'll get that right out!"

The waitress left. Nina said:

"April, I need to talk to you about these letters."

"You mean concerning new Special Education appointments?"

"Is that what we're calling them now? 'Appointments?'"

"Well, that's what they are."

"Nina, these students are falling far behind in their classes. They're holding everybody back."

There was a pause; finally Nina said:

"We're labeling these students as learning disabled because we don't want them to take the tests, aren't we?"

"Special ed students are not tested. Nor should they be."

The waitress arrived, holding a purple headband.

"Ma'am?"

"Yes?"

"The other night when the basketball girls were in here?"

"Yes?"

"One of them left this. Thought maybe you might take it to her."

"Sure. I'm not certain which one it was, but we'll figure it out."

"Good."

She set the band down and asked:

"Y'all want anything else?"

"No. Thank you," answered Nina.

The waitress left.

April van Osdale was staring at the band.

"What was she talking about?"

"A few nights ago the team ate dinner here."

"The team?"

"The women's basketball team. They came here and had dinner after the Portageville game."

"At whose expense?"

Oh God, thought Nina.

"Don't worry, April. The school didn't pay for it."

"Then who did?"

Oh God, re-thought Nina.

"Jackson Bennett."

"Bennett…the school board president?"

"Yes. He's also a parent of one of the players."

"And the coach let this happen?"

Oh God, thought Nina, for the third time.

It just gets worse and worse and worse.

"Well, the coach…"

"Who is the coach? What is his name?"

"Her name is Meg Brennan."

"Was this Ms. Brennan not aware that financial benefits paid to student athletes are strictly forbidden? And that meals count as financial benefits? Nina, we could be placed on athletic probation because of something like this! Now once again, was Mr. Brennan not aware of the rules?"

"She…"

"Surely she must have known that. Did she not protest? How could she have let it happen?"

"Actually, she wasn't here."

"She what?"

"She wasn't here."

"Then where in Heaven's name was she?"

And what could Nina say?

What could she say?

Nina, you idiot you idiot you idiot.

"She had left after the game."

"Left?"

"Left why? To go where?"

"I don't..."

"She just left the student athletes to get home from Portageville on their own?"

"It was a special occasion. Jackson came home with them, driving just behind. They were perfectly safe."

"No thanks to Ms. Brennan! And what was this occasion?"

Don't answer don't answer don't answer...

...but you have to answer, don't you, Nina?

Because you're an idiot.

"She was driving to New Mexico. To get married."

"Why New Mexico? Does her husband live there?"

Well, that's about enough for one lunch.

Let's just let it go, shall we?

"I don't know."

"You don't know why she went to New Mexico?"

"There were special circumstances involved."

"Special circumstances."

"Yes."

"Do you realize, Nina, what could have happened to us if one of the students had somehow been injured? No coach present?"

"I guess I didn't think about it. Jackson..."

"This is not Jackson's affair."

"I just..."

"And it's not your affair now, Nina. It's mine."

"April. I'm truly sorry if I've..."

"You've told me what happened, to the best of your ability. That's your job. I'll look into the matter now. But...you must excuse me. I'm late for a one o'clock appointment."

"Sure."

"Thank you for the lunch. And once again, I'm sorry for not getting with you before the letters went out."

"It's all right."

"Good day."

"Good day."

April van Osdale left the restaurant.

The waitress approached the table, looked down at the untouched salad, and said:

"She don't eat no meat, does she?"

Nina shook her head and said:

"Don't you believe it. She's a cannibal."

Then she looked at her meal for a while, took several deep breaths, cursed herself, and went back to school.

"It's because I'm alone... If I could just feel it, it would be different, because I would not be alone. But if I were not alone, everybody would know it. And he could do so much for me, and then I would not be alone. Then I could be all right alone."

—William Faulkner, *As I Lay Dying*

"Sometimes I lose faith in human nature for a time; I am assailed by doubt."

—William Faulkner, *As I Lay Dying*

It was slightly after dark when she reached Elementals: Treasure from the Earth and Sea.

The place was locked, of course, Margot having left two days earlier for The Candles, where she spent most of her time these days.

That did not matter.

Nina needed, if not the presence of her best friend, at least the ambiance of that friend.

So she walked up the darkened stairs, rammed her fist down the metal cylinder labeled 'Bannister Canister,' took out the key that had been made especially for her, and unlocked the door.

The shop gaped at her.

There were only shapes hanging from the ceiling, standing by the windows, and sparkling softly in pale moonlight that filtered through the blinds.

She walked in, made her way to the cash register counter, and flipped the light switch.

An aura of orange light glowed around her.

She walked on, happy to be if not home again, then at least home-away-from home again.

Here were the tables, the desks, the ferns, the treasures, most leased from artists in the area or other shops in Bay St. Lucy, to be sold on consignment:

Handmade clay sculptures by Jennie McCardill, who first opened her business in The French Quarter in New Orleans in 1980. Pieces sculpted from white clay, hand painted and fired twice in a high temperature kiln.

And:

Six assorted white-shell boxes from Joyce's Shells and Gifts, along with Four Cyprian Moneta Center Cut Shells.

And:

From Judy Trice at Tuesday Morning:

Hummel Keeping Time; Hummel Little Miss Mail Carrier; Hummel Chimney Sweep; Hummel Forty Winks.

And:

From Bay Breeze:

Hermann Traditional Mohair Bear; Hermann Little Starlight Mohair Bear

And:

From Denise, at M&L Gifts:

Limoges: Hinged Chef Hat; Hinged Delft Mini Duck; Swarovski Duck—Fancy Felicia

And more objects, more of the lovely things she had learned to love working around:

Pickle Casters. Meridian Basket. Pin Inverted Thumbprint.

Ruffled and Quilted Peach Bowl Art Glass Sweetmeat Server

She made her way out to the garden, where she and Margot had shared so many cups of coffee or tea, or, at the end of the day, the occasional glass of sherry.

And now Margot was to marry.

The shop would be sold.

No more mornings chatting around the cash register with someone who was paying for the latest Ramoula Peters seascape.

Nina sat at one of the tables and let her hand wurgle around in her purse until her fingers found the letter of resignation.

She took it out, held it up, and read by the pale blue light buzzing around her, the name typed on the envelope.

TO JACKSON BENNETT

Then she laid it on the table in front of her.

My God, the things that were happening.

Forty-seven students labeled Special Education.

Learning Disabled.

Separate classrooms.

All of the grades entered into computer by Bay St. Lucy teachers now immediately available for access by…by whom?

Anyone with a bit of power who wanted to read them.

Forty seven students, their lives changed permanently.

So the test scores could go up.

"I can't beat these people," she found herself whispering. "Margot, I can't beat these people."

Monsters. Everywhere monsters.

"Nina, I have funds at my disposal. If these February test scores, are, say, an average of twenty-three points higher, why, that would put the school in the 'Exemplary' range. A great many people would be very pleased if that should happen. There would also be, I can promise you, significant bonuses all around."

Significant bonuses.

What did that mean?

A thousand dollars for each teacher?

Ten thousand dollars?

Could she ignore that prospect?

And then there was Meg.

What in God's name were you thinking, Nina?

"The team ate dinner here."

Of *course* she should never have mentioned that!

What was Jackson, the smartest man in Bay St. Lucy, even thinking?

Well, he wasn't thinking, of course.

He was doting-fathering.

But that was not the worst.

"Where *was* the coach, anyway?"

Out getting married.

"Her husband is from New Mexico?"

No, April, her husband is her wife.

She's gay, April.

The coach of our women's basketball team is gay.

"Margot, I can't beat these…all these things. I'm an old woman. What am I supposed to do, Margot? I want so much to resign—but this is my town. They're my teachers. My students. Meg and Jennifer are my friends. I can't resign, Margot, can I? Can I, Frank?"

She waited.

Of course, Margot, being in love and thus absent, did not speak.

Her best friend was gone.

Nor did her husband speak.

For, despite all the comforting walks along the beach and all the imaginary conversations, he was gone, too.

She was alone.

CHAPTER 12: THE POINT GUARD

The following afternoon Meg Brennan was fired.

This was done carefully, and with as much sensitivity as possible.

At 1:15, two Mississippi State Patrolmen entered Bay St. Lucy High School, showed their badges at the front desk, walked down the main corridor, entered the room where Meg was teaching fourth period Health and Wellness, and said:

"Ma'am, are you Ms. Brennan?"

"Yes."

"You need to come with us."

"Where?"

"We're under instructions to escort you from the building, ma'am."

"What?"

"You need to get your things together."

It was at this point that Nina Bannister, who'd been showing one of the maintenance men a cracked window in the ladies' restroom, came running down the hall, her face flushed, her short brown hair disheveled by the fact that she'd been running her fingers through it.

"What the hell is going on here?" she is said to have asked.

(Reports concerning all of these matters differ slightly.)

"Ma'am, I'm Patrolman Bartkowski. This is Patrolman Davis."

"I'm very glad to know you both. Now, what the hell is going on?"

"We have instructions to escort Ms. Brennan out of the building and to her vehicle. She is to leave the campus immediately."

At this point, the students, seven of whom were on the women's basketball team, are said to have entered the discussion.

"Who *are* you creeps?"

"Is this a joke?"

"Are you guys from Hattiesburg or something?"

"What are you doing with our coach?"

The patrolmen, on the other hand, remained consistent in their approach:

"It would be better if you came now, Ms. Brennan. We need to go."

"But what is going on?"

"All we know, ma'am, is that you are to leave the building immediately. It's our job to make sure there's no chance of an incident."

"Nina?"

"I don't know what's happening, Meg."

"Am I being arrested?"

Patrolman Bartkowski:

"No, ma'am. This is not an arrest procedure. You simply need to leave the premises. Now."

"Says who?"

"Who are you creeps?"

"You leave our coach alone."

Etc., etc.

"Please, officers, please! I'm Nina Bannister! I'm the principal here; I have to know what's going on!"

"We're simply acting on orders, ma'am."

"But whose orders?"

"It would be best if Ms. Brennan would come with us immediately. We have to insist on that. Now, Ms. Brennan, please assemble your belongings."

"Nina, what's happening?"

What was in actuality happening at that point was that the hallways were filling up, both with teachers and with students, all of whom were standing and staring, open mouthed, at Room 153 where the confrontation was taking place.

Out of one of these rooms (102 to be exact), came Max Lirpa, who'd been moderating a very loud and completely chaotic discussion of the film *Inherit the Wind.*

"What the bloody hell is going on here?"

"Sir, you need to step back."

"Who the---are you?"

"Sir…"

"What are you bleedin' Nazis gonna do if I don't bloody choose to bloody step back?"

"Sir…"

"Max. Go back to your room."

"Who are these damned goons, Nina?"

"Policemen. That' all you need to know."

"They've got no rights here!"

"Well, actually, they do. They're Mississippi State Troopers. And this is Mississippi. Ergo…"

"They're not 'state troopers'! They're---Nazis!"

"Sir, will you please moderate your language?"

"Who *are* you people, anyway?"

"What are you doing with our coach?"

"Are you creeps from Hattiesburg?"

"Nina, what is happening?"

"I'm going to find out, Meg."

"Are they firing me? Am I under arrest?"

"You bleedin' bloody pigs!"

"Sir, please step back into the corridor."

"Make me! Come on! Make me!"

"Yeaahhhh! Go, Mr. Lirpa!"

"Max, please go back to your room."

"The hell I will!"

"Sir, please don't make us arrest you."

"Try to arrest me! Just try!"

And at that time, the record of events becomes somewhat difficult to follow.

What is agreed upon by all though is that Max Lirpa, if he did not actually return to his room, at least stepped back far enough to allow the patrolmen to lead Meg Brennan away, and at least moderated his language sufficiently as to avoid being led away in handcuffs himself.

The students did pour out into the corridor, where they were joined by two hundred or so other students, who followed their coach and their principal and the law enforcement arm of their home state through and then out of their school, finally standing in a tight mass in the parking lot and bellowing:

SCREW YOU COPS! SCREW YOU COPS! SCREW YOU COPS!

Until Meg had gotten into her van, along with Nina, and the black vehicle had inched its way through the crowd, the patrol car close behind it, the students still shouting and now beginning to throw handfuls of pea gravel.

It was in this way that an "incident" was avoided.

"What is happening, Nina?"

Meg was in tears, and hardly able to drive.

Nina thought about telling her to pull into the nearest parking lot, so that Nina herself could drive.

But Nina was frantically yelling into her cell phone with one breath and trying to pacify Meg with the next.

Both of these goals were proving difficult to accomplish, because: a) neither of the parties she'd been attempting to reach for the past mile and a half (Dr. April van Osdale and Jackson Bennett) were in their offices, and b) she had no idea how to answer Meg's incessant question "What's going on?" because she had no idea what was going on.

Except that she did.

Meg was obviously being fired.

Had been fired.

True, it might have been better if someone—she, Jackson, Meg, *someone*—had been informed of this fact, either orally or in writing, before a police presence had been thought necessary—but life was imperfect, and the secret of maturity lay in dealing with small setbacks with grace and as much aplomb as possible.

"Where is she? Where in God's name is April van Osdale?"

"Ms. Bannister, Dr. van Osdale has been in Jackson all day."

"Doing what? Doing what?"

"I don't know."

"There has to be a way to reach her!"

"I've been trying to call her on her private line; she doesn't pick up."

"Give me her private number! *I'll* try to call her!"

"I'm sorry, but I'm not allowed to do that."

"But we have an emergency here!"

"I'm sorry, but…"

Nina flipped the phone shut.

"Nina! I think I'm going crazy!"

"We both are, Meg."

"Why did the students have to see that?"

"I don't know."

"I feel like a criminal!"

"Just try to take it easy; we'll figure it out."

"How?"

The cell phone buzzed.

"Jackson?"

"Yeah."

"Jackson, have you heard?"

"Heard what? I've been huddled with a client."

"Two patrolmen just came and escorted Meg Brennan out of the high school."

"What?"

"Two patrolmen…"

"Okay, I heard! That's crazy!"

"You better know it's crazy!"

"Where's Meg now?"

"I'm with her! We're driving in her van."

"Where?"

Nina looked at Meg, who was shaking her head and muttering inaudible sounds.

"Meg, where are we driving to?"

"I don't know."

"We don't know."

"You don't know where you're going?"

"No."

"Then come here. Drive to my office. I'll be waiting for you."

They did.

He was.

Three p.m. signaled the beginning of rush hour in downtown Bay St Lucy. Nothing much happened in downtown Bay St. Lucy in the winter (or in the summer either, if one wanted to be scrupulously accurate), and so designations such as rush hour, mid-morning coffee break hour, early morning rush hour, and evening quiet time, did not mean very much.

But there they were, if one wanted to deal with them.

Meg and Nina parked in front of the red brick two-story building that housed Jackson's current (and Frank's once upon a time) law firm. They clambered out of the van and somehow got round to the sidewalk, Nina keeping her arm around Meg, who was still sobbing quietly, this being due to the fact that women are overly emotional, and sometimes react quite strongly to small events, such as losing a career and being humiliated by state troopers in front of two or three hundred of their students.

"I don't understand this."

"It's all right, Meg."

"No, Nina, it isn't!"

And of course it wasn't, so there remained little to say to that.

They approached the door and Nina pressed the appropriate button beside Jackson's name. There followed an immediate 'buzz,' then a reassuring 'click,' then a strange and almost indescribable 'quaat,' then the door swung upon.

The stairs stared down at them.

"Come on, Meg. Let's go up."

"How am I going to tell Jenny about this?"

"We don't even know what's going on yet."

"I'm fired, Nina! They've fired me!"

"Maybe not."

"My God, those policemen! And right in front of everybody!"

"I know."

"We're not going to have enough money to live on! Jenny's shop brings in a little, but that's mostly in summer. We don't have that much savings!"

The door at the top of the stairs swung open, and Jackson appeared in it, his form outlined in yellow, glowing background light.

"Come on up. Come up here. Let's get the two of you inside."

They climbed the narrow stairwell, which was just wide enough for the two of them to pass side by side, Nina's arm still tight around Meg's waist.

She kept it there for fear Meg would turn around, peer down the ten steps they'd already climbed, decide to end it all, and jump.

'Despairing lesbian coach kills self with plunge down stairwell of prominent attorney.'

Not good publicity.

They reached the top of the stairs.

"Come in! Come on in, Meg. Nina, you sit over there. Can I get coffee for the two of you?"

Meg shook her head:

"I can't drink anything!"

"Jackson," Nina said, "why don't you get a cup for each of us?"

It was, she had found, a universal truth that a little coffee never made things any worse.

And these things were about to get a lot worse.

"Sure! Sure, both of you have a seat. Little cream?"

"Yes."

"No."

"Sugar?"

"No."

"Yes."

"Splenda?"

"NO!"

"NO!"

Things were already getting better.

Nina, seated now in one of the imposing green leather chairs (She could remember when Frank had bought the chairs from a downtown furniture store. She had doubted the possibility of getting themt up the stairwell.)

But miracles of all kinds happened in those days; new clients showing up, victories in court, chairs fitting into impossible places and turning absurd angles…

….a long time ago.

"Here. Here's a cup for both of you."

"Thanks."

"Thanks."

So, finally, they were all seated, coffeed, deep breathed, and miserable.

"Jackson," Nina said, "do you know anything about this?"

He nodded:

"Yes, I do. I've been on the phone with the capital for the last fifteen minutes, ever since I got your call."

"And?"

He shook his head, then said quietly:

"Meg, I'm afraid you've been terminated."

"Oh, God! Oh, God, no.!"

"Why, Jackson?" asked Nina.

"Because of me."

"You?"

"Yes, Nina, because of me. Because I behaved like an idiot. I followed those girls home in the bus, and I bought them dinner. I'm a professional attorney. I'm a school board member. If anybody should have known that such things are against the rules, it's me."

Meg looked at him.

"I knew you were going to follow them home in the bus. But I thought that would be okay. And as for the meal…I thought the players were going to pay for their own food."

"They should have. But I…I just wanted to do something special for them. I must have been out of my senses."

"But…"

Meg was stammering.

"…but that seems like such a small thing. Okay, we broke the rules. Couldn't they just give me a slap on the wrist? I'd be happy to write an apology and promise never to do it again!"

Silence in the room.

A huge gorilla—probably a male silverback, weighing at least eight hundred pounds—wandered in, leapt upon the littered mahogany desk, and simply sat there, staring at each of the three of them in turn, saying in gorilla-speak:

"You can't ignore me, can you? I'm the eight-hundred-pound gorilla in the room, and sooner or later you've got to acknowledge me."

Meg did.

"This woman. This new 'coordinator' or whatever."

"April van Osdale," whispered Nina.

"Did she know about this?"

"Yes," Nina continued to whisper. "I told her."

"Why?"

"Because I'm stupid."

"You told her about the meal?"

"Yes."

"But did you tell her…"

"About New Mexico? Yes. I told her you'd gone to New Mexico after the game."

"To get married.?"

"Yes."

"To Jenney?"

"I didn't go quite that far; but I'm sure she found out quickly enough."

The gorilla jumped off the desk, said 'Thank you!'—again in gorilla—and walked out of the room.

"So," said Meg, 'that's the real reason, isn't it?"

"Two of your best friends," Jackson said, quietly, "have just gotten you fired."

The room was silent.

It was better, Nina decided, with a gorilla in it.

"But I can try it. I can try to do it."

—William Faulkner, *Light in August*

Between the hours of 3:30 and 8 p.m., too many things happened in Bay St. Lucy to be described.

So no attempt will be made.

It is possible to report, though, that a secondary conference room in the city hall was reserved for a small group of people, and that Edie Towler, the mayor, Jackson Bennett, the attorney, and Nina Bannister, the principal, all found themselves in it, when April van Osdale entered and threw a leather briefcase on the table before them.

"I have been," she said, "in Jackson. All afternoon."

No reply.

"Do any of you know," she continued, "how close we came to incurring sanctions?"

"Dr. van Osdale…"

"Mr. Bennett, you are an attorney. You are a school board member. How could you have been a party to this?"

"I made a terrible mistake."

April van Osdale shook her head.

"No, Mr. Bennett. You made several terrible mistakes. You gave what amounts to a cash reward to student athletes. You might as well have slipped each of them a fifty dollar bill and said 'Good job!' Then you took charge of them, herded them into a bus, and pretended to be their official escort during a fifty mile bus trip. If anything had happened during that trip, the school—as I'm certain you must know—would have been liable for millions of dollars in lawsuits."

"I understand all of that, Dr. van Osdale. But, as I've already said, it's my fault."

Again, a shake of the head.

"No. It's Ms. Brennan's fault. Those student athletes were her responsibility. Now, as for what she did after the game, where she went, and whom she married, those are her concerns, not mine. And I don't worry about them."

You're lying you're lying you're lying You're lying you're lying you're lying You're lying you're lying you're lying You're lying you're lying you're lying You're lying you're lying you're lying You're lying you're lying you're lying You're lying you're lying you're lying You're lying you're lying you're lying...

...thought Nina.

But she did not say anything.

"But when she left those kiddoes to, in effect, find their way home, and allowed monies to be doled out to them—she put our entire athletic department at risk."

Edie Towler, always the voice of reason, said quietly:

"We all have just been wondering, Dr. van Osdale: is there no way she could be let off with a reprimand?"

A shake of the head.

"Apparently the three of you do not understand—and perhaps no one else in the town understands—just how passionately I have had to plead this entire afternoon, and with the heads of how many disciplinary committees, just to make this thing go away. A number of people came close to losing their positions this afternoon. Now I'm sorry that this happened the way it did. I know it seemed rather sudden. The presence of the patrolmen was—well, unfortunate. But Ms. Brennan had to be taken from the school immediately. And she was."

"There is no way," Jackson asked, "for her to keep her job?"

"Absolutely none. No one is going to thank me for keeping every one of our teams: football, track, baseball, boys' basketball, all of them—from having been put on probation for at least one year. But I did so. And the cost of one coach's job was, if regrettable, still the best possible alternative."

More silence.

It was Edie's turn to talk.

"So. The girls should not have to suffer for this. Who will be their new coach?"

"As far as I can tell," answered April van Osdale, "no one."

"What?" asked Nina, Jackson and Edie, in complete simultaneity.

"We have no one to spare at the school to take over those duties. Not at this point."

"But…" stammered Jackson. "One of the assistant boys' coaches?"

"Those coaches already have a full slate of duties, both in the gym and in the classroom. To ask them to take on an entire new coaching responsibility would be unfair to them. Also, I'm very uncomfortable with men coaching a women's team."

"But that's done all the time!"

"And it might be done here, in the future. I don't know. I'm sure the search for our new coach will be a careful one. We'll interview a great many candidates."

"But," asked Jackson, "what will happen to the team now?"

"Nothing."

"What is that supposed to mean?"

"We have no team. Our basketball season is over. For this year, anyway."

Jackson's mouth fell open.

He could only stammer.

Edie was stammering, too, but more intelligibly.

"Can't we bring in someone from outside simply for the interim?"

"And pay that person out of what funding source? Everyone in this community seems to think the school is made of money. We aren't."

"But…"

"The long and short of it is, there is no woman currently employed at the high school, who understands women's basketball, and whom I would feel comfortable asking, on a purely volunteer basis, to coach this team."

"I'll coach them," said Nina.

All eyes turned to her.

All of them asked:

"What?"

"I'll coach them."

April van Osdale leaned forward:

"You're the principal! You don't have time to do this!"

"Yes, I do."

"But Nina—you don't know anything about basketball."

"I was an all district point guard for the Bay St Lucy Mariners my last three years in high school."

Silence for a time.

Finally, April rose, saying:

"Well. Let me think about it."

"That's all I ask," said Nina.

"All right then. I'm sorry for the events of this day. I wish none of it had happened."

And so saying, she left the room.

"Nina," said Jackson. "You never played basketball a day in your life."

Nina nodded, then replied:

"No. But April van Osdale doesn't know that."

Then someone smiled.

It might have been Nina.

CHAPTER 13: THE PLAY BOOK

The following day winter returned to Bay St. Lucy.

The balmy breezes and improbable January picnics on the beach were replaced by north winds, scudding clouds, and pelicans that sat shivering on pier posts, their gray feathers ruffling and their implacable eyes staring toward the sea.

Things at school had gotten somewhat better.

At least no more state patrolmen showed up.

Classes resumed.

A substitute was found to teach Health and Wellness.

The parents who visited the school, faces flushed, fists pumping, and obscene comments either muffled or not muffled, were divided into those who hated April van Osdale for labeling their children as retarded and those who hated her for firing a winning basketball coach.

Just things as usual, things as usual.

At 3:00, Nina—having left school a bit early—found herself in the living room of Meg Brennan and Jennifer Warren, a cup of steamy hot chocolate in front of her, a picture window rattling in the north wind at her elbow.

"This is not that bad," Jennifer was saying. "We're going to deal with it."

The newlywed couple had for several years rented an old frame house only blocks from the city center, and, consequently, Jenny's Art Treasures. Rental property was easily found in Bay St. Lucy, most of the older houses being owned by shop owners, who liked the ability to walk or bicycle to work. Nina had walked through the area on several occasions, always remembering the neighborhood, a mile or so distant, where she and Frank had spent so many years. She always found herself wandering wistfully from block to block, gazing at flower boxes on the dormer windows and remembering a former life.

"The shop is not doing that badly. We have some savings."

Jennifer was tall and slender. Her page boy haircut glistened black in the yellow light cast by an overhead ceiling light.

She wore a sweater and jeans, and thus was dressed almost exactly as her spouse was dressed, except her gray sweater bore an image of Bob Dylan, and the sweatshirt of Meg Brennan bore an image of Goofy.

A small fire crackled and sputtered blue-orange in the fireplace.

Tiny marshmallows floated in the chocolate, resembling mini-icebergs adrift in a kelp-brown sea.

"I'm sorry I overreacted yesterday, Nina," Meg was saying between slurps. "It was all just so unexpected."

"You can't let that bother you. Anyone would have been thrown off balance."

There was a movement from a glassed-in front porch. Nina turned and saw a white form lumbering toward them, its tongue, like an obscenely red garden hose, hanging halfway to the ground and spraying saliva as though it were an extremely slow flying crop dusting plane with short, white fur.

The animal looked occasionally from side to side but kept its attention riveted for the most part on Nina's knee, until that bodily part was directly beneath It and needed slobbering on.

She put her hand upon the dog's broad back, the effect being something like a small Cessna landing on an aircraft carrier.

"Borg," said Jennifer. "Don't bother Nina."

Borg remained implacable, lying at Nina's feet with as much restlessness and potential movement as The Spitsbergen Ice Glacier.

Borg wasn't going anywhere.

"Oh, he's all right," said Nina, quietly, sipping her hot chocolate and waiting while warm moist dog-drool soaked its way through her skirt and turned cold, which she knew it would, upon contacting her skin.

"He's a good dog."

A big dog, she found herself thinking.

An exceptionally big dog to be an indoor dog.

But a good dog.

He owned her now, had taken possession of her, and would not let her move a step without planting his toad frog-sized front paw upon her brown leather pump.

"Yes, Borg's a good dog."

Pat pat pat along the back white fur.

Ecstasy, thought Borg, his eyes now tightly closed, his heart chugging along at perhaps two beats per half hour.

"I can't believe," Meg said, "that she wanted to close down the team."

"It was that close, Meg."

"All that work…"

"Well, it didn't happen. That's the main thing."

"You saved us."

"I was desperate."

"And you really don't know anything about basketball, Nina?"

"I like it."

"Well, that's something."

"And I know…"

She paused.

The fire continued to crackle.

The wind continued to howl, rattling the window.

Borg continued to exist.

"…well, that's all I know. I like it."

"Okay. That's something. You'll be meeting the team for practice today?"

"I guess so. Three-thirty, isn't it?"

"That's right. I've got a copy of the playbook I need to give you."

"It probably won't make much sense to me, Meg."

"Still, I want you to have it. It's got clear diagrams as well as a step-by-step narrative describing the various formations and plays. I've also got a practice schedule. First, we do laps, then bleachers, then layups, then free throw drills, then dribbling practice, then five on five, and finally wind sprints."

"Okay, that's clear."

The two women sitting across from her smiled.

"The players," Meg said, quietly, "should know this stuff by now. They won't expect too much from you. Just be a calm presence."

"That's me all over."

They sat for a time.

Finally, Jennifer asked:

"Nina, why did this woman fire Meg?"

"Because Meg's gay."

Nina was surprised at the forthrightness of her statement.

But there it was.

"If it had been any other coach, there would have been a reprimand."

"So all of this story van Osdale told you about various disciplinary committees…"

"Bullshit."

Jennifer and Meg looked at each other over the coffee table and smiled.

"You know that for sure?" asked Meg.

"No. I just like saying 'bullshit.' It relieves me."

"Well," said Jennifer, "if that's the way of things, then it seems we're all being covered by tons and tons of pure relief."

They all laughed at this.

"What?" asked Borg, looking up.

They did not answer him.

By the time Nina had Vespa'ed back to the gym, the players had already changed into their practice jerseys and were doing shoot arounds on the south court. There was the pum-pum-pummeling of dribbled basketballs, the odor that is only found in gymnasiums and locker rooms and that cannot be described (it being the only smell of its kind in the world and thus comparable to nothing), the quiet banter of athletes going about their business, the rattle/whirr of huge ceiling fans in the high, vaguely transparent ceiling above, and the grim-visaged back and forth of one custodian and two male student helpers polishing the gym floor with six foot wide mops.

She stood in the gym door, watching.

She felt like she needed a ticket.

Where were the guys from the Rotary Club?

Why wasn't it all light and bright and festive and aroma-filled and party-down?

Where was all that, huh?

Nowhere to be found, of course.

Because this was the nuts and bolts of sports. Gray dust floating in the soft-filtered light of a weekday afternoon. Empty stands. A jump shot from the corner; a jump shot from the free throw line; dribble with the left hand dribble with the left hand dribble with the left hand…

…now switch and…

dribble with the right hand dribble with the right hand dribble with the right hand …

NOW STOP AND SHOOT!

Clang.

So do it again.

"Way to look, Sonia!"

"You the girl, Alyssha!"

"Go, Amanda!"

"Haley Haley Haley HAY! Haley Haley Haley Hay!"

For possibly the first time in her adult life, Nina Bannister walked into a gymnasium without a ticket.

She walked to the bench area, took off her Land's End dark red jacket, placed upon the flat surface beside her the playbook and practice schedule she'd been given, and looked out at the court.

The players had stopped; they were now standing stock still, all eleven of them, their faces glistening and sweat covered.

"Come on; huddle up!" she shouted.

Wow.

They did so!

Here they all were, circled tight around her.

She was a coach!

Damned straight!

"You probably all know I'm Nina Bannister."

Nods.

"Yes, ma'am."

"We know, Ms. Bannister."

More nods.

Okay, so that went all right.

Probably need to say something more though.

So here goes.

"I'm going to be your coach for a while."

More nods.

"We know that, too," said Alyssha Bennett.

"Did Meg email you?"

Because Meg was now forbidden to have contact with any of the girls.

"No, ma'am. We haven't heard anything from co—from Me—from…"

"…we haven't heard anything that's, like, official or anything."

"So where did you hear that I was going to be your coach?"

"The Coffee Niche."

"McDonalds."

"My boyfriend told me."

"That's all right," Nina said. "I get it."

She took a deep breath.

Haley Stephens, young, fresh-faced, hair pulled back—

—of course, they were all young and fresh-faced and hair pulled back, so why bother even to mention that?

—asked:

"Is Coach Brennan really fired?"

Nina nodded.

She knew, of course, that there would be this moment.

So why not just get it over with?

"Meg has been administratively suspended for the time being."

"So, fired?

"Yes."

"That sucks."

"Yes."

Questions were coming from all the players now, while what had been youthful expressions of joyous exuberance only moments ago were growing into the dark, threatening, and ultimately dangerous scowls that would mark their passage into adulthood.

"What did she do?"

"Is this really about that dinner at Dee Tee's?"

"We went back on the bus…so what?"

"Is that really the reason she was fired?"

Have to put a stop to this, obviously.

"Ladies…"

Nina held up a palm. The ladies quietened.

"Ladies, I know you have questions about what happened to Meg."

"Just one thing, Ms. Bannister…"

This from Alyssha Bennett:

"Did this new administrative some thing or other, this Dr. van Osdale fire Meg?"

"Yes."

"Can we kill her?"

"No."

"Can anybody kill her?"

"No. And this really isn't very funny."

"We didn't," said Haley, or Stephanie, or Megan, or Taylor—or maybe all of them at once:

"….mean it to be funny."

And they didn't.

Nina's first practice session went surprisingly well, probably due to the fact that she had to do nothing at all more than sit in the stands and watch it. The players knew that they were supposed to do laps, then bleachers, then layups, then free throw drills, then dribbling practice, then five on five, and finally wind sprints.

By the time they'd done all of these things it was precisely 5 p.m.

So there would have been nothing left to do except be sure no belongings had been left in the locker room, but that was a chore handled routinely by the student manager, Clancy Gail, or be sure the gym was locked, but it wasn't and didn't need to be, because the men's team had begun arriving at five o'clock, since this was one of the days when they practiced late.

No, there would have been nothing to do except go home and fix dinner.

Except that Moon Rivard had arrived.

She saw him as he appeared in the doorway.

He waved at her, all gray uniformed and unkempt and hair sprouting out of everywhere on him and blue eyes a twinkle.

She waved him up to the spot in the stands she'd singled out for her coach's lair, and she watched him approach while she watched the players disappear into the locker room.

"Ms. Bannister!"

"Hey, Moon!"

"Our new coach!"

"Looks like it!"

"How's it going?"

She gestured for him to sit down, and he did so, looking at the papers spread out beside her.

"It's going well. We just finished the first practice."

He beamed.

"Wonderful! Is that your play book?"

"Yes, it is."

"Know anything about it?"

"No, I don't."

He laughed.

"Well, it'll be all right. You just tell them to put the ball in the basket."

"I think I can do that."

"Bet you can! Bet you can!"

He watched the court below them, as it began to fill with slender, gawky, gangling, guffawing young men.

Finally he said:

"Nina, this thing yesterday. I was real sorry to hear about it."

"Well. It wasn't handled very well."

"The State Patrol…I don't know how that could have happened."

Nina shrugged:

"There were a lot of committees meeting in Jackson, I guess. Somebody decided that Meg had to be removed quickly, before an incident took place. And so an incident happened."

"I know. I feel like it was my fault somehow."

"I don't see how it could be your fault, Moon."

"If I could have been there first, I could have broken it to her easier, gotten her out of there by a back way or something."

"Well, don't beat yourself up."

"Anyway, a lot of people are upset by it."

"Yes, they are. That and a lot of other things. The players just asked me if they could kill April van Osdale."

Nina smiled as she said this.

Moon Rivard did not.

They sat for a time.

The men's team began its layups.

"Is there," Nina finally said, "something I should know?"

"Yes, ma'am. You probably should know it."

"Okay. What is it?"

"The town is very upset. Up until two weeks ago they didn't even know this what's her name woman existed. Now apparently people are worried about losing our money for the school. Kids are getting told they're retarded. The coach gets fired…"

"And?"

"Well, this van Osdale woman came to see me a couple of hours ago."

"Why?"

"She's been getting some letters. Bad words. Even a few threats."

And so there it was again.

The old semi-nauseated feeling in the pit of her stomach.

She had it upon meeting Eve Ivory for the first time; she had it upon seeing Helen Reddington slapped viciously by her husband.

Someone is going to get hurt, it warned her.

Someone is going to get killed.

And they come in threes, don't they?

Movie stars die in threes.

Sports figures die in threes.

There had been two murders in Bay St. Lucy…

…but no.

No, that was crazy.

The Eve Ivory affair involved huge sums of money, and the very existence of the town was threatened; and besides, Eve Ivory was killed by the sins of a horrid and violent past. Helen Reddington's murder involved passion, affairs of the heart, cruelty and villainy and morbid passion.

This was school.

This was *just school*!

Tests and records and a basketball team.

School for God's sakes!

Nobody was murdered because of school!

"So, Moon…what should we do about these letters?"

He shook his head and rose.

"Just keep your eyes open, Ms. Bannister."

"Okay. I will."

"I know you will. And good luck with your play book!"

He laughed.

She laughed.

He left.

"It's school," she found herself whispering to the play clock, which hung inert and lifeless across the court in front of her.

"Nobody gets murdered because of school."

So saying, she rose and left the building.

CHAPTER 14: A TOUCH OF JANE AUSTEN, A TOUCH OF ALFRED HITCHCOCK

"You intend to kiss me and yet you are going to all this damn trouble about it."

—William Faulkner

The following evening was a special one in The Little Hobbit House by the Sea, which was the name Nina had invented for the place where she lived, Tolkien's term being so much friendlier and so much more poetic than 'the old shack where Nina lived.'

She'd awakened early to do her chores, but had included as one of those tasks the insertion of a pot roast—along with quartered new potatoes—into her crock pot.

The meat had been cooking all day, simmering in two cans of French onion soup.

So that when she arrived home at a quarter until six, rejoicing inwardly that for an entire school day no outraged parents had stormed the main office, no storm troopers had invaded the cafeteria, no athletic teams had been eliminated, no teachers had been fired, no new standardized testing ultimatums had been handed down, Max Lirpa had not started the French Revolution, and April van Osdale had neither been seen nor heard from…

…when she arrived with her mind filled only with these reveries, and opened the door, she was greeted, in fact engulfed, by succulent aromas and the prospect of an excellent dinner.

"Yes!"

Just what she needed!

"Hi, Furl."

"Rrrggggh," answered Furl, rubbing against her leg to re-establish territoriality.

"Anything bad happen today?"

"Rrrgggh."

"Good. Any interesting national news?"

"Rrrggh."

"I didn't think so. What about domestic news?"

"Rrrgggh."

"Well, that's just the Republicans and Democrats for you. Smell the roast?"

"Rrrrrggh."

"I thought so. We'll make this a special meal."

And she set about doing so. She took off her winter clothes and hung them up, lay her school papers on the desk that sat just inside the bedroom door, walked into the kitchen, turned on the light—for it was already growing dark outside—and flipped on the Boze radio/CD player.

What should she listen to?

An Evening with the Boston Pops.

Hello, Arthur Fiedler!

And so, while she busied herself inserting the corkscrew into a bottle of Pinot Noir—she was going to have two glasses of red wine tonight despite her vows that she would not do so on a school night—the lush tones of Rimsky-Korsakov danced around her.

She turned the corkscrew, withdrew the cork, smelled it, tossed it on the counter, poured herself a large glass of Lindemann's (the world's most elegant bottle of wine for under five dollars) and sat at the kitchen table.

Furl curled (she liked the phrase 'Furlcurled') into an orange and white ball on the chair next to her.

Outside the sliding window, the lights in the offshore drilling rig had just begun to sparkle; a pale half-moon hung low over the ocean, and the great breakers roiled and crashed a quarter of a mile seaward before dissipating in eddying currents and frothing ashore as white tracery.

So what the hell was she to do?

How was she going to take arms against the sea of troubles that, like the sea that was The Gulf of Mexico, seemed to be rushing up to engulf her?

Well…

...the first thing to do was coach the Lady Mariners. Tomorrow night they were to go to Donaldsonville. Her first outing. But Donaldsonville was not that tough. The Mariners had won by 23 a month ago.

The girls knew what to do.

She would sit primly on the bench and watch. All she had to do was not run off to New Mexico and get married, and not let Jackson Bennett escort the girls home to Bay St. Lucy and then into Dee Tee's, and not buy them dinner, and not tell April van Osdale that she had done these things, and not subsequently be fired and then led from the building by state troopers.

These were all things that she could pretty easily not do.

Couldn't she? Not?

Of course she could not.

But then there were the other things.

There was the fact that she had pretty much promised to use the MOCKMACES to help get the school's scores up.

One MOCKMACE per week.

The students would be MOCKMACED to death.

And there would be more MOCKMACES, and more still, until the school became 'exemplary.'

A better idea? Why not just cheat?

How might it work?

Let's see.

Well, just find out what the questions were going to be, tell the teachers what the questions were going to be, and then instruct the teachers to, in turn, tell the students what the questions were going to be—and of course, what the answers were going to be—and what letters corresponded to the right answers.

So it would sound like:

"Students, question number 22 will be, 'Name the author of the essay, 'Nature.' The answer is 'Emerson,' (Ralph Waldo but don't bother with that because first names aren't on the test nor is anything concerning the content of the essay) and the appropriate letter will be 'b.' So write 'b' as the answer to question number 22."

She could do that.

And that wouldn't be cheating, would it?

Would that be cheating?

Certainly not!

Of course, the teachers could also just walk up and down the rows, looking over the students' shoulders and going 'tap tap tap' with pencils on the appropriate answer circles, and it might be easier.

There would be less chance of a mistake.

"That wouldn't be cheating, would it, Furl?"

"Rrrrgggh."

"You think so?"

"Rrrrggggh."

"Well, I'm not sure. I'm not sure; I think it's a very gray area."

"Rrrrgggh."

"Sure, but that's only if you see it in a Kantian way. You would see it that way because you believe in the CAT-egorical imperative. Get it? CAT-egorical imperative?"

No sound from Furl.

"Well, I thought it was pretty funny."

Still no sound.

"Okay then, let's have some salad."

She rose, turned, and opened the refrigerator.

Fresh head of lettuce, nice and tightly wrapped.

Around her, the tunes of Arabia frolicked and soared, dancing in the moonlight and glutting themselves with the smells coming out of the crock pot.

There was a flash of light on the beach below, and then another in the parking lot.

HONK.

A car horn.

Damn.

Who would be visiting her tonight?

NO!

This was the one day when everything had gone relatively smoothly. And was it to be disturbed?

She thought of all the possibilities, all the people who could have been down there blowing that horn. Moon Rivard? No, she didn't want to see him. Jackson Bennett?

No, she didn't want to see him, nice a man as he was. Alanna Delafosse? No, she had nothing suitable to wear. Tom Broussard? No she had not enough to drink. Max Lirpa? No, for so many reasons that it was unnecessary to name any one in particular. Penelope Royale? No, because she didn't want Furl hearing that kind of language.

"Just a minute!" she shouted uselessly at the closed window.

She made her way through the living room, reached the door that led to the stairwell landing, put her hand on the knob, and whispered:

"Whoever you are, I don't want to see you tonight."

Then she opened the door and looked down.

"Margot!"

"Nina!"

And, hurtling down the stairs, she threw herself into the arms of her best friend, fighting back the tears of joy as she did so.

An hour later, the three of them—Margot, Nina, and Goldmann Bristow, who was to be Margot's new husband—had devoured the roast and were sitting in a tight circle in the living room, a candle glowing on the small table, the second bottle of Lindemann's now sitting half full.

There had been introductions, of course. There had been some shock in the realization that Mr. Bristow was a somewhat elfin man, fully six inches shorter than the decidedly non-elfin Margot; but then joy in the equally clear and powerful realization that he was a shrewd and witty man, too, and that he did not laugh at his own jokes, and that he did not make the kind of jokes that elicited a required and not natural laugh, and that he might have fit quite well in one of Jane Austen's drawing rooms, and that Margot had—oh good for you, Margot, good for you indeed!—made a wonderful choice.

Nina kept thinking, during all the hugs and all the kisses and all the "We just got back from Candles today!" and all the "I hope we're not interrupting but Goldmann had to meet you's"—about Emma, and Miss Taylor, and Mr. Weston.

‘Some sadness there must be…”

For Miss Taylor, who had been Emma’s lifelong friend, had in fact married Mr. Weston, and was now to live at Randall’s, and no more at Hartsfield.

A sad thing for Emma.

But wonderful for Miss Taylor!

And wonderful for Mr. Weston, who, after having made his fortune and acquired his wife (splendid neo-classical Jane Austen!) was now to experience the pleasures that an amiable and well-judging woman could provide.

Margot, amiable?

Well, ninety percent of the time, certainly.

And well-judging?

Yes.

Or Nina would not have enjoyed her presence so thoroughly during the last two years.

Would not be enjoying it so thoroughly now.

Listening to Bristow reminisce:

“I suppose the first time Margot and I ever met was at a fund raiser. It must have been in the late seventies.”

“Nineteen seventy nine.”

“How do you remember that, Margot?”

“I marked it on my calendar.”

“You did no such thing!”

“No, but doesn’t it sound romantic, dear?”

Margot saying ‘dear’ to someone.

How strange it all was!

“It sounds romantic. But the truth is, you hated me, Margot!”

“I did not hate you! I didn’t even notice you!”

“Are you certain? I could have sworn that you hated me!”

“Not in the least! You were much too short to be worth bothering about!”

“Do you promise? Because I always felt you hated me!”

“Then why didn’t you tell me? I would have asked you what your name was again, and you would have been utterly convinced that I had not noticed you!”

“I would have been ecstatic, and I would have called you immediately.”

"Oh, by then I would have forgotten you again; but I'm sure I would have appreciated the effort!"

"And you are," said Nina, realizing that she had no business in a Jane Austen novel, but feeling the need to be a hostess, "a psychologist?"

The man across from her nodded, his coal bright eyes sparkling, and the tufts of silver gray hair circling tightly around his ears doing nothing at all, but still adding to a touch of leprechaunity that seemed to emanate from him.

"Clinical psychology. I had a practice for a number of years."

"Goldmann," said Margot, "was one of Chicago's most eminent psychologists."

He laughed.

"That's complete rubbish."

"I know that," Margot countered. "But Nina doesn't."

"Then I was," he said, nodding. "And you're very lucky, Ms. Bannister, ever to have made my acquaintance. By the way, I love your bungalow."

"Thank you for calling it a bungalow."

"What do most people call it?"

"Most people," Margot interjected, "don't come here, so it doesn't become a problem. Nina?"

"Yes?"

"You going to ask about our wedding plans?"

"No."

"Then it's time I told you."

"Tell me."

"May first."

"You're celebrating spring."

"No, it's Mayday and we're celebrating Communism."

"Margot," said her fiancé, putting a small and delicate palm over her rawboned and dangerous knee, "is not a romantic."

"I do love sex though," she said, putting her own palm atop the one already lying there, and obliviating it. "Sex and Karl Marx. Will you stand with me as Best Woman?"

"What?"

"I asked, Nina, if you would stand with me at the altar."

Nina began to speak (because one had to speak quickly in these fashionable novels or one would not be read), found that she could not, gagged a bit to get the lump out of her throat, and then stammered:

"I would love to be your maid of honor, Margot. I will be so honored."

"We," said Goldmann Bristow quietly, "are the ones who will be honored."

And then April van Osdale arrived.

The thing was so unexpected, so improbable, that it could only have coincided exactly with an equally improbable event, that is, the display of fireworks visible through Nina's plate glass window, and originating, apparently, from one of the half mile distant off shore drilling rigs.

There was no reason for the workers in such an installation to be setting off, at 8 PM on a cold useless night in late January, a fanfare of green, red, and golden rocket trails that exploded into the sky like rays in a peacock's tale, hung there for a quivering few instants, and then began to dissipate into stubborn sticks of wistful smoke.

But they had set off such a display, and there it was for all to see, and there its remnants would remain, until the cold night air swallowed them and they were left as a memory for small boys and offshore poets.

There was, equally, no reason for April van Osdale to have parked her big dark limousine directly behind Margot's outgunned and outshone Volkswagen, crossed the oyster shell parking area, made her high-heeled way up the rickety stairs of Nina's shack—which could certainly not have been The Hobbit House by the Sea to her but simply the Nina-Unsuitable Shack—and knocked at the door.

But there she was, as improbable and inexplicable as the skyrockets, differing from them not at all in color—for she was red and green and golden and orange too—but in her longevity.

She did not dissolve in the sea air and hang up in the sea air a mile or so off shore.

She stood right there, seemingly surprised that Nina had heard her knock and opened the door.

Of course, Nina was surprised, too.

"April!"

"Nina!"

Well, there was that, out of the way.

"April, come in! What a surprise!"

"Nina, I'm so sorry to come barging in like this!"

"Not at all, come in, come in!"

She did so, mincingly, staring at the hardwood floor to avoid stepping in something.

Her long blonde hair still glowed radiantly, shining an obscene peroxide gold. She had begun her Bay St. Lucy sojourn dressed as a cake; then she had become a flower; then she had become a nebula; and now she was an image of the Great Coral Reef, all a twinkle with buttons that were fishes, and hemlines of aqua anemone.

"You have guests; I should have called."

"It's all right. April, this is Margot Gavin. She owns Elementals, the shop where I've been working."

"How do you do, Ms. Gavin?"

Margot and her fiancé were standing now, neither open-mouthed nor gaping, since they could be these things later, but the pictures of social aplomb, acting as though they'd expected all along for the front door to open and The Great Painted Desert to come sauntering in.

"I'm well, thank you. This is my fiancé, Goldmann Bristow."

"Mr. Bristow."

"Very happy to meet you."

"Dr. van Osdale," Nina said, leading the natural phenomenon into her living room as fast as decompression procedures would allow, "is the Coordinator for Public Schools in Southwest Mississippi. She has offices here in Bay St. Lucy—as well as other cities—and she's been working with us at the high school in an effort to raise our test scores."

She's also a cheat and a homophobic bitch.

"She's also helping us with some budgetary matters."

Well, that was nice and weren't they honored to have her here with them and if they or anyone else in Bay St. Lucy could bladeblah blahdeblah blahdeblah.

De blah.

"So. Won't you sit down, April?"

"I can't, I really can't. I've got a late dinner with some of the folks from Seaway."

Nina was ashamed to admit that she had no idea what Seaway was—a steamship line, a hotel, a newly formed country, or a corporation of some sort—so she didn't.

"I just felt I needed to come by."

"Well. We're glad you did."

Otherwise, we would have been forced to have a good time.

"First, I should tell you that your contract as coach is ready to sign."

"I didn't know I needed a separate contract."

"Well, technically you might not have, but I managed to squeeze a bit of a financial bonus into it for you."

"That wasn't necessary."

"I know, but...well, it's an admirable thing for you to do, after all, with your other duties."

"I'm looking forward to it."

"And also..."

The woman was wringing her hands, Nina noticed.

She also noticed that Furl, who'd been hiding behind a couch in the corner of the room, now was in the process of shooting like a bi-furred meteor out from his seclusion and, at speeds beyond that of light, into first the kitchen and then—the counters not providing enough protection—the deeper recesses of the pantry.

"I...I hardly know how to say this."

"What, April? What is it?"

"It's just that I know the last days have been difficult for you. The matter of Special Education; the sudden termination of Ms. Brennan..."

"Well, those things have been difficult for us all."

"I simply wanted to say that you have comported yourself admirably. And I appreciate it."

"It's nice of you to say that. It truly is."

April's glance—for she only glanced and did not gaze or stare, such actions presaging a quality of lastingness, of permanence, which she clearly would have no truck with—that glance hardened like a split second crystallization, and she said, too quietly to be ominous and too audible to be truly conspiratorial:

"It saddens me that everyone in the community does not have your understanding."

Margot, who was not as impatient as April, gazed.

So did her fiancé.

"I have received certain letters."

I know, Nina did not say, because she'd learned her lesson, and would no longer say things around April that were, to put it one way, uncircumspect, and, to put it another way, dumb as dirt.

So she said nothing, predicting in her mind that April would go on anyway.

Which she did.

First she pursed her lips.

Her hands continued to wrangle and snake together in mortal combat like Sumo fingers.

"I don't mind the letters so much. There is another matter. A personal one. I shouldn't be mentioning it."

"What is it, April?"

"Well. There is, and has been, a man in my life. He became a part of my life while I was still at university. The relationship subsided for a time. A long time. That was good, because we have always been…how shall I say it? Fire and water. Complete opposites. Often through the years I've thought myself rid of him. But he always returns in some capacity. I found out recently that he wishes—"

She shook her head:

"I don't know exactly what he wishes. I never have, not entirely."

Nina knew nothing to say.

This woman, this confection, this joyless being.

It was hard to imagine her having a relationship at all.

"I wanted you to know about it—if something should happen."

"I'm glad you told me."

"Yes. Well, at any rate, congratulations on your basketball position. It's been so nice to meet you, Ms. Gavin. Mr. Bristow."

"The pleasure," said Margot, "is ours."

"And so, I'll leave you now; good night."

"Good night."

"Good night."

"Good night."

The door closing.

The high heel steps descending.

The oyster shells crunching.

The front car door opening and closing.

The engine starting.

The limousine pulling away.

Pause pause…

Finally, Nina:

"Well. That was April van Osdale. She's…"

But she was interrupted by Goldmann Bristow, who shook his head quietly and said:

"I know who she is."

Both women in the room looked at him.

"You know who she is?" asked Margot.

He nodded, continuing to speak quietly.

"She's a classic paranoid schizophrenic."

Nina looked at him:

"She thinks somebody may be trying to kill her."

Bristow continued to nod:

"And someone is."

"Who?" asked Nina.

"She is."

And for a time, there seemed nothing more to say.

CHAPTER 15: THE THRILL OF VICTORY, AND…

"Battles lost not alone because of superior numbers and failing ammunition and stores, but because of generals who should not have been generals."

—William Faulkner

The following afternoon at five o'clock, she arrived at the gym to board the bus for Donaldsonville.

Most of the players—Alyssha, Sonia, Amanda, Sarah, Haley—were already there, and getting aboard.

They all had bags of athletic gear.

She knew what to expect. She'd ridden the band bus decades ago to Bay St. Lucy's away games. There would be high spirits, singing, hand clapping…

She had spent the day looking forward to it.

NOW THIRTY NINE KIDS ALL CALL ME MAAAAAWWW

FROM SIPPING CIDER THROUGH A STRAAAAAWWWW!

And…

CHEER CHEER FOR ST LUCY HIGH!

BRING ON THE WHISKEY BRING ON THE RYE!

She secured the Vespa to the metal bike rack in front of the main door, waved to the bus driver, made sure of the contents of her own bag, slung it over her shoulder, and boarded the bus.

"Hi, ladies!"

"Hey, Ms. Bannister!"

"Hey, Coach!"

She turned to Arnie Johnson, the balding and perpetually smiling driver who ran a swamp excursion as his primary source of income, and asked:

"So when do we arrive in Donaldsonville?"

His smile never disappeared, and his humor was thus measured by the width of it.

Medium width.

"About an hour. It's thirty-five miles away. We got to go through Abbeyport, Smithville, couple of other little places."

"That should exhaust their supply of songs and chants."

"Ma'am?"

"I've been on band and sports busses. I know how wild the kids can be."

"How long has it been since you was on a bus?"

"Doesn't matter. some things never change."

Then she turned.

All of the twelve players had boarded the bus, as well as the two team managers.

Each of them had sprawled into a separate seat row.

Each of them wore headphones.

Each of them held in her hand a glowing device of some kind, and was typing on it with her thumbs.

None spoke.

They were completely silent. There was no sound in the bus except the grinding of gears, the low howl of the motor, and the soft tapping of incessant and nonstop text messaging—and it was clear that there would be no other sound or movement for the entire thirty five miles.

I'm very old, thought Nina, going to sleep.

Gyms, Nina had decided years earlier, like music, were decade things. All music from the sixties was the same, all music from the seventies was the same, all music from the eighties…etc., etc. Correspondingly, all gyms built in the sixties were the same, all gyms built and so on and so on.

Donaldsville's gym looked like the other gyms of its era, whichever decade that might have been. It was bright, cheery, polished, and the soul of mutability. Nothing about it was meant to be permanently in one place for, seemingly, more than a few hours. The stands were portable sliding things and could be folded like Formica accordions should there be a need for more court space. Four baskets and backboards hung uselessly over exit signs, and would hang so until needed for PE classes the following day and cranked into suitable positions.

The whole place, Nina decided while walking into it, might have been rolled up into suitcases and packed on circus wagons if the need had arisen.

The players walked in single file in front of her, seemingly unaware of their surroundings, following a sixth and lemming-like sense toward the visitors' dressing room but never looking away from their palms, which glowed as though radioactive.

"Hey, Coach!"

A beefy man was walking across the court toward her, one arm extended.

"Coach! I'm Coach Johnson!"

Who came in? she found herself asking for an instant.

Then she realized that she was the coach.

She turned and walked out onto the court, peering up at her counterpart, who smiled down at her:

"Ma'am, I don't believe I know you."

"I'm Nina Bannister."

"Paul Johnson. We were expecting to see Coach Brennan."

Well, you won't, Nina found herself thinking, *and 'why' is none of your damned business.*

Oh well, you'll probably hear it soon enough anyway.

But not tonight.

"She's a little under the weather," lied Nina.

"I'm sorry to hear that," said Paul Johnson, who, with a sweat through white shirt and golden tie—Donaldsonville's colors were gold and white—looked more like a minister than a coach.

Of course, those things were dangerously similar.

"I'm a great admirer of Coach Brennan. I also know some of y'all's football staff: Coach Hargoty, Coach Polaskus, Coach Smith, Coach Drayton—y'all have a fine overall program down there!"

"We're proud of it."

"So are you the assistant coach now, Ms. Bannister?"

"Actually, I'm the principal."

"Oh! Well, we're honored to have you here!"

"Thank you very much!"

"Y'all spanked us pretty good last time down at your place."

"Well, every game is different."

Nina the sports philosopher.

"That's true! That's true. Anyway, we're gonna try and give a better account of ourselves this time. We'd like at least to make it kind of interesting for you!"

"I'm sure you will!"

"Looks like your players know where their dressing rooms are."

"Most of them were here last year."

"Okay then. Anything we can do for you, just let us know. And good luck!"

"Same to you, Coach!"

And, with a small, coach's wave, she walked off to follow her team down into the bowels of dressingroomdom.

The gym may have been bright and polished, but there was something murky and cave-like about the dressing room: glistening tile floors, steam in the air, and the clanging of locker doors as the players spread their deep blue road jerseys on benches beside them and slipped into sports bras.

Nina walked behind them, wondering how many times they'd gone through this ritual, and wishing she were getting ready to address an English and not a basketball class.

"All right," she said. "This is your last district game before Logansport, then Hattiesburg. Don't be nervous. Just play your individual games, and you'll be all right. There's going to be a crowd out there trying to give you a hard time; don't let them. Just remember to concentrate and do the things Meg has taught you. And remember also: you're representing your school, and your community. We're all very proud of you. Now: any questions?"

There was no response at all for a second or so.

Finally, Alyssha Bennett, who'd finished dressing first, turned.

She took off her headphones.

"Ms. Bannister?"

"Yes?"

"Were you saying something?"

Nina shook her head.

"No."

Then she walked out of the dressing room and up into the gym.

From that point, everything went fine for fifteen minutes or so. The players filed out onto the court, the mangers distributed basketballs, the layup lines were formed, the free throw drills got done, the familiar omnipresent thumpthumpthump of dribbling drummed its reassuring background undertone, and, on the other end of the court, a dozen or so ponytailed and gold-jerseyed figures went about doing the same thing.

The stands were two-thirds filled on the home side, practically empty on the visitors' side.

Except for a few parents who'd driven up from Bay St. Lucy.

And, of course, Jackson Bennett.

"GO MARINERS! GO MARINERS!"

The Donaldsonville pep band struck up, playing the same thing that the Bay St. Lucy pep band always played:

"BLAAAAAAAAHHHHHH DE
BLAAAAAAAAHHH DE BLAAAAAAAHH!"

Rest rest—

"BLAAAAAAAAAAAIIHH DE
BLAAAAAAAAHHH DE BLAAAAAAAHH!"

Then came the fight song.

Donaldsonville's team called itself The Pirates.

The University of Wisconsin had stolen their fight song, too.

ON YOU PIE-RUTS, ON YOU PIE-RUTS
FAT FAT FAT FAT FAAAAT!
(BUM BUM BUM BUM BUM)

The scoreboard clock clicked down over the south basket:

One minute forty-five seconds.

One minute ten seconds.

Players huddled.

My God, thought Nina. No headphones!

Well, they must be somewhere.

Starters in game jerseys now, bench players sitting down, warm-ups still pulled around them…

Everybody out on the court.

Star Spangled Banner.

AND THE HOOOME OF THE BRAVE!

Cheers.

Clapping.

Fans on their feet.

And the jump ball!

For a minute or so things went normally.

It all reminded Nina of the Pass Christian game:

Donaldsonville won the tip.

Trouble there. They had a six-foot tall girl.

(Why did all the opposing teams always have a six-foot-tall girl?)

Still, there was hope. Bay St. Lucy stole a pass, worked the ball down the court, and began a fancy outside semi-circular weave, Alyssha Bennett, dribbling hard to the right, slipping it behind the back to Sarah Gray barreling left over the top of the key, Sonia Ramirez taking it right back in the other direction, Haley Stephens right there on another switch, everyone milling inside, screening, turning, heading out, then back in, then the ball back in Haley's hands, shot clock now at ten seconds, now at eight seconds, back to Sonia and then—

Bullet pass under the basket!

Alyssha! All alone! Uncontested layup!

Inbound Pass by Donaldsonville—

Stolen ball?

What was the call?

Bay St. Lucy ball!

Long pass—

Haley open from the three-point line, then a long, arching shot, soft, soft—

SWISH!

THREE POINTS!

Bay St. Lucy five, Donaldsonville nothing!

One minute into the game…

…two minutes into the game…

Haley off to Alyssha over to—nope, ball stolen by the tall red-haired girl from Donaldsonville down court to the slender girl with glowing ebony skin over to the feisty blonde who was built like a fire plug and who hurtled over everything in her path then her pass re-stolen by Sarah across to Sonia and then—OH NO BAD PASS knocked away by tall Hispanic girl with ponytail taken by fireplug girl—my god, she's everywhere—down court to red head over to frizz hair number 32—who'd just checked into the ball game—and bounce pass to ponytail back to frizz over to taller-than-anybody-on-our-team, then back to fireplug—

—and two points.

Then things began to go badly.

The weave worked imperfectly. The Mariners seemed to stop communicating effectively. They began yelling at each other:

"Take her! Take 32!"

"No, I've got 54!"

"They're zoning, don't you see that?"

"They're not, it's man-to-man!"

"I'm open!"

"Get out of the middle!"

"Post her up, post her up!"

"Switch! Switch!"

"Double down, now!"

Two minutes left in the first quarter; Donaldsonville 15, Mariners 9.

And then:

Alyssha Bennett dribbled hard to the right, slipped it behind the back to Sarah Gray barreling left over the top of the key and she ran SMACK into Sonia Ramirez and they fell down like two sacks of wet cement.

"OhmyGod!" screamed the whole bench.

And Nina found herself out on the floor, kneeling inside a circle of players, all of them looking down at Alyssha and Sonia, who, dazed, were sitting on their knees.

"Are you two okay?" she asked the girls.

They nodded, woozily.

"I think so."

"I think so."

"What happened?"

Alyssha pursed her lips and said:

"They were going 2-1-2. We had to adjust, and…"

Sonia shook her head:

"It wasn't 2-1-2, Leesh! They had switched back to 1-3-1, didn't you catch that? The middle was completely closed!"

"They don't play 1-3-1! They never use that! It's a disguised 2-1-2 with number 54 back in the paint to clog things up!"

"No, no, she was doubling down on the baseline!"

Sarah Gray:

"Guys, it's man-to-man! They're just softening it, don't you see that?"

The two girls got to their feet and made their way to the sideline, replaced by two bench players, while Nina found herself thinking:

They don't know what the hell is going on out there.

Which was, of course, unfortunate, given the fact that she didn't either.

And that was the way it went for the rest of the game, except it got worse.

Shots that usually went in for the Lady Mariners clanged off the rim, or, worse, were partially blocked.

There was no open space on the court in which to maneuver.

Every patch of floor that should have been used as a jump shot's launching pad was, impossibly, occupied by two beefy young women in yellow jerseys, snarling and snatching the ball away.

Halftime score: Donaldsonville 32—Bay St. Lucy 17.

"...and victory is an illusion of philosophers and fools."
—William Faulkner

There was nothing to say at halftime—or rather, there was probably a lot to say and Nina didn't know what it was.

The Lady Mariners spent their fifteen minute break doing unladylike things, such as banging their balled up fists into the lockers and screaming into each other's faces:

"CAN'T YOU SEE I'M OPEN! I'VE BEEN OPEN THE WHOLE HALF!"

"NOBODY'S OPEN! WHAT THE HELL KIND OF A DEFENSE ARE THEY RUNNING!"

"IT'S A MATCH UP ZONE, DON'T YOU SEE THAT, DOESN'T ANYBODY SEE THAT?"

"IT'S NOT A ZONE AT ALL, THAT'S THE PROBLEM!"

And then, of course, there was the inevitable realization that the game was being lost for the same reason that all athletic events are lost, and that, when one thought long and hard about it, all potential joy, success, and happiness in life itself were lost:

"THESE REFEREES ARE CHEATING!"

"THESE ARE THE WORST DAMN REFEREES I'VE EVER SEEN!"

"THIS GAME NEEDS TO BE PLAYED UNDER PROTEST!"

It was not played under protest, of course, nor would any subsequent in-depth investigation reveal a cunningly concealed plot among the two officials—one a hardware store owner from Cape Hatteras and the other an insurance agent from Sedonia—among these two men, the school administration of Donaldsonville, The Warren Commission, and the Cuban government.

There was no such plot.

There were just twenty more minutes of ugly and sordid basketball on court, accompanied off court by blaring pep band fanfares and delirious cheers from the home side of the gymnasium, and complete silence from the other side, unless one counted Jackson Bennett, who stood for most of the time bellowing alternatively the *C* word, the *R* word, the *E* word, the *H* word, the *S* word, the *P* word, and other words, so loudly that he would have been thrown bodily out of the building, had he been less than six foot five in height, and lighter than two hundred and eighty pounds in weight.

So that he got to stay.

But it wasn't much fun.

Not for anyone connected to Bay St. Lucy Basketball.

Final score: Donaldsonville 64-Bay St. Lucy 41.

And it wasn't really as close as the score made it seem.

The events following the game resembled the events following any well run funeral. Some tears, a few mutual assurances that it was all for the best and was part of a plan that we do not understand now but will at a later date, the packing of any food that remained uneaten, and everybody finally going home.

By ten o'clock they were all on the bus.

Nina had shaken hands again with Paul Johnson, of course, and had congratulated him on his victory.

"Your girls played great tonight, Coach Johnson."

"Well, we got lucky. Your bunch never quit; they kept fighting."

Da da da da and so on and so on.

She was last onto the darkened, sepulchral bus.

The players lay motionless and silent across their seats, decorating them as angels decorate tombstones.

She got into her seat.

Her travel bag lay at her feet.

She looked out of the bus.

She burned within.

Somehow, deep down, she realized this was her own fault.

Her team had been outcoached.

That big fat jackass from Donaldsonville had outsmarted her.

Well, it would not happen again.

She put her nose ball against the cold bus window, and squinted out into the night.

The sky was on fire. Atlanta was burning.

She had no head phones, but the music was playing quite clearly in her head:

Ta taaa ta ta…"

Tara's theme.

All the city was ablaze around her, but…

"Tomorrow," she whispered, "is another day."

Tara might be in blazes, but…

Ta taa ta ta…"

"I'll *never* be beaten again!"

She turned on the small reading light overhead.

Then she reached into her bag, pulled out the playbook, and began reading it.

"Read, read, read. Read everything—trash, classics, good and bad, and see how they do it."

—William Faulkner

"When it's a matter of not-do, I reckon a man can trust himself for advice. But when it comes to a matter of doing, I reckon a fellow had better listen to all the advice he can get."

—William Faulkner, *Light in August*

The following morning—Saturday—she rose, ate breakfast, went back to bed, curled up, and continued to read the playbook.

She finished the playbook at 9:30, then began re-reading it.

She finished a second reading at 11:00, then took out her notebook and re-drew the playbook until she knew every diagram by heart.

She finished this task at 1 p.m., when she had a salami sandwich for lunch. She also fed Furl and changed his litter.

At two o'clock, she went to the Bay City Public Library and affixed herself to one of its computers.

A short time later, she approached the main desk, carrying one book *(You Haven't Taught Until They have Learned: John Wooden's Teaching Principles and Practices*), and a list of ten others, which she requested to be ordered as quickly as possible, this being an emergency situation. The list included: *Dan Meyer, Basketball the Dan*

Meyer Way; (by, obviously, Dan Meyer, who, according to the computer, was a coaching legend); *The Game of Basketball: Basketball Fundamentals, Intangibles, and Finer Points for Coaches, Players, and Fans* by Kevin Sivils; *Basketball Skills and Drills, 3rd Edition* by Jerry Krause; *The Complete Handbook of Rebounding Fundamentals* by Swen Nater; *The Physics of Basketball* by Joseph Fontanella; and *My Philosophy of Basketball* by Bobby Knight, and any possible bit of information about Muffet McGraw (who reminded Nina of herself).

For the next four days she immersed herself in these books and interviews.

(Two of them came to the library on Tuesday afternoon, the others the following day.)

She most appreciated the literary style of John Wooden, whose work, for some strange reason, reminded her of Eudora Welty. Don Meyer was not bad, and came across with a touch of Stephen Vincent Benet. Kevin Sivils was John Cheever, Joseph Fontanella had in him a bit of Spinoza, Jerry Krauss was Tacitus, and for most of the Bobby Knight book, she just marked through the dirty words.

She also borrowed from Jackson Bennett, the films he'd taken of all the girls' games, including last year's loss against Hattiesburg.

She also, being a good southern woman, realized that preparations for battle demanded knowledge of the arts of war: so she checked out a book on The Battle of Gettysburg, whispering, "This time we're going to win."

At practice on Monday and Tuesday, she did nothing but sit high in the stands and watch, paying particular attention to the five on five scrimmage that took up the final thirty minutes of each session.

And on Wednesday afternoon, at precisely 3:30, she was ready.

She called the players into a tight circle and spoke to them:

"All right, ladies. We lost to Donaldsonville for the following reasons: we did not recognize that they had switched from the matchup zone they employed during the first three and a half minutes to an alternating diamond and two and box in one, with number 32 shadowing Alyssha on alternate possessions and number 54 fronting Sonia when the ball was on the left side of the court, or when Amanda threatened to go baseline. Furthermore, we consistently misread their offensive configurations and so were unable to penetrate the screens they set for number 23, who, because of her shot-making ability and tendency to go left-handed with alternate dribbles, and her sagacity in choice of shots behind multiple picks—burned our collective little butts."

The players stared at her, open mouthed.

She was to continue for fifteen minutes.

Then it was time to get to work.

Having done nothing for the rest of Wednesday's practice and all of Thursday's practice but five on five scrimmage, they felt prepared for their home game against Logansport.

The last game before Hattiesburg.

Nina showed up in her best beige suit, and two-inch high heels.

The best women coaches, she'd noticed by watching Jackson's films, always wore high heels.

The Bay St. Lucy gym was aglow, as always, with the snack bar doing land office business, Rotary Club and Masons passing out programs and directing people to their seats, band blaring, cheerleaders hurling themselves into the air, and Jackson Bennett alternately screaming encouragement and glowering at the world.

Nina noticed none of these things.

She simply stared at the Logansport players as they ran through pre-game drills.

Number 13 is only good with her right hand; she cannot dribble left. Number 24 has a hitch in her shot. Number 40 does not miss, from any range—keep the ball out of her hands. Number 4 will be their go-to girl inside—front her with Amanda. Keep Sonia darting at her like a sparrow, don't let her turn and go to the basket.

Keep number 6 off the baseline.

School song.

Star Spangled Banner.

Blare of the horn; two minutes until tip-off.

"Okay, huddle up!"

Nina was kneeling in the middle of the circle of players now, drawing frantically on the gym floor with a piece of chalk she had brought from one of the school classrooms.

"We're going to open up man to man, Sonia you take 6, Alyssha 13, Amanda 24, Hayley number 40 AND DENY HER THE BALL. SHE DOESN'T MISS, HAYLEY. WE'RE DEPENDING ON YOU. DON'T LET THE BALL GET INTO HER HANDS!"

"I won't, Coach."

"Good. Now we're not going to go plodding around with this team like we did at Donaldsonville. We have more speed and quickness than they do; so it's what we worked on the last two days, a three-quarter court zone press every time we score, if they beat that press to half-court then get back, but relapse into an alternate half-court zone press and man-to-man press depending on their offensive configuration and who's handling the ball out front. Now look, look here…"

She was drawing madly now, oblivious to the crowd noise behind her or the fact that Logansport's green-clad players had already taken the court, and were standing, hands on hips, awaiting the jump ball.

"They're too slow to guard us man-to-man so they'll go zone, but Sonia you've got to see this when you first bring the ball down court, even front zone we attack with odd front offense, and vice versa, if they're odd front, we go even."

"Now every time we switch zones or offensive attacks, I'm going to scream: GAME CHANGE! Ya'll got it?"

"WE GOT IT!"

"THEN GET ON OUT THERE AND WHIP THEIR TAILS!"

"YEEAAAHHH!"

And the game began.

Nina was able to sit quietly on the bench for perhaps a minute and a half. Then she sprang to her feet and followed the basketball up and down the court, ignoring the people sitting at the scorer's table, and fixated only on the tangle of green-clad and white-clad bodies hurtling against each other, weaving through each other, and jumping over each other.

"Front her, Sonya! No, closer! Atta girl! Move in behind, Alyssha! NO! NO! Dammit ref, she's all over her get her off her back. MOVE AMANDA! That's right. That's….OH COME ON REF. ARE YOU BLIND? Now…now get into the press *now* DOUBLE TEAM DOUBLE TEAM DOUBLE TEAM…

"GAME CHANGE!"

"THAT'S RIGHT TAKE IT FROM HER TAKE IT FROM HER TAKE IT FROM HER! YES YES YES YES …TWO! TWO! TWO! TWO!"

On you Mare ners On you Mare ners

FAT FAT FAT FAT FAAAT!

"Get back get back double down double down on her KEEPPRESSINGKEEPPRESSING…

"GAME CHANGE!"

"WATCH THAT BASELINE DO *NOT* LET HER TAKE YOU DEEP HAYLEY STAY IN FRONT OF HER!"

"MOVE HER DOWN MOVE HER DOWN WATCH THE PICK WATCH THE PICK OK OK NICE PASS NOW SCREEN AND ROLL SCREEN AND ROLL SHOT SHOT SHOT! TWO TWO TWO ATTAGIRL ATTAGIRL!

Cheer cheer for St. Luuucy Hiiiigh!

Bring on the whiskey bring on the rye!

Ever loyal to those mare ners

Fighting for victory

Baddadadadadda…

"NO DON'T LET HER SLIP BACK DOOR ON YOU BABY FRONT HER POST HER UP POST HER…OH!"

"GAME CHANGE! GAME CHANGE!"

"YES! YES, WAY TO PICK IT UP YOU MARINERS! NOW THREE QUARTER WATCH CENTER COURT WATCH THE SNOWBIRD WATCH THE SNOWBIRD THAT'S GOOD ALYSSHA HAWK HER HAWK HER PRESS PRESS PRESS PRESS…"

"GAME CHANGE!"

Foul.

"WHAT? THAT'S RIDICULOUS! THE OFFENSE INITIATED CONTACT REF!"

Swish.

Swish.

"THAT'S OK THAT'S OK STAY AGGRESSIVE STAY AGGRESSIVE! MAN DEFENSE NOW SLIP INTO NUMBER TWO ATTACK NUMBER TWO WAY TO MOVE SONIA TAKE IT TAKE IT TAKE IT YES YES YES NOW..."

"GAME CHANGE!"

"GREAT STEAL SHE'S OPEN DOWN COURT HIT HER HIT HER NICE PASS LAYUP YES!"

"GAME CHANGE"

"NOW DOUBLE DOWN POST HER UP POST HER UP POST HER..."

"Coach?"

"What is it, ref?"

"You've got to stay in the bench area."

"Okay, okay, but, keep number twenty four off Amanda's back, will you?"

"Just stay in the bench area."

"Yeah, all right but look at the game some time, will you?"

"This is a warning, Coach. I don't want to have to warn you again."

"Right. I got it."

And then ball thrown in by Logansport.

More switching.

More pressing.

"GAME CHANGE! GAME CHANGE!"

The game began to move from a canter to a sprint, and the players hurled themselves up and down the court at a frenetic pace.

WATERMELON WATERMELON
WATERMELON RIND!
LOOK AT THE SCOREBOARD
AND SEE WHO'S BEHIND!

Four minutes to go in the half. Mariners 36-Logansport 18.

It was then that it happened.

"STAY BEHIND HER DON'T LET HER DOUBLE DOWN ON YOU LIKE THAT WATCH THE PICK AND ROLL DON'T SET THAT STATIONARY SCREEN GET THROUGH IT GET THROUGH IT GET…OH! OH BEAUTIFUL PICK NOW…"

"GAME CHANGE! GAME CHANGE!"

Tweeeeeet.

Whistle.

"Coach!"

"What is it, ref?"

"I've warned you about staying in the bench area."

"Okay, I heard you."

"No, this is it! I'm tired of having to stop the game like this."

"Then don't stop the game, dammit! Let 'em play. But will you get number 34 off my nose guard's back?"

"That's it, Coach!"

"What?"

The black and white zebra'd referee bent back, then javelined his arm over his head and bellowed:

"YOU'RE GONE!"

"WHAT?"

The crowd bellowed back:

They did not say "what?"

Fourteen men, several of them coaches, ran as fast as they could up into the stands where they threw themselves on Jackson Bennett, who did not notice them.

'YOU…….! ARE YOU…….!"

The only person in Bay St. Lucy who could have restrained him physically or matched profanity with him was Penelope Royale, and she was not there.

In a short time, another fourteen men had surrounded him, and somehow they kept him from committing what, given his rage and lack of self control, would probably have been considered manslaughter in the second degree, or "Man Two."

Nina, of course, took no notice of anything that was happening in the stands.

"Are you serious?"

"You're gone!"

"I haven't done anything!"

"You've got to leave the court area! Now!"

"You can't throw me out of this game! I've got a right to coach this team!"

"Leave! Leave the court area! Right now!"

And then the state patrolmen came.

Amazing.

Every time Nina looked up these days there seemed to be state patrolmen around.

Were these the same two who'd led Meg from the building?

Oh, it probably didn't matter. One state patrolman, another state patrolman...

...pretty much all the same thing, when one thought about it.

"Coach, you need to come with us."

"But but but but..."

"Now."

"Oh, come on!"

The players were circled around, staring open-mouthed.

She looked at them and said:

"Game change."

Then she left the court.

She spent the second half in the dressing room, being consoled by this parent or that who came down to tell her she was doing a wonderful job and that they had no right to treat her this way.

Finally, with perhaps a minute left in the game, Jackson Bennett appeared.

It was of course the women's dressing room, but nobody was going to throw Jackson Bennett out of it.

He stood massively in the doorway.

Then he took two steps toward her and said:

"I've never seen anything like that in my life."

She tried to answer but could think of nothing to say.

He continued:

"I'm so proud of you. And Frank would have been, too."

Then they embraced.

Then he told her the final score: Bay St. Lucy 68, Logansport 41.

Then they embraced again.

CHAPTER 16: MOCKMACE!

"...how false the most profound book turns out to be when applied to life."

—William Faulkner, *Light in August*

"The displacement of water is equal to the something of something."

—William Faulkner

The following Friday, Bay St. Lucy High School took the MOCK MACE.

This did not happen quite as expected, though.

The tests—in English, math, social studies, and Spanish—were to be administered at precisely 10 a.m., taken with Number 2 pencils, and finished by 11:50.

Except that at 9:35 a.m., a fight broke out.

This was not one of the after school fights that took place ever so often, and that Nina had broken up on her first day back.

This was a fight in school.

"Ms. Bannister?"

"Yes," Nina answered, taking her nose out of the English literature MOCKMACE she was reading over and hoping that the students would remember that *Huckleberry Finn* was not written by Nathaniel Hawthorne. "What is it?"

"There's something going on down the hall!"

"What? What's going on?"

"I don't know; there's just a lot of yelling!"

She got to her feet, left the office, took off down the hall, and glanced around for state troopers.

None in sight.

Well, that was something, anyway.

The shouting was coming from Max Lirpa's room.

Room 102.

Chairs, she could hear, were being thrown around.

"NO! NO! NO!"

She approached the door, which was closed, and put her hand on the handle.

Several people who worked in the office had clustered behind her.

She opened the door.

All of the students were standing, but two in particular had faced off in the middle of the room; the others had formed a kind of semi-circle around them.

The two who'd been shouting, and who now stood glaring at each other, were football players.

She'd spent so much time recently with the women's basketball team that she'd forgotten what male football players looked like.

They were very big.

On one side of an imaginary 'x' that one could visualize in the floor's middle, stood LaMarcus Johnson, a defensive tackle. Facing him, red faced, was linebacker Thomas Swinson.

LaMarcus, at six feet five, was somewhat the bigger of the two; but Thomas was no stripling, and the potential clash between them promised broken furniture at the least, and perhaps a shattered wall of windows.

"All he had to do," LaMarcus bellowed, "was get out of the road!"

"He *couldn't!"*

"Why couldn't he?"

Nina took two steps forward into the room. The small entourage behind her followed.

"The way he was brought up, man!"

"What are you talking about? What does that have to do with anything?"

Max Lirpa was nowhere to be seen.

Probably off drinking, Nina surmised, with Tom Broussard.

One of the girls from the back of the room—Susan Alexander, to be exact, five foot four and short brown haired, so that she seemed a perfect imitation of Nina herself years and years and even decades ago—made her way into the combatants' circle, and, with a show of great bravery, piped up:

"He was a prince! He was raised to be a prince!"

But LaMarcus was having none of it, and continued to roar at the half of the room that was facing him:

"Don't mean nothing! The Dude has got to…move, man!"

"But he can't!"

"What you tellin' me that for?"

"What is going on here?" said Nina.

No one heard her.

No one even seemed aware that the door had opened.

A slender boy with black-rimmed glasses—clearly not a football player but probably quite proficient with computers and deeply involved in social networking—shouted:

"It's self defense!"

Then everyone seemed to want to talk at once:

"It's *not* self defense!"

"What was he gonna do? They attacked him, man! And they was four of them."

"But it's not like they came looking for him. They just told him to move!"

"Would *you* have moved?"

"For a king? You better know it!"

"He didn't know that was a king!"

"Don't matter who it was, common sense be tellin' you to move!"

"But they didn't see it that way in those days!"

"Those days, these days, it's all the same thing, man!"

"If you're walking along the sidewalk and some dude comes up and pushes you off it, what are you gonna do?"

"I'm gonna fight him, man."

"See?"

"But that's *me!* I ain't *him!*"

The room was bathed in the half light of a winter Mississippi mid-afternoon, For some reason, Nina allowed her eyes to rest upon a monstrous and grotesque piñata, which was used when Spanish was taught in the room, but which, proving far too great a distraction for other students in other classes, had been bolted tight to the ceiling.

The walls were covered with posters announcing various Shakespearian plays, for Max Lirpa was a lover of theater and was constantly in the habit of switching from one character's voice to another as he taught.

How boring, he said constantly, to be trapped in the body and mind of one being.

The students loved it.

There! There in the back of the room was power forward—how strange that she now saw certain students only in terms of their position on the court—Amanda Billingsley.

She was waving her hand.

Don't worry about getting called on, Amanda, Nina told herself, and, at least mentally, Amanda. *Just jump right in there; nobody's here to call on you anyway.*

Where was Max Lirpa?

"It's not a question of self defense or not self defense."

"What is it a question of, then?"

"Fate."

"What?"

"It's a play about fate. The gods told him he was going to have to do this; he had no choice."

"That's not right! We all have choices! It's not like God *makes* us do stuff!"

This from the boy with the black-rimmed glasses.

Do not do not do not label him a nerd, Nina.

He's a young individual with multiple tastes and strengths, and he should not be labeled as a geek or a nerd.

Amanda responded:

"But these are different gods! This was like two thousand years ago!"

"It doesn't matter," the nerd responded. "Gods are gods! It's a question of free will versus determinism!"

LaMarcus was not to be moved away from his original point;

"He still had no business blocking the road!"

Amanda:

"But that was his decision!"

Somebody else she didn't know:

"Listen, you guys!"

None of the 'guys' seemed particularly ready to listen, but the new speaker, a chunky girl with a red ponytail, was loud:

"He's supposed to be wise, right? But he doesn't *act* wise! You're told by the gods that you're going to marry your mother. So what do you *not* do? You do *not* marry somebody old enough to be your mother! Like, how smart is that?"

"But he had to marry her! He was the new king and she was queen! He had no choice!"

"But what about Tiresias?"

"Who?"

"The blind guy! Oedipus is going to have him executed! For nothing!"

"Yeah but if Creon…"

At this point, Max Lirpa stepped out from behind a movie screen in the corner of the room, and yelled:

"All right! Enough!"

Everyone looked at him.

"You have to go!" he repeated. "The bell's ready to ring!"

Everybody looked up at the clock.

Someone said:

"It's time already?"

Twenty-three students, Nina found herself thinking, do not realize that fifty minutes have passed. Unbelievable.

And they weren't even talking about phallic imagery.

Amanda tried to make herself heard above the din of people getting backpacks together.

"Mr. Lirpa?"

"Yes, Amanda dear?"

"What do we do for tomorrow?"

"We vote! The jury votes! Oedipus: guilty or not guilty!"

Responses came like popcorn from a sea of exiting bodies:

"Guilty!"

"Not guilty!"

"The Dude is toast!"

"Guilty but not of murder!"

Max Lirpa shook his head:

"Get out of here get out of here get out of here YOU'RE LATE FOR THIRD PERIOD! Now be off with you, you rabble!"

He finally saw Nina.

"Headmistress! You've come! So good of you!"

"Max…"

Both of them approached the desk in the front of the room.

"Max, what were they yelling about?"

"Oedipus."

"You're teaching Sophocles?"

He shook his head, while raffling through an impossible mixture of multi-colored papers and dog-shaggy paperback books.

"No, I've nothing to teach Sophocles. But Sophocles, on the contrary, is doing a beautiful job of teaching our students."

"Max, Oedipus is not on the MOCK MACE. Or in the real MACE! We have to teach what's on the MACES!"

"Oh yes, I meant to ask you about that."

"About the MOCK MACE?"

"Yes, yes, that…can we go to your office?"

"But your next class is at ten o'clock! That's when you're supposed to be MOCKMACEING!"

"Yes, yes, I know but I shall only need a second."

"All right."

"I have this packet of tests. Where is it? Ah, here. I'll just grab it up, and…off we go!"

The two of them left Room 102 and hurled themselves into the whitewater rampage that was the hall between bells.

"I love the term MOCKMACE, don't you? It reminds me of Lewis Carroll's Mock Turtle. His school teaches 'reeling' and 'writing,' remember? Well, just look at this hallway! Completely appropriate, what?"

"I suppose. But Max, the tests…"

"Yes, yes, I've got them right here. Ah, here we are!"

They entered her office.

He closed the door behind them.

"The tests are extremely important, Max."

"Oh yes, I know! By the way, I've heard that there exists this crow of a witch named April or May or June or some month nomenclature, who has offices downtown and is making everyone's life holy hell. That it was in fact she who was responsible for the disgraceful Nazi-like ouster of our lovely lesbian, the Sappho of Health and Recreation, our dear Queen Meg. Is this true?"

"No, Max. There is no such woman as April van Osdale. She does not have offices anywhere; and everything that's happened is our own fault because the somebody that you describe doesn't exist."

"Fie, there's no such creature! It's impossible! But of course, there is, you know. Iago does exist. As does, I assume, this woman. I should like very much to speak with her. Would that be possible?"

"No no no no no no no no no no no no not ever! Never never never never never are you even to be in the same building with this woman!"

"Well, we shall see. Now, as for this packet of—what are they called, 'standardized examinations,' that I am to give next period?"

"Yes?"

"Well, I simply…oh! Oh my god, they seem to have fallen into your wastebasket! Can you imagine such a thing?"

"Max, YOU HAVE TO GIVE THE TESTS!"

"And I would love to do so with all my heart, dear lady headmistress mine, with eyes a-shining…but as you can see, they are quite irrevocably lost."

"Max…"

The door opened; a student, out of breath, stuck her head in and gasped:

"Mr. Lirpa, LaMarcus and Thomas are in the hall!"

"What a lovely place for them!"

"They're getting ready to fight about Oedipus!"

Max Lirpa's hands flew up to cover his face, then fell to his side.

"How delightful!" he shouted.

Then, to Nina:

"My God, I love your students!"

He ran toward the doorway, passed through it, then turned abruptly and said to Nina:

"By the way, word has it you were tossed from the pitch last night."

"Tossed from the pitch?"

"Yes, everyone is saying you were thrown from the pitch."

"It's a court, not a pitch."

"Of course it is, of course it is, and what of any slightest importance happens anywhere at all except at court—but were you indeed tossed from it?"

"Yes," she sighed, "I was tossed from it."

He smiled broadly and said:

"Good show, old girl! Jolly good show!"

And he was gone.

She had no time to worry about disciplining Max Lirpa, who probably could not be disciplined anyway, and who, if everything were considered, was proving to be the most effective teacher in the high school.

She had no time for anything, actually, except being sure that the tests were administered properly.

As it happened, they were.

They were collected promptly at 11:45, graded by Scantron machines by two o'clock, and back in their packets by mid-afternoon.

At the end of the school day, Nina had the grades.

They were not good.

This was hardly surprising; what was surprising was the elegantly written letter she found in the mail holder that had been affixed on the wall beside her office door.

Dear Nina:

By now you should have the results of your first set of MOCKMACES. I sincerely hope they reflect all the hard work I know you and your staff have been putting in.

I'd like to invite you over for dinner tonight, at, say, 7:30. We can go over the scores together and drink a glass of wine with some boiled shrimp. The address is 2245 Fairway Drive.

PS: Sorry I haven't invited you over before now. I'll try to make up for it in the future.

April.

Where had this letter come from?

Ask the people in the office:

"Have any of you seen Dr. van Osdale? Was she in the building today? Did she leave a letter?"

No.

No, haven't seen her.

"Anybody here from city hall?"

No.

Nobody.

"Then how did this letter get here?"

...well. No way to know. Somebody obviously brought it by and dropped it off.

Now it's here and must be acted upon.

Okay.

Bad scores.

An invitation from April, so that the two of them can go over the bad scores.

And eat shrimp.

Well. There was nothing to do but do it.

And so she did.

"From that night the thousand streets ran as one street, with imperceptible corners and changes of scene"

—William Faulkner, *Light in August*

Seven-twenty p.m.

Her Vespa seemed out of place on Fairway Drive. It was fine along the beach, and it fit well with the bicycles, skateboards, Mini-Coopers, and bandaged pickup trucks that populated the rest of Bay St. Lucy.

But this was the land of true foreign exports: Mercedes, BMW, Porsche…this was oil and gas money, political clout money, Big Fishery money…and anyone able to live here had to be one of the shining stars of the Southern Riviera.

Which, of course, any friend or ally of the senator was.

Still, she wondered, was he that powerful in the state?

She'd never been in one of these homes before.

And she wondered, as she braked, accelerated, scanned addresses, peered beneath the just-now-illuminating blue street lamps, and cautiously urged her little cycle over speed bumps…whether April would have been housed in a porched and pillared plantation home, magnolias dropping huge oily-green leaves on the lawn and rocking chairs sitting motionless on the second floor verandas…or if she would have opted modern, living in a one-story brick ranch house, giving up in historicity and charm what it gained in having bathrooms that actually worked.

The streets grew smaller. Jack Nicklaus Way; Arnold Palmer Trail; Tiger Woods Drive…and the vast low hanging pines obscuring the houses thickened, so that she could see only patches of yellow light seeping through the great picture windows behind them. The automobiles too became, not larger, but blacker and greyer and shinier and more redolent of old money.

She turned again, this time merely a slight curve to the right, but the street changed names yet again and narrowed still further, only allowing room now for one car at a time to pass between those few vehicles parked on the street.

What was this street?

Fairway Drive.

And, yes, there was the fairway, and the greens, and the perfectly sculpted hundred or so acres set aside for the truly rich. The golf course, meandering through evergreens that towered above the steep and slate gray roofs, not reaching all the way to the sky, but brushing just slightly a moon that seemed particularly round and improbably jocund.

Twenty-two-forty-one; twenty-two-forty-three…

There it was. Twenty-three-forty-five.

She pulled meekly into the driveway, feeling a need either to ask permission to be here or to reach out and take a parking ticket from an automatic vendor.

Immediately before her sat a car the size of her beach shack, but cleaner, and with more dining space inside. She inched her way to within a few feet of it, so that the Vespa's front bumper just extended a foot beneath an overhanging wooden roof which protected the car that mattered.

She killed the engine and got off, slinging her purse over her shoulder. Night had actually fallen now, but golden illumination from the high windows of the house itself, the yard lights standing sentinel along manicured clay walkways…all of it made her feel that she was in a private midway, and that, only a few yards farther along, arcades would have been set up and it would be possible to throw balls for Kewpie dolls.

She glanced at her watch and read the luminous dial: 7:30

Exactly on time.

She walked around a corner of the house, skirted a hedge that seemed to have been trimmed to the exact rectangular dimensions of a densely limbed and web-infested cracker box—and approached the main door.

"The clock tick-tocked, solemn and profound. It might have been the dry pulse of the house itself, after a while it whirred and cleared its throat and struck six times."
—William Faulkner, *The Sound and the Fury*

It was slightly ajar.

Strange.

She pressed the doorbell and heard, very clearly through the open door, a cascade of chimes detonate throughout the house.

Then silence.

Nothing except a few winter-hardy cicadas complaining in the trees back over the street.

She waited.

Finally, she said, not really shouting, but still in a tone that seemed to her intrusively loud:

"April?"

No response.

The door stood open before her.

She rang the bell again.

Same response.

Dong *DONG* dong *DOOOOOONG*!

She became aware of the ticking of a clock in the room before her.

No one was at home.

She reached once more for the doorbell, which glowed reassuringly pink, and seemed to draw her index finger to it by a warmth that, if it did not really exist, at least produced a kind of imaginary antidote to this world of stillness and shadow.

Ring again?

Why bother?

The door had ornate glass designs, backed by wisps of hanging curtains, dark now like everything else…and a black space of slightly more than an inch separated it from the door jamb.

She peered through the glass and could see nothing.

Reaching forward, she felt the smooth mahogany of the door frame scratch the tip of the same finger she would have used to press thc doorbell button.

Go home. Go home. Just go home. Something's not right here. Just go home.

She pushed.

The ponderous, lead-weighted door swung inward, brushing over a throw-rug lying just inside, the door itself now two inches open, now four, now six…

A vast and dimly lighted room spread before her like the set of a movie. Plate glass window far across the Angora carpet…she did not know what an Angora carpet was, but if there was such a thing, soft and giving and firm and colorless and never-spilled on at all…this thing sponging beneath her shoes was it; furniture of dark green leather and black-iron tubing, books like soldiers guarding every inch of wall space, separated from other books only by paintings, which hung perfectly straight, like windows with Dutch sailors and English ships looking out of them.

She could hear behind her the sound of a plane overhead, probably on a landing approach to Bay St. Lucy's small airport. Far down the street there was the occasional baying of a dog; and beyond that she could make out traffic noise, muffled and distant, on the Interstate circling the city.

Why was the door unlocked?

The room stared back at her, grey and inert, its sharpened corners and clear lines blurred now by darkness and near silence. But the clock, almost as tall as the ceiling itself, stood watch, pendulum swinging easily within its panel-casing, a face surrounded by Old English numbers.

Seven thirty-five.

She stepped further inside.

The room grew more distinct as her eyes accustomed themselves to its half-light. A staircase beyond and to the right, leading up into complete darkness; a decorative cupboard on the wall opposite, circular shapes that must have been dishes gazing out into the center of the room; several feet beyond that, the doorway leading into the kitchen, where she could see counter, shelves, refrigerator, a table.

In her purse was a cell phone.

She felt a mad desire to call the police.

And tell them what?

She had been stood up?

There was no one here. And that was all.

"April?" she shouted.

Her voice echoed back at her.

But there was no response, of course.

Was there something wrong here?

No.

No, of course not!

This was completely like April van Osdale. Nina did not exist to her.

Someone important had called. Someone from the state educational center, perhaps flying into Bay St. Lucy on the very plane that she had heard only moments ago.

April had received a dinner invitation and had simply forgotten once more about little Nina, the woman she'd met years earlier at The University of Mississippi and not retained the slightest memory of.

This was the nature of Aprils. To completely forget Ninas.

And that had happened once again.

Nothing was wrong here.

No need to call the police.

But, why was the door open?

The door was open, she told herself, because April had simply forgotten to close it securely.

Happens all the time.

She took a deep breath, then another.

Then she turned, walked out of the house, closed the door firmly behind her, and pushed on it.

It had locked itself.

"Just one of those things," she whispered to the knob. "Wasn't in a mood for shrimp anyway."

She walked away, wondering what April would have to say to her the following day.

She did not know that she was not to see April the following day.

Or any other day.

Ever.

CHAPTER 17: THE WILDS OF MISSISSIPPI

"Before us the thick dark current runs. It talks up to us in a murmur, becomes ceaseless and myriad, the yellow surface dimpled monstrously into fading swirls travelling along the surface for an instant, silent, impermanent and profoundly significant, as though just beneath the surface something huge and alive waked for a moment of lazy alertness out of and into light slumber again."

—William Faulkner, *As I Lay Dying*

The following morning, Saturday, Meg Brennan arrived at Nina's shack driving a recreational vehicle with two kayaks on it, announcing: "Great weather! Love this weather! Dramatic!"

Nina, who'd arisen some time earlier, stepped out onto her porch and sniffed the air.

It was not great weather, but somber, wet, gray weather.

Still, Meg's exuberance seemed to warm it up and dry it out.

"You had breakfast, Nina?"

"Yep. Bacon and eggs. What's going on, Meg?"

"Congratulations on the Logansport game! I heard all about it!"

"Thanks!"

"Can't believe you got tossed! Took me two years coaching before I had my first ejection!"

"Yeah, well, I'm a fast learner!"

"You sure are! Hey, wanna talk about Hattiesburg?"

"Of course I do!"

"I'll tell you everything I know. I've only got about a hundred or so pages of notes and play diagrams to use against them."

"Ok then, come on up."

"I've got a better idea; let's go kayaking!"

Nina shook her head:

"I don't know how to kayak."

"You don't know how to coach basketball, either. But somehow, you do. You're wonder woman."

"I don't want to drown."

"You won't drown. I'll teach you how to kayak—and we'll talk Hattiesburg!"

She thought about it; what was the harm?

It would get her mind off April van Osdale, off being stood up, and off the ridiculous examinations that she'd been forced to administer the day before.

"All right. What do I wear?"

"Wear your kayaking stuff!"

"Got it."

She went back inside, changed into her 'kayaking stuff'—which consisted of a pair of Nikes, a pair of blue jeans, and a pair of sweatshirts, one worn over the other—and in five minutes, Meg was sliding open for her the door of the van.

Nina felt as though she was staring into a sporting goods store.

There were tennis rackets, bowling shoes, golf clubs, kayak paddles—two of which Meg grabbed casually and threw behind her out on the driveway—and softballs. There were running shoes and running shoes and more running shoes. There were dumbbells and barbells and hats and caps and sunglasses and tubes of suntan lotion (which, thought Nina, neither of them could ever have needed).

"My God, you've got everything in here!"

"Jenn and I like to be ready for all emergencies, sport wise."

"Where is Jennifer?"

"She's running the shop."

"I must say, Meg, you guys seem to be taking this pretty well."

The two women had climbed into the van by now; Meg started the engine, backing carefully out of the driveway while nodding and saying:

"We've been through worse. We've been through a lot worse. I was just caught off balance the other day at school. But I'll get another job. In a way, I'm kind of glad to be out of this one. I loved working for Paul, but this…"

"Don't say it."

"I know. Hey, let's talk Hattiesburg."

And they did.

They talked about nothing but zones, pick and rolls, press strategies, psychological ploys, players' strengths and weaknesses, and every other possible matter, while pine forests grew denser on either side of the two lane road as they wound their way north.

They also talked, of course, about the McNulty sisters.

"They're both six four, Nina. And believe me, they're mucho tough. Theresa and Nicki. One of them slapped 24 points on us last year; the other 18."

"How do you stop them?"

"You don't stop them. Nobody stops them. That's why Hattiesburg won state last year. All you can do, maybe, is slow them down. But when they alternate down low and move the way they can from free throw line to baseline—and given the fact that Hattiesburg has superb guard play as well, it's just tough."

"How much did you lose by last year?"

"We lost by eighteen, but it felt like more. Of course, we were at their place; this year they have to come to us."

"Well. That's something."

"You plan to get thrown out again?"

"No, but I'll have my say."

"You know the whole town's talking about you."

"It seems like that's happened before. Twice in fact."

"Yeah, but that was about solving murders. This is about sports; it's serious. You're everybody's hero. I can tell you, the gym's going to be packed Friday night. Oops! Here's our cutoff!"

Meg braked and turned into what appeared little more than a cow path. The van bounced for half a mile or so, and came to a stop at the edge of a clearing.

"The stream's down there! It's almost white water for two miles or so, then it flows into a small lake. We'll kayak down into the lake, then hike back and get the van. There's a way to drive back to the lake where we'll pick up the kayaks so that we don't have to carry them back. This kayak trail was the first one Jenny and I tried after we'd moved to Bay St. Lucy. Come on! Help me get these kayaks off the roof of the van!"

She did so to the best of her ability. There were two kayak beasts for them to battle against, one bright yellow and the other an even brighter red.

The fight was uncertain for a time but ultimately they won. Finally, the boats lay begging at their feet. The two women passed a quiet moment of mental exultation, after which Meg clapped a palm on Nina's shoulder and said:

"Now we have to get you outfitted. Primary rule among kayakers: life jacket. Here's one that fits me pretty well. We're about the same size. Put it on."

Nina took it in her hand, unclamped a few elastic bands, slipped it around her, snugged it back down to her, thumped her palms once or twice on her now greatly expanded chest, and deemed herself ready.

"It's good."

"Not too tight?"

"Nope."

"All right. Try this helmet."

The helmet was a good thing too, because rain was starting—she could hear droplets spattering on its vinyl surface—and because it, along with the jacket now protecting and enlarging her torso, made her feel like a football player.

She almost wanted to take off running toward the stream, which she could hear running beneath them, somewhere hidden in the dense forest.

But that was impossible, of course, because of the kayak lying there.

"First," shouted Meg, above the roar of an increasing wind, "stretch a bit. Do what I do; you don't want to pull a back muscle."

She could not do what Meg did, of course, but she could do half of it, bending halfway to the ground, twisting halfway into a pretzel, etc.

But finally it was time to attempt the job at hand:

"Have you ever picked up and carried a kayak?"

"No."

"It's not that hard. This one just weighs forty pounds. So, stand right in the center of it."

"Here?"

"Yeah, that's good. Now crouch down, and pull it up so that the cockpit opening is against you."

"Cockpit?"

"The hole in the middle where you're going to sit."

"Why don't they just call it a hole?"

"I don't know. But do it."

"Okay."

"There you go, that's good. You've got it snug against you. Now bend down low and get your shoulder under the edge of the kayak. When you feel that edge cutting into your shoulder just a little bit, then plant your feet, take a deep breath, and stand up."

"Can I do this?"

"Sure you can! All the lifting's going to be done with your legs. You'd be amazed at how strong they are. Nina, you could probably lift a double kayak. Come on now, do it!"

She braced herself, took a deep breath, counted one, two…

…and stood up!

And she could do it!

She was doing it!

"Hoorah for Nina!"

"Wow," she said, rocking back and forth from one foot to another, "it's not that bad!"

"Told you so!"

The weight of the kayak was cutting slightly into her shoulder, but all in all the boat seemed much lighter than she'd expected.

"Wait for me a second…"

Meg hoisted her own load as though it were a sack of groceries and said:

"The stream is down there to our right. I'm pretty sure I remember the path; it's a little overgrown but not too bad. Now come on, follow me."

And off the two of them trekked.

Nina had not gone ten feet before the forest had surrounded them. The already dark morning closed in, rain spattering on dense foliage, and the ground springy and soft beneath her sneakers.

She fell into a march rhythm, one two one two behind the steadily pacing form in front of her, and she began to realize a sense of—what was it?

It was near exultation.

The wind, strong as it was, was not actually cold, and the rain was movie rain: she could watch it and hear it but not feel it. It had no effect on her.

What did have an effect on her was the adventure of the thing, though. She was not feeding her cat, nor sipping tea in Margot's garden, nor reading a book, nor walking idly along the beach.

She was doing this entirely outrageous and unplanned thing, a thing she'd never done before or even dreamed of doing, a thing that other people did, bizarre people, people who squinted against the sun and climbed mountains and sailed around the world and caught marlin and—well, those kind of folks.

Just like two nights ago.

She was a basketball coach…and she was a kayaker?

What would Frank have thought?

"How you doing?"

"Good! Doing good!"

"Maybe a hundred yards more and we're there! You up for it, Nina?"

"Sure!"

"All right then!"

They trudged on.

She could not free her mind of April van Osdale, though, despite the excitement this new world was supplying her with. What an outrageous thing to do to her. Invite her for dinner and simply not show up! And then, of course, there was the matter of Max Lirpa. He could not be allowed simply to ignore the tests. Someday April would find out, and then there would be more state troopers.

"Okay, here we are!"

Her reverie was shattered by the appearance of the stream, which hardly looked like a mere stream.

It may not have been the Mississippi River, being perhaps no more than fifteen feet wide.

But it was a pretty significant current of water at that, foaming and frothing, bits of branches and leaves spinning in tight, miniature whirlpools that sucked them under into the gray/green mud water, then spewed them up again a few yards farther along...

…yes, it was a pretty good little water stream at that.

And in a minute or so she was going to be on it.

Like one of those tiny branches.

Sucked under, spewed up.

Well, so be it!

"Okay, we'll enter the stream here. Crouch down, and let the kayak slide off your shoulder."

She did as she was told.

In a second, they were sitting together, their breaths coming faster, whether because of what they'd done or were about to do Nina did not know.

"Now, here we go…"

Meg was forced to shout, to be heard over the noise of the wind, the rain, and the fast flowing water.

"Put your left foot into the cockpit first, then be sure you're balanced and slide over into it. I'll give you a shove."

"What do I do then?"

"The stream will take you. So go ahead, slide on in."

All right, Nina told herself.

Left foot over, and in.

Now, slide on, slide on over…

…and in!

Knees cramped in front, leather seat behind, get straight get straight.

"Got your paddle?"

"Got it!"

"You're off!"

A great push from behind and the stream had her, hissing along, sky now a slight band of open gray as the canopy of trees opened up.

She was aware of several things simultaneously: the undergrowth on either side of her blurring slightly as her speed increased; droplets of spray kicking up from her paddle as she dipped it—almost pointlessly since the stream was carrying her so fast anyway—first to the right and then to the left of the kayak; and two black crows flying directly above her, stationary now, their speed matched precisely by hers.

There was a sound behind her: Meg shouting something.

She could not make it out, her ears already too jammed with rushing water, roaring wind, paddle banging on vinyl kayak side, and bird yammering from the wall of forest sliding past.

Certain landmarks did stand out: a gnarled tree that had fallen into the stream and was now reaching out with dead and rain-soaked limbs to grab her as she shot by; a huge rock, moss-covered and sodden, looking on dour and sullen; a fish that jumped, flat and shining-silver at a spot just five feet to her left as she took the paddle from the water and attempted to change sides.

"RRRgggg!"

The shout again.

Could she turn around?

She laid the paddle across the cockpit in front of her and did so.

The world reversed itself, with the creek now thundering away behind her and a bright yellow collaboration of human and vinyl that was now Meg Brennan motioning thumbs up.

She did the same, then turned back.

God this was fun!

She did become aware, at least momentarily, that she had no idea what to do in case she flipped over. She had read something about it, she knew that.

There was one thing you did have to do, and it was relatively simple. There was another thing you absolutely were not supposed to do, and it was simple too, and if you did it you would drown.

But she could not for the life of her remember what these things were.

And on and on they went, she and the little craft beneath her and the benignly hissing water and the twin crows that were her pilots, all navigating a straight course for the Great Gulf of Mexico.

Occasionally, there were rocks, the slime-green upper curves of them breaking the current, which shot past them uncaring, as it would have gone by statues of dead sea turtles; but Nina realized quickly that she could turn the boat with some dexterity, a few degrees right, a few left; so that, given time to see the obstacles approaching, she could contrive to miss them.

Unseen obstacles…

…well that was for another time.

If she hit something unseen she would tip over into the water and either drown or be rescued by the woman following behind her.

The rest be damned.

This lusciousness went on for an indeterminate amount of time, since time, in the middle of a fast flowing stream, alters its own flow, becoming something to match the perceptions of birds tree frogs snakes rocks crows ripples leaping fish and swirling eddies—and not the perceptions of human beings.

But after whatever the amount of minutes or seconds or hours or years it actually was, something did finally change.

The current, she could tell, began to slow.

The banks were farther from her now.

The entire stream turned itself to the right, and then continued to curve on, moving now at a forty-five degree angle to the straight northerly flow of the clouds.

And in front of her, opening like a window, was a kind of lake, its water slow-moving and placid, its surface dotted with what seemed like jagged cypress knees rising amid rugs of green moss and lichen.

The boat slowed, slowed, slowed; the trees lost their blur and regained edges to their leaves; frogs, twin humps above their eyes giving away their position, squatted in an inch or so of water just at the shore line—

And Meg, pulling hard on her paddle, came abreast, shouting:

"How was it?"

"Great!"

"Exciting?"

"Incredible!"

"We have to paddle over to the right, now. We'll beach the kayaks and rest for a while."

They did beach, and within a minute they were sitting on the shore of a lake perhaps a hundred feet across, getting their breath, the boats sitting like psychedelic hunting dogs beside them.

As she bent forward and wrapped her arms around her knees a chorus of bullfrogs began to go off, the guttural groans mixing with all the other noises of this forgotten little jungle, unexplored for god knows how long.

Sometime later, their sense of intimacy having grown enormously out of basketball bonding, Nina surprised herself by asking:

"How was it for you two, at the first? When you first got to know each other and became…partners?"

Meg shook her head slowly, the bottom of her chin just touching each wing of her tightly closed life jacket.

"Not too bad. When you consider people's attitudes back in those days. There were problems; but we had a lot going for us as a couple. We got through them."

"Did you always know that you were gay?"

"Oh God, no! Girl Scout normal, both of us. Jenny growing up in Vermont, me in northern Mississippi. We both thought we had the perfect marriage. Then…it just went crazy. Hers and mine. Crazy."

"What happened?"

"Everything started being miserable. Even the little things, the trips to the grocery store. Just hateful. Yelling at our husbands, our husbands yelling at us. And then we were divorced—I don't even want to go into that—and then each of us was just floating around like something out on that lake. Somehow we each wound up getting jobs at a bank in a suburb of Vicksburg. Don't even ask how we got to there. But we were working right beside each other, and, of course, we commiserated, and that led to lunches together, still no idea—well, you know. And then one day it happened. God I was shocked. I'm still not sure about Jenny. I think she may have seen it coming more than I did."

"Was it tough for you, being a couple?"

"Not so much. We both knew what the world was like. So we were discreet. For a while we had separate apartments. It's not like we went parading around naked in the park yelling, 'We're glad we're gay!' like some people do now. We were especially careful in the bank, and so both of us kept getting promoted. We were making pretty good money. And we discovered Bay St. Lucy on a vacation trip. Jenny had always dreamed of running a boutique. I had always been a jock, and had a degree in physical education. So I got the coaching job here, and Jenny bought her place. It's been good ever since. Despite April van Whatshername."

"Don't worry about her, Meg. We'll find a way around her. She's not going to torment Bay St. Lucy forever. The town won't stand for it. By the way, where in New Mexico did you get married?"

"The county courthouse in Roswell. We wrote our own vows. I suppose we've been writing them for a long time, living them really. But it means a lot to do this. It means an awful lot."

There was, of course, no silence, for the cacophony of the rising winds and the caws squawks and rattles of the wilderness prevented that; but there was a lull in the tumult that was Wilderness Mississippi, and in the middle of it, Meg said, smiling:

"It's funny. When we had the wonderful shower at Margot's place…"

"Yes?"

"We laughed because she almost missed it. She was off chasing ghosts."

"Yes. I remember that."

"It's just that, for so many years that seemed exactly what Jenn and I were doing."

Then the sounds of the forests resumed, and the two women simply sat and listened.

CHAPTER 18: PROPOSALS

The afternoon cleared gradually, so that by six o'clock, when Meg's van pulled onto Breakers Boulevard and then onto the small lane leading down to Nina's shack, Bay St. Lucy had turned golden and shimmered like a painting done in luminescent colors. The sun, almost ready to dip its solar toe into the ocean down shore and to her right as she made her way up the staircase, looked as big as a basketball. She'd have been surprised that it reminded her of a basketball, except that now everything in the world—ball point pens, cattle, love poems, dishwashing detergent—reminded her of some aspect of basketball, so she simply made herself ignore the phenomenon.

The stairs rocked and groaned with her weight as she made her way up them.

Her calves were already sore from the afternoon's kayaking.

Sunlight shone on the window panes, and made it look as if her living room had burst into flame.

She was high enough now to see out over Bay St. Lucy. The tops of waving palm trees looked as though some careless celestial chef had over-plopped an egg on each one, the yokes breaking and spilling out over the town, which had thus been transformed from seaside hamlet to seaside omelet and was ready to be eaten, along with the green salad that was its treescape.

"Oh, come on. Not again."

A sheet of paper had been stuck between the screen door and its facing.

"Why can't I just come and go inside? Why is everybody always writing me letters and sticking them in my door?"

The door did not answer.

The letter though, after she opened it, did:

Nina,

Thanks so much for the lovely pot roast dinner. Goldmann and I are driving back up to The Candles tomorrow, but we wanted to see you one more time before we left.

We have a proposal to make to you. We think it's a very interesting notion, and we'd like to discuss it with you.

We're going to walk along the beach for a while and then go out on the pier. It's five thirty now; we should be somewhere on the pier, or near it, for the next hour or so. If you don't find us there, come on over to Elementals.

Hope to see you soon!

Margot.

Well. Good news.

She put the sheet of paper in her pocket and walked back down the stairway, cursing at the pain in her calves, and wondering if a similar affliction was starting to affect her shoulders.

Damned exercise.

But, she remembered, the feeling of flying down the river!

Maybe it was worth it.

She straddled the Vespa, started it, and puttered off toward the setting sun, which had now turned blood red and appeared as romantic and beautiful as a nuclear device exploding.

Within a mile, she could see the pier, and shortly thereafter she was walking toward it.

The ocean pier was a new feature to Bay St. Lucy, constructed with funds the town had recovered from the Robinson estate. For decades there had been no access to the ocean except for the flat and frothy beachfront, and the stone jetty that was constantly wave-splashed and crabclaw spattered. But now, here, stretching before her and a quarter of a mile into the Gulf of Mexico, was this twenty foot high elongated platform, with solid belt high stair bannisters that led not upward but outward, along which the infirm could steady themselves, and on top of which children could terrify their parents by preparing to fall into the ocean.

The air was fresh and cool; two stars could be seen in the twilight sky, and the waves frothed and billowed, churning around the long pier posts and scudding a miniature storm surge that could just be seen through cracks in the pier's flooring.

Few people were out here: a fisherman, lone and desolate, his baseball cap pulled low over beetling eyebrows, a cigar stub sticking cold and forgotten from his lips, which also seemed cold and forgotten, having nothing to do with the fishing process.

A young couple.

A father with two children.

The wave surge was changing now, more majestic, deeper, roaring as it crested and spread and shallowed and rebuilt itself, the grand sweep of the thing stunning in both its simplicity and inscrutability.

"Hey! Nina!"

There they were. All the way at the end.

"Margot! Goldmann!"

"Come on out! It's marvelous out here!"

"I'm coming!"

Within a minute, she'd reached the end of the pier, beyond which lay the string of yellow lights that was the offshore drilling rig, beyond which lay the Great Gulf of Mexico, beyond which lay the Great Atlantic Ocean, beyond which lay if one were to believe all one reads some other continents and other people but if one really thought about it and used common sense nothing at all except The Great Eternal Universe and The Never Changing Mind of God.

"Good to see you guys!"

"Yeah! We couldn't go," said Margot, now embracing Nina, "without saying good bye!"

"I should hope not."

The two of them, Margot and Goldmann, were dressed almost identically in London Fog trench coats and floppy Rex Harrison My Fair Lady hounds-tooth hats.

Goldmann Bristow spread his arms and shouted:

"Look at all this! Isn't it wonderful?"

Nina, who'd always thought that, nodded.

"It is."

Nothing more to say.

Bristow took a step toward her and said:

"We heard about you!"

Oh God.

"Yeah."

"Nina," said Margot, leaning down just a bit so that she was closer to the two five feet four people she had to address:

"Nina, is it true?"

"It's true."

"How could you get thrown out of the game?"

"It's easier than you might think."

"It's just so…not you!"

"It was me. All me."

"What did you say to the referee to make him do that?"

Nina thought for a time and answered:

"I told him I felt his decision making, while evincing perspicacity and aplomb, and certainly demonstrating an impressive knowledge of detail, might have been lacking in balance, sensitivity, and—well, the kind of 'panache' and ebullience that would have lifted his performance even beyond those standards that the community had come to expect from him."

"And what did he say?"

"Oh, he said 'Get the…….out of the game."

Goldmann Bristow roared.

"Marvelous!"

"Everyone," Nina said, quietly, "seems to like that part."

The waves laughed.

So did the klatch of seagulls screeching low overhead, and so did a giant manta ray, which, like a brown dishcloth, was floating some fifty yards out in the ocean.

All of this laughter continued until Creation sobered itself up, and, between deep breaths and sighs and smiles and whatever, Margot said:

"Nina, Goldmann and I have had an idea."

Aha.

So this was the proposal.

"What idea, Margot?"

"How would you like to work full time at Elementals?"

This was a bit of a shock.

"I don't understand."

Margot leaned forward:

"Nina, do you really want to keep being principal…I mean, after this year?"

"I don't know. Probably not."

Because that was true.

She would fight the battles that she now perceived were raging around her.

But more? Another year? Another five years?

No.

"Probably not."

"Well…Goldmann and I are going to be at Candles a good bit of the time. But Elementals is such a joyous place. And I have such lovely memories of our cups of coffee or tea or brandy or whatever there, while people shopped and puttered and perhaps bought a seascape or a bit of earthenware…"

"I have those memories too, Margot."

"Then let's not give them up entirely. We can easily find someone to run the shop until May, perhaps cutting back on hours open—say from ten until two, a little more on weekends. But starting in June, you could manage it full time. You have marvelous taste, and we would, of course, trust you to find things to be sold on consignment. Either I, or Goldmann and I together, could drive back down to Bay St. Lucy every weekend or so, and we could all hang out together in the shop. You wouldn't have to worry about living on commission, or such things. We could pay you quite a decent salary."

"Wow."

The sun, not wishing to deal with such problems, disappeared below the horizon.

A pelican swooped low and defecated on the pier.

"You don't have to answer now, of course."

"That's very interesting, you guys. It really is."

"We know you're caught up in a great many matters at the school now. But—well, if you would just think about it."

"I will. I truly will. And as for school now—I can't tell you how much I wish I could just quit tomorrow. Not the basketball, of course, but everything else."

"I'm sure," said Goldmann Bristow, "it must all be terribly difficult."

Nina nodded:

"It would all be okay. I could do it. But this woman. This van Osdale."

Silence for a time.

A speedboat cut across the water, roared its way west, and finally disappeared, falling into the hole left by the setting sun.

"Goldmann…"

It seemed strange calling him that.

But she would get used to it.

"Yes?"

"I just wanted—well, now that we're out here—"

"Go on, Nina."

"The other night, when you met her. You said those things about her."

"I shouldn't say a great deal. After all, I was around the woman for no more than five minutes."

"But you formed an opinion."

He paused, then nodded:

"Yes. I formed an opinion."

"Could you tell it to me again?"

He shook his head:

"Like I say, perhaps it would be wrong of me."

"Please. I have to deal with this woman. Bay St. Lucy has to deal with her."

Silence.

Margot spoke quietly to her fiancé:

"Go ahead, dear."

To which Goldmann Bristow shrugged:

"She has all the symptoms of paranoid schizophrenia. She impresses me as a woman who has been, well, 'driven,' for a great deal of her life."

"Yes. That's April."

"Such a desire for perfection is, on the one hand, laudable. On the other, though, it can be quite destructive."

"In what way?"

"In the way that perfection is simply impossible. In neither ourselves nor in others."

"We can't all," Nina heard herself whispering, "be exemplary."

"Pardon?"

"Nothing. People who develop this trait—they like measuring things, don't they?"

"Oh, immensely. They are 'quantitative' people, not 'qualitative.' Deeply distrustful of themselves, of their identities, they require mathematical proofs of their excellence."

"Without which," Nina continued, "they wouldn't exist at all."

Bristow nodded.

"You might say that. The middle stages of such paranoia result in intense self loathing."

"And the advanced stages?"

"Self denial. Not self discipline, but the denial of one's own existence."

"Suicide?"

"That is one possible outcome. There are others, many entirely unpredictable. It's like, out there, in the gulf, if one went deep enough or far enough."

"How do you mean?"

"Uncharted waters."

The waves continued to pound.

The night continued to deepen.

Nina said that she would think about Margot's proposal.

They walked back to shore.

Uncharted waters.

She went back home and tried to think about something other than April van Osdale.

This was basketball of course, her new passion.

She had a small cave made in her bedroom: chairs, end tables, bookshelves—all of these had been pulled into a tight circle. She had pasted play diagrams on every available space.

The lights were turned out.

A cup of hot chocolate steamed in front of her as she watched again and again the tapes of two Hattiesburg games. There they were, always. Therese and Nicki McNulty.

No one could stop them.

Each of them six foot four.

Long, blonde hair, broad shoulders.

Identical twins.

And no one could stop them.

Ball down low, Theresa goes for basket, slips ball to sister.

Layup.

Ball over the top.

Layup.

What to do? What to do?

And then…

And then…

Tara's theme. The Civil War.

She kept thinking about the Civil War. And Pickett's Charge.

No sense, but there it was.

And what had Meg forgotten to do?

Why did Meg lose to Hattiesburg?

And then…

And then…

"She didn't use her whole army," Nina whispered, her breath making small ripples in the hot chocolate.

The wind outside grew stronger, rattling the shack's windows. Saturday night faded into Sunday morning.

"She didn't use her whole army."

And we will.

We will use the entire army

Some of us will be sacrificed.

Half of us will be sacrificed.

But we will use our whole army.

By Monday afternoon's practice, the plan had been perfected.

She called the team around her:

"Ladies, we're going to win this game that's coming up on Friday night. We're going to beat Hattiesburg."

No answer.

No cheers.

Everyone remembered the McNulty sisters.

It was easy for a coach to talk about victory, but…

"I'm going to tell you right now just how we plan to do it."

"How, Coach? We've never been able to stop those two girls."

"I know, but we will this time."

"How?"

Nina shook her head:

"When you met them before, you failed to weaken their center. You didn't put enough infantry fire on Hancock's men."

Blank stares.

"Well, we're going to weaken that center. We'll have to sacrifice half our team to do it. But it will get done. We will weaken their center; and then we'll hit them with Pickett's Charge. Only this time, it will work."

Two girls at once:

"Pickett's Charge?"

Nina:

"Yes. Pickett's Charge."

Pause, pause, and then:

"Is that going to be on the MACE?"

Nina shook her head:

"No. Thank God."

And then:

"Now, let's get to work."

And they did.

CHAPTER 19: WHAT IS TESTED IS TAUGHT

The first part of Tuesday morning Nina spent in limbo. She had in her desk the results of the first MOCKMACE examinations given the previous Friday morning. These were results that she'd been expected to share with April van Osdale on Friday evening, at dinner.

Except that April van Osdale had not been present for dinner; present had been only a well decorated house on a golf course.

An empty house.

April had also not answered her phone on Monday morning or Monday afternoon.

"Dr. van Osdale is not in the office," the secretary had said.

Twice.

She could have been in Jackson, with the senator.

Or she could have been at her alternate office in Hattiesburg.

At any rate, she was not reachable, and Nina did not know what to do about the test results.

Make careful notes of all missed questions and re-test?

Forget these tests and order new ones?

Why could she not simply coach the basketball team? In that area, things were at least beginning to make sense.

And it was in this state of mind, asking herself these questions, that she spent Tuesday morning running around like a chicken with its head cut off, doing this errand and that errand, dealing with a milk money crisis in the lunchroom and fifteen lost volumes in the book depository.

She was in a bad mood when she returned to her office.

Stuck in the mail slot was yet another standardized test.

"Who left this damned thing here?" she shouted at no one.

No one answered.

She opened the office door, fuming, and took inside the manila envelope containing what she assumed was yet another mock test, this one also having come from the inscrutable April van Osdale.

She sat down, ripped it open, and read:

OFFICIAL EXAMINATION DOCUMENT

NOT TO BE OPENED UNTIL DATE OF ADMINISTRATION

ANSWER SHEET IS TO BE COMPLETED WITH NUMBER 2 PENCIL ONLY

TIME LIMIT: FIFTY FIVE MINUTES

MARK CLEARLY ONE AND ONE ANSWER ONLY

"Okay, okay," she said to herself.

Then she read further:

PART ONE

ANSWER THE QUESTIONS IN PART ONE TO THE BEST OF YOUR ABILITY. YOU ARE TO READ THE QUESTION CAREFULLY, FORMULATE YOUR ANSWER, AND THEN MOVE ON. YOU ARE URGED NOT TO TAKE AN EXCESSIVE AMOUNT OF TIME ON ANY ONE QUESTION. PLEASE NOTE THAT EACH SECTION OF THE EXAMINATION IS STRICTLY TIMED.

DO NOT UNDER ANY CIRCUMSTANCE BEGIN THE EXAMINATION BEFORE THE OFFICIAL MONITORING AGENT SIGNALS YOU TO DO SO.

WHEN GIVEN THE APPROPRIATE 'START' COMMAND, YOU MAY BEGIN.

GOOD LUCK!

Then the questions:

Dr. April van Osdale is:

a) Dead

b) Alive

c) Missing

Nina stared at the document in her hands:

"Oh my God," she whispered.

There was a knock on her door.

"What?" she said, automatically.

The door opened; a student assistant stuck her head in:

"Ma'am?"

"Yes?" her voice still on automatic pilot.

"Are you busy?"

She looked up and said:

"What?"

"Are you busy right now?"

Then she looked down at the examination, which lay upon her lap like a flat, white cobra.

"I think," she whispered, "that I'm going to be busy for some time."

"All right. I'll see that you're not disturbed."

The whisper continued, almost automatically.

"Thank you."

The door closed.

The examination refused to go away and continued to hiss, silently.

She read the first question again:

1. Dr. April van Osdale is:

a) Dead

b) Alive

c) Missing

She found herself continuing to whisper, and she wondered who might be listening.

"Statistics show that if you don't know," the whispering said, "you should choose 'c'."

The questions continued:

2. If you show anyone your work, or share the questions with your neighbor, you will be:

a) Not practicing good citizenship

b) Failing to comply with the stated rules and regulations pertaining to The Mississippi Academic Skills Examination, Regulation 4298-Part B.

c) All of the above

…and the last question:

3. Your next step should be:

a) Act rashly and impulsively

b) Panic

c) Act prudently, go home, and wait to hear from a friend.

…then:

THANK YOU FOR COMPLETING THIS PORTION OF THE MISSISSIPPI ACADEMIC SKILLS EXAMINATION.

PLEASE PASS FORWARD YOUR NUMBER TWO WEIGHT PENCILS, OR GIVE THEM TO THE PERSON MONITORING THE EXAMINATION.

YOU WILL RECEIVE THE RESULTS OF YOUR EXAMINATION IN SIX WEEKS OR LESS.

IF YOU FEEL YOU HAVE BEEN DISCRIMINATED AGAINST IN TAKING THE EXAMINATION, YOU MAY REQUEST, IN WRITING, THE OPPORTUNITY TO BE TESTED AGAIN.

THANK YOU AGAIN FOR YOUR COMPLIANCE.

And that was that.

Nina thought for a time.

Then she carefully put the test back into its folder.

Then she went home, without speaking to anyone.

The next ten hours were pure hell.

She could do nothing but sit in her bedroom and look out of the window.

Her cell phone remained in her hand. She should call Moon Rivard, should call the state police, should call *somebody*!

But whoever had put this thing in her mailbox would know it.

And what could Moon Rivard do?

Begin a search for April van Osdale?

Who had probably been abducted?

It was too chancy, was it not?

And when had April been abducted? The only answer was, Friday night, just before Nina had arrived at Fairway Drive.

She had been told to go to her shack and wait: a friend was to arrive.

What friend?

She waited. And waited. And waited.

At 7:00 PM, just after sundown, Penelope Royale drove up in her jeep.

She went downstairs just as Penelope was getting out.

"Nina?"

"Penn, what's up?"

"I got this letter. Got it about an hour ago; don't even know where it came from."

"Yeah, that's the way things seem to be happening. Let me see."

She read:

"Dear Ms. Royale. Please take Ms. Nina Bannister to the following GPS coordinates as soon as possible this evening. You will find a five hundred dollar bill enclosed as partial payment for your services. As soon as you and Ms. Bannister have returned to Bay St. Lucy, another thousand dollars will be forthcoming."

Penelope looked at Nina.

"Do you know what this is about?"

"No, Penn, I don't. Not exactly. I know some things. But I can't talk about them."

"Do you want to go?"

"Where are these coordinates?"

"Petit Bois Island. Maybe ten miles from here. Have to go by boat. It's wild grass and marshland, with a few trees and fishing sheds."

"I think I have to go."

"All right; I can use the money."

"Penn—this may be dangerous."

Penn approached Nina, laid a palm gently on her shoulder, and said:

"I'll promise you something, Nina. And I mean this. I wouldn't lie to you."

"What?"

"I won't hurt anybody."

Nina thought for a time, then said:

"Well. If you're sure."

And the two women drove off.

CHAPTER 20: PETITE BOIS ISLAND

"And I will look down and see my murmuring bones and the deep water like wind, like a roof of wind, and after a long time they cannot distinguish even bones upon the lonely and inviolate sand."

—William Faulkner, *The Sound and the Fury*

At 8:30 p.m., Nina and Penelope approached Petit Bois Island, a part of the Gulf Islands National Park Reserve. The moon was in the absolute middle of the sky above them; shallow grass water shimmered beneath it, as though the air were filled with phosphorescent particles.

"Is there anything out here, Penn?"

"I don't know. I guess we'll find out."

Penn, wearing a bulky fatigue jacket and combat boots, turned the keel slightly; she increased power on the small outboard motor, which chugged and purred enough to disturb the water slightly, their wake flat after ten feet. Her nervousness could be measured by the fact that she'd refrained from cursing.

This almost never happened.

"Come here."

"Okay."

Nina stood carefully and made her way from the metal seat she had taken…as much for ballast as any other reason…back to where a black box in the stern was glowing green, flashing, going dark, then blinking again.

"Look at the radar screen."

"It's just a bunch of green splotches."

"That's land, islets and such. The dark is the water."

"Where are we?"

"Here. We're always in the center of the screen. Z653x…those are our GPS coordinates."

"What about the others?"

"X869r. That's where we're going."

"How far?"

"Half a mile more. There's a narrow little river, not much more than a stream, that runs into the island."

Soon they had gone from open water to what seemed little more than swamp, the boat slowing as they made their way under moss that hung down like spider webs, and Penelope navigating carefully through the white jutting knees that seemed to grow up through the water like stalagmites. Overhead an occasional owl thrashed about in the tangled branches, and standing, sometimes no more than a few feet from them, herons and egrets, absolutely motionless, gazed into the water, hunting, waiting.

The island sang to them as they drifted. The marshes to her left were covered with blue radiance.

Penn said quietly:

"Gas. Nitrogen. Bubbles up through the reeds. They call it swamp fire."

She watched its filmy curtain rise, quiver, and evaporate.

Finally Penn whispered:

"We're there."

Nina looked around. They were in a lagoon, the swamp encircling them, shadowy and impenetrable. Here and there she saw logs, glistening in what was still a daylight bright night.

Double humps with yellow spots for eyes ringed the boat, half-submerged in marsh water and cattails, croaking gutturally in a kind of unearthly syncopation.

"Frogs out here," Penn whispered, "size of a basketball."

Beyond the boat's prow Nina saw, for the first time, a kind of man made structure.

It stood stork-like on spindly poles that seemed much too emaciated to hold anything larger that one of the monster frogs that kept croaking in anti-harmony, or one of the turtles that she could see floating like black and patterned dinner plates beside the boat.

"What is that thing?" she whispered, her voice sounding unnaturally loud.

"A kind of shelter."

"Does anybody live there?"

"No. You see them sometimes on these deserted islands. They're just fishing shacks."

She focused more clearly on the structure now, on the clapboard room and its rusted metal roof. Nothing about it was straight, the boards themselves running at odd angles as though they'd been fixed to its precarious frame by nails in a hurricane

Penn killed the engine of the boat, which began to drift through eddying moss across the lagoon. She took Nina's hand and whispered:

"When we get there, I'll go up and see what's in that shack. You wait here; stay by the motor."

Penn stood, gazed up at the shack hovering ten feet over them, then sighed heavily:

"Okay, here goes," she said, and started up the stairs.

They creaked and wavered with each of her steps.

Within a minute, she'd topped the stairway and pushed open what passed for a door. It's screeching seemed to quieten for a second the marsh birds, crickets, frogs, cicadas, and, as far as she knew, bears that bellowed from the vines encircling them…but the sound disappeared with Penn, and, after only an instant, the swamp was the same singing chorus and the shelter stood dark.

In a second she reappeared and beckoned.

"Come on."

"What did you find?"

"Not much. The stairs are okay, I think. So is the floor."

Nina made her way out of the boat and onto a half rotted step. She touched lightly on it then moved on, gripping the banister to steady herself as she climbed.

"Come on in. Not much here."

She entered the shack.

The room she found herself in was perhaps ten to twelve feet square, and empty except for one or two beer cans that lay against the baseboards. Dust was everywhere, floating in the air, covering the table on which Penelope had left her flashlight, thick on the soft boards beneath their feet, and weighing down even the spider webs that hung ponderously like gigantic fans from cracked boards on the ceiling.

Nina began to make her way around the room, wondering what had been planned, what was to happen here.

Then she glanced down at the seat of the chair.

There was a piece of paper.

"Is that trash?" asked Penn.

"Maybe. It's been here a while. There's dust on it."

"Open it."

"All right."

Nina did so.

It had once been typing paper but had now begun to darken and crack.

The words, typed on what seemed to be a word processor, were still clear, though:

APRIL IS THE CRUELLEST MONTH.

"What does that mean?" asked Penn.

"It's Eliot."

"Eliot who?"

"Don't worry about it."

They walked around the room. Several of the window panes were broken. The jagged glass remaining was so deeply filmed by dust as to be impossible to see through.

"Nina, come here."

"What?"

"Come here to the porch. Look down there, in the water. And tied here on the porch rail."

Nina crossed the room, stepped out onto the porch, and looked down.

She saw a thick rope, securely tied, taut.

"There's something down there."

"What?"

"I don't know. But I will."

Penn grasped the rope and began to pull, hand over hand.

Finally she said:

"Bring the light here."

She retrieved the flashlight, returned, and centered the beam on the spot where the rope entered a tangle of black moss.

Penelope continued to pull, hand over hand, hand over hand…

"There. Look…"

"What is that thing?"

"Wire. It's some kind of a cage. Here…let me wipe that moss off…"

The cage continued to rise from the water. Nina could see within it now: there were saturated rags that had once been clothes. There was also what seemed at first to be a tangle of colorless hair.

"What are those things, Nina?"

"Those were," Nina answered, "April's clothes."

"And that other thing? It looks like the hide of a cat that's been skinned."

"It's a wig. A blond wig."

"Look. There's a little locket of some kind."

"Yes."

It was a locket. Circular and silver.

It opened easily, revealing a note, which said:

"This is the last of April van Osdale. RIP."

The two women looked at each other.

After some minutes, they descended the stairs, made their way back onto the boat, and went back to Bay St. Lucy.

CHAPTER 21: THE WOMAN WHO WASN'T THERE

"...the reason for living was to get ready to stay dead a long time."

—William Faulkner, *As I Lay Dying*

There was no thought, of course, of further confidentiality.

Something had happened to April van Osdale, and the authorities had to be informed.

Nina chastised herself mercilessly during the boat ride back to Bay St. Lucy harbor, saying every five minutes or so to Penelope Royale:

"I should have gone to Moon the minute I got that stupid "standardized test."

"But, Nina, if I understood you right, whoever wrote the test told you not to."

"Yes, but whoever wrote the test must have done something to April."

"That's just the point, Nina. If you had told somebody, maybe April van Osdale would be dead by now."

"She might be anyway, for all we know."

"Maybe. But all we found were two dresses and a wig."

"That's not all we found."

"We found a note saying 'RIP.'"

"Oh. Well, there's that."

By nine o'clock, Nina was sitting in the office of Moon Rivard, who was studying the 'examination' she had received, the letter to Penelope, and the soaked garments and wig.

"Now what time did this, this 'test' come to you, Nina?"

"I got it about ten this morning."

"How did you get it?"

"It was in the mailbox on the door of my office at school."

"And you have no idea who put it there?"

"No. There's so much hustle and bustle around a school principal's office. I was in and out. Teachers come and go, and so do parents and students. We try to make sure that no complete strangers come in, but sometimes…"

"I understand. And you chose not to bring this thing to me immediately?"

"I know. It was stupid. I just thought, whoever left the thing seems to know everything I do, anyway. If I tell someone…"

"Yeah, well, that's the way kidnappers usually work."

"You think April has been kidnapped?"

"I don't know what to think right now. You say you were invited over to her house for dinner on Friday night?"

"Yes."

"She wasn't there, and the door was open?"

"Just slightly ajar, yes."

"You went inside?"

"I did, Moon, but nothing seemed wrong. No sign of a struggle or anything. April is—well, she's got important friends, and she doesn't care a whole lot about somebody like me. I just assumed she'd forgotten the dinner invitation, gone out with friends, and failed to close the door properly."

"And you didn't try to get in touch with her."

"I did on Monday. Twice. I called her office here in town, her office in Hattiesburg, and her office in Jackson. No one had seen her."

"That seems strange."

Nina shook her head:

"Not really, considering that it's April. She has friends in very high places. She's on committees we don't even know about. Most of the time her offices have no idea where she is."

"I see. Well, the bad thing about this, is that she got all those angry letters."

"There's something else, Moon."

"What?"

"April was at my place the other night. She talked about some man coming into her life."

"In what way?"

"I don't know. She was vague. But she said they had been in a relationship for a long time. A love-hate relationship."

"You didn't see this man?"

"No."

"Any strangers been hanging around the school?"

"Not that I've noticed."

"Well, it's like I say, ma'am, I don't know what to think."

"Moon, I have to tell you, Margot Gavin's fiancé is a psychiatrist."

"I think I heard that somewhere around town."

"He met April. Just briefly, but he met her."

"And?"

Nina shook her head:

"He thinks she has some pretty bad problems. She's a classic…"

"No, ma'am. Don't tell me any of those big words."

"Okay, but he held out the possibility that she might consider suicide."

Moon shook his head.

"Maybe. But as far as I know, folks who want to commit suicide just do it. They don't go sending people on treasure hunts to pick up their clothing."

"No, I guess not."

"But, Miss Nina, I got to say one thing to you."

"Okay, go ahead."

"It was really wrong for you to go out to that island. Anything could have happened."

"I had Penn with me."

"Well, that makes me feel some comfort. And of course, we have some people going out there now, just to search all that water around the little shack."

"Again, Moon, Penn and I didn't find anything wrong in the shack."

"No blood, nothing like that?"

"Nothing. It was pretty dirty, like nobody had been there for a while…but no signs of a struggle."

"This is the damndest thing I ever saw. It's like the woman just disappeared."

"Yes."

"Okay, then you go home and try to get some sleep. We're gonna treat this as a missing person's case. We're trying to get a lowdown on all the contacts that might know something about this."

"I've given you all the numbers I have, all the offices, her secretaries' names."

"That's good. Now we're going to have a car take you back home. You understand: if anybody calls you again, or contacts you in any way, you don't try to be no hero. Just call me immediately."

"I understand."

And so ended the conversation.

The following day meant school as usual.

It was hardly 'as usual,' of course, because Nina's mind was filled with a thousand frantically working ants, all digging tunnels in the soft clay of reality.

She could not keep her eyes off the mail holder affixed to her door.

She knew that a statewide 'woman hunt' must be going on; that the senator had to have been informed by now of April's disappearance; that all of her offices in the southwest part of the state were being gone through, that her phone records were being checked, that her car was being gone over, that her home was being examined with the utmost care, that neighbors were being questioned, that the writers of all critical letters were being interviewed…

…and yet she also knew that a strict blanket of confidentiality was being spread over the entire matter.

The press knew nothing.

The school knew nothing.

Occasionally, a teacher would ask Nina about the results of MOCKMACES. Nina knew of no choice but to reveal those results.

But she did not bring up the subject of April van Osdale's reaction, and she simply changed the subject as soon as possible.

In short, whatever was being done about the disappearance of April van Osdale was being done without her knowledge.

This did not make the matter a great deal easier.

True, she did not like the woman.

But somehow, she felt she had failed.

There had been some attempts at fraternization.

She had done nothing to further them.

Perhaps, if the Friday night dinner had taken place, April would have confided in her.

But confided what?

No, the thing preyed on her mind and would not let her rest.

It preyed on her mind during Wednesday's basketball practice.

It preyed on her mind during the school day Thursday.

And it was preying on her mind Thursday afternoon when the phone rang and Jackson Bennett said:

"Nina?"

"Yes?"

"There's been a development in the matter of van Osdale."

Ominous.

She almost did not want to continue with the conversation.

But she did, saying:

"What is it, Jackson?"

A pause.

"We need to talk about it."

"Who?"

"Edie Towler wants to meet with you and me and Moon. Town Hall, her office, seven tonight. You can be there, can't you?"

"Sure. That's right after practice."

"All right then."

"Jackson, is April…"

"I'm not sure what it is. I'll see you tonight, Nina."

And he hung up.

Some hours later she entered City Hall.

The three others—Moon, Edie, and Jackson—were waiting for her.

Once all of them were seated, Edie said:

"We just got word about four hours ago…"

Silence.

Only the sound of the ventilation system.

Nina felt on the verge of tears.

Say it, Edie. Say it.

"Here."

Edie passed around several copies of what appeared to be a letter.

Nina forced herself to look at it. It appeared to have been written out on an older typewriter.

It said:

TO THE SENATOR:

IT IS WITH TRUE REGRET THAT I MUST RESIGN FROM THE POSITION TO WHICH YOU HAVE APPOINTED ME. THE CHALLENGES FACING OUR EDUCATIONAL ESTABLISHMENT ARE GREAT INDEED, BUT AT THIS TIME I DO NOT FEEL CAPABLE OF MEETING THEM. I HAVE IN THE LAST DAYS SUFFERED A DECLINE IN MY HEALTH, AND I FEEL THE NEED TO GO AWAY AND ENTER UPON A PERIOD OF REST AND RECOVERY.

AGAIN, WITH TRUE REGRETS,

APRIL VAN OSDALE.

They looked at each other over the table.

"I'll be damned," growled Jackson.

Silence for a time.

Nina looked at Edie:

"What do you think?"

Edie could only shake her head.

"I don't know."

"Edie, when was this delivered?"

"Apparently early this morning. But there was only one copy, and it was sent to the senator's office. The senator gets a lot of mail. This was almost overlooked."

Moon Rivard:

"What does this do for our investigation here?"

Again, Edie shook her head:

"Moon, as far as I can tell, no one knows exactly what to do about this. The letter's hard to authenticate. It seems to have been written on an old typewriter. But it could be true. The woman had strange habits, and, apparently, had been under a great deal of pressure. Maybe the letter is the real thing."

Nina shook her head:

"It's not the real thing."

Everyone looked at her.

She could only repeat:

"It's not the real thing. It can't be."

"But Nina…"

"April's dead."

The words sounded as though they were clanging around in a tomb.

She surprised herself by saying them yet again:

"April van Osdale is dead. Someone has murdered her."

Jackson:

"How do you know that, Nina?"

She shook her head:

"That insane 'test,' that cage in the water, those clothes; all those things didn't just happen by chance. Someone took April. And someone murdered her."

Questions from all around the table:

"*When* did someone take her, Nina?"

"Sometime late Friday afternoon."

"How? Somebody just came in, said, 'Please come with me!' and left?"

"I don't know."

"You think this was someone April knew?"

"I don't know that either. A lot of people didn't like what she was doing at the school; and there was a man she told me about."

"But, Nina, if this had been a kidnapping, wouldn't there be a ransom note?"

"It wasn't a kidnapping. It was an execution."

"Who in Bay St. Lucy hated her that much?"

"Someone."

"Who?"

"I don't know."

Nina got to her feet.

"But I promise you we're all going to find out. I don't know when, and I don't know how. But we're all going to find out."

They were staring at her.

She was staring at her.

Tired of being stared at by so many people, she turned, said:

"Right now I've got a basketball game to get ready for."

And left the room.

CHAPTER 22: PICKETT'S CHARGE!

"You can't. You just have to."
—William Faulkner

The evening of the big contest with Hattiesburg fell with balmy winds and clear skies over a Bay St. Lucy that was oblivious to murder and obsessed with basketball.

People had been talking about it all day.

(The live event, not the dead woman.)

In "Sadie's by the Sea:"

"You think we really have a chance?"

"I don't know! We might! Anything can happen!"

In "The Stink Shoppe:"

"How are we going to stop those big girls?"

"I don't know."

In "Sergio's by the Sea":

"What's the point spread?"

"They're ten point favorites!"

And so on and so on.

Very little work got done.

This was in stark contrast to the high school, where *no* work got done, except that there was a pep rally at ten o'clock, where Haley Stephenson announced that the team was not going to be satisfied with giving one hundred percent effort (as they had against Logansport), but had decided to give two hundred percent effort.

YEEEEEEAAAAAH!

ON YOU MARE NERS ON YOU MARE NERS

FAT FAT FAT FAT FAAAAAAT!

Nina watched the pep rally from the back row of the auditorium, her mind fixed on other things.

Someone in Bay St. Lucy was a murderer.

And that person, at least once in the past week, had gotten access to the mail rack on her door.

Once.

How many other times?

There is nothing you can do about this, Nina.

Think of other things.

So she thought about the game.

People came and went, bells clanged and were silent, coaches charged up and down the halls. My God, *she* was a coach now, why wasn't *she* charging up and down the halls?

Oh, well, perhaps that would come.

The week's healthy lunch of hot dogs and tater tots was served…

…the afternoon was endured…

…the busses rolled up, gorged themselves on students, rolled away.

All those teachers left in the building ate the last of whatever food had been brought and then, waving and screeching like chickens, took plates and platters out to their cars and left.

Nina was left alone in the building.

Light filtered gold through the front windows.

She was seated at her desk, a row of play diagrams before her.

April. The McNulty Girls.

RIP. Hancock's Middle.

She is a) Dead; b) Missing; c) All of the Above.

Use all of the army. Use all of the army.

Are you using all of the army, Nina?

What are you missing?

What are you missing?

It was five o'clock before she left the building.

Forty minutes before game time, the gym was completely packed. Four busses had arrived from Hattiesburg, one carrying the team, three others carrying fans. These people filed sullenly in through the foyer, looked around cynically, remarked to themselves how quaint things were in small towns, eschewed the snack bar's offerings, found seats on the visitors' side, dusted off the benches, sprayed them with anti-pollutants, and settled in.

At twenty minutes before tip off, the Lady Eagles filed regally onto the floor.

They were clad in black and gold, and, like Richard Cory (who was not a basketball player) they glittered when they walked.

They had the bearings of champions. Nina wondered as she watched them from her place on the bench just how the process of winning and winning and winning and winning created that aura which turned the average offspring of normal people into Greek Gods. How had they all learned how to turn the collars of their black warm-up jackets in just that special way? What were the forces that had acted on Nicki McNulty, who was just at that time scooping in a warm-up lay up with insolent ease, in such a way as to make Grace Kelly seem small and weevilly beside her, and completely devoid of confidence?

Out came the Lady Mariners, through the twin lines of fans who had formed a tunnel for them.

The band blasted forth:

BLAAAAAHHHH DE BLAAAAAAAHHHHH DE BLAAAAAH!

The gym went wild. Everyone was standing now.

Drills. Shot practice.

Lay-up lines.

Nina did not move from where she was sitting.

Five minutes before tip off.

Alyssha and Amanda left the court and went to one of the exits, where someone handed each of them a three foot high, bright orange, traffic cone. They placed these cones just inside the out-of-bounds lines, approximately fifteen feet apart, so as to demarcate NINABOUNDARIES.

Both players approached her and said, earnestly:

"Whatever you do, Coach, you cannot go beyond those cones!"

"I know. I know."

Alyssha gestured:

"Dad!"

"Yes, honey!"

Jackson Bennett made his way down through the stands, and, in a moment, was standing in the midst of them.

"Dad, you have to stand down here right at that cone over there."

"I know, Leesh Baby."

"Do *not* let her go past that cone!"

"She won't get past me."

"And Mamma?"

"Mamma will be at the other cone."

"All right. Now, you promise you won't swear?"

"I never swear, Baby."

"And you won't get into any fights?"

"I promise."

"I'm counting on you, Dad; make me proud!"

"I will, Alyssha."

"OK, I've got to go finish warming up!"

And she ran back on the court.

Jackson Bennett, his hand lying menacingly on the metal ringed top of the cone, glowered down at Nina and said:

"Don't make me have to get rough."

"I won't."

"All right then."

Five minutes to tip off.

The horn blared.

The players began their tight circle, but Nina gestured to five of them:

"You five come here; others take a seat on the bench for just a minute."

The others did.

They were the starters.

But Nina had ringed into a tight circle now another group.

Her bench players.

Patricia Donaldson, Emily Crowder, Maggie St. Clair, LaToya Peterson, and Patty Jones.

These were the young women who seldom got to play.

But they were not bad, and they played their hearts out every day at practice, and they formed the loyal opposition for the starting team.

They were the rest of the army.

"All right," she whispered to them, their faces all close together now. "This is your biggest game. You're going to weaken Hancock's Middle, just like we worked on. You understand that?"

"YEAH!"

"You're going to win this game for us. You understand that?"

"YEAH!

"You may be gone when the battle's over; but the flag is going to be flying for *you*, do you understand that?"

"YEAH!"

"Ok then; Emily and Maggie start; at the six minute mark, LaToya and Maggie. Three minutes later, Patricia. And don't hold back, Mariners; you're our infantry! Now go out there and get 'em!"

Another blare of the horn.

And the players took the court.

"All right," Nina whispered. "Game Change!"

Jump ball.

Ball goes easily to Hattiesburg, one pass two passes into Theresa McNulty who turns and lays it in.

Two nothing.

Fierce cheering from the visitors' side.

Bay St. Lucy inbounds.

No press.

"They don't think," said Nina softly, "they need to press us. We'll see."

Ball across the half court line.

Alyssha Bennett dribbles hard to the right, slips it behind the back to Sarah Gray barreling left over the top of the key; Sonia Ramirez takes it right back in the other direction…

…then over to Patty Jones.

Work it, Patty, work it, watch for an opening...

...there it is...

"Charge," Nina whispers.

Patty sees the opening, barrels through it, hurtles herself at the basket flying through the air. SHOT SHOT SHOT SHOT…

TWEET!

Foul!

Number 32.

Foul on Patty, who is now sitting dazed on the court.

"That's all right, Patty. That's all right."

Ball brought in by Hattiesburg.

Across center court.

Pass, pass, inside.

Theresa McNulty, high above everybody, arching hook.

Swish.

Four nothing.

"That's all right, girls," Nina whispers.

Bay St. Lucy brings the ball down.

Haley Stephens on another switch, everyone milling inside, screening, turning, heading out…

…ball in the hands of Latoya Peterson.

"Look for it, LaToya, look for the opening…"

…there it is.

Nina:

"Charge."

Latoya barrels through the opening, top of key free throw line, fakes right, then back…

TWEET!

"Foul!"

Pause.

"Number 54! You're blocking her!"

Howls from the Hattiesburg bench.

WHAT ARE YOU TALKING ABOUT!

SHE WAS CHARGING!

Latoya at the line.

Clang.

Swish.

One of two.

Four to one.

Hattiesburg ball.

Cross court.

Ball inside STOLEN by Haley fast break, down court one on two…

"Slow it down," whispers Nina.

Haley does.

Work it, work it, then the ball back in Haley's hands, shot clock now at ten seconds, now at eight seconds, Maggie again…

Charge.

TWEET!

Foul! Number 34, blue!"

"That's all right."

Hattiesburg's ball. Missed shot, long rebound…

Take it slow, Mariners…

Weave, weave, watch for it…

Charge.

"Foul!"

ON WHO REF?

"Number 51, you're blocking her!"

OH FOR GODS SAKE REF!

Shots for LaToya.

Swish.

Swish.

Four to three.

But more important:

One foul on each of the McNulty sisters.

One each on Maggie and LaToya.

Nina looked at her bench: Patricia, Emily, Patty…

Her five reserves had twenty-five fouls to give. Her four starters had sixteen, and they would still be in the game.

Forty-one fouls.

"And you two," she whispered at the McNulty girls, who were taking their place under the basket on defense, standing their ground, waiting for the next attack, "you two have eight left."

Move the ball move the ball move the ball there's the opening there's the opening DRIVE DRIVE DRIVE FAKE LEFT MAKE HER SLAP AT YOU…

TWEET!

"Number 52, you're blocking!"

"Two on you, Nicki McNulty," whispered Nina. "Three to go."

Time out.

What are they going to do now?

They're going to fall back into the middle.

Okay, let them try.

Nina in the circle, scribbling madly with chalk on the gym floor.

"Starters back in! Great job, Maggie and LaToya!"

Instructions given.

Ball thrown in.

Bring it on down…

Yep, there they are, all back, all knotted up under the basket.

Okay, try that and see what it gets you.

Weave outside weave outside weave outside use the clock use the clock use the clock then the ball back in Haley's hands, shot clock now at ten seconds, now at eight seconds, back to Sonia for the long, arching…

SWISH!

THREE!

BLAAAAAHHHH DE BLAAAAH DEBLAAAAH.

CHEER CHEER FOR ST LUCY HIGH

BRING ON THE WHISKEY BRING ON THE RYE!

Steal.

Slow it down.

Weave outside weave outside weave outside use the clock use the clock use the clock then the ball back in Sonia's hands, shot clock now at ten seconds, now at eight seconds, back to Amanda for the long, arching…

SWISH!

THREE!

And Nina whispering:

"You just stay sucked up inside there. See what it gets you."

Time out.

Hattiesburg fans bellowing at the referee.

Is that the same referee who threw Nina out?

Yep.

But now Nina is standing stock still, staring straight in front of her.

Ball in play.

Hattiesburg in a normal defense.

"Okay, Patricia, Emily, you both know what to do."

"Yes, ma'am!"

"Go get 'em!"

Subs in.

Hattiesburg brings the ball up.

Nicki McNulty up for an easy two.

"That's okay, that's okay…"

Haley off to Alyssha over Emily…

"Charge."

Emily explodes into the paint hurtles at one of the blonde bodies in front of her fakes right fakes left comes up under SLAP ball blocked away…

TWEET!

OH COME ON REF!

"Number 16, you're charging her!

YES!

NOW YOU'RE CALLING THE GAME REF!

That's okay. One on Patricia, one on LaToya, one on Maggie…

Three on the McNultys.

Twelve minutes left in the half.

Nick McNulty spin shot.

Clang.

"You getting tired of playing defense, Nicki McNulty?"

Bay St. Lucy ball.

Weave weave weave weave…

Charge!

TWEET!

"Blocking on number 51!

YOU IDIOT YOU IDIOT

Paper cups raining down on the court.

The battle progresses.

Eleven minutes to go in the half.

Hattiesburg 23, Bay St. Lucy 12.

Patricia: three fouls
Emily: three fouls
Latoya: two fouls
Patty: three fouls.
Hattiesburg in the bonus.
"Can you hit free throws?"
Clang.
Clang.
No. Okay for you then.
Weave weave weave..
"Charge."
TWEET!
"Number 51, you're blocking her!"
More howls, more cups.
Nina whispers:
"That's number three, Nicki. And your sister has three also."
Steal!
Shot by Bay St. Lucy!
Swish!
Three!
Up and down the court, up and down the court…
Use the whole army.
"Patty, in for Samantha!"
Amanda over to Sonia, in to Patty…
Charge.
Patty hurling herself again at the basket, whap, sprawled on the floor ball batted away…
TWEET!
"Blocking, number 51."
"And that," Nina whispers, "is number four on you."
Coach in the face of the referee, bellowing, screaming:
"THEY'RE TARGETING OUR GIRLS! THEY'RE TARGETING OUR GIRLS!"
Referee approaching Nina.
Nina standing stock still, simply staring across the court.
"Coach…"
"Yes, Ref?"
"He says you're targeting his players!"

Nina looks at the referee.

"Yes, we are."

And the ref smiles.

"Well. That's your prerogative."

"Yes, it is."

Game on again.

Back and forth, back and forth.

Five minutes left in the half.

Hattiesburg 37, Bay St. Lucy 21.

Charge.

Charge.

Charge.

TWEET!

"Number 51, you're blocking her."

Four fouls.

Four.

"So what are you going to do now, Coach?" Nina whispers. "She has four. You want to take her out?"

Time out.

Nicki McNulty out of the game.

And Nina shaking her head.

"That's a big mistake."

Her players circle around her.

"You know who to take it to now."

"YEAAH!"

Game on.

Weave weave weave weave…

Maggie St. Clair launches herself like a missile at Theresa McNulty.

Foul on Maggie.

Next possession.

LaToya attacks.

Foul on LaToya.

Next possession.

Emily attacks.

And feints left.

Foul…

…on Theresa McNulty.

Four on her.

Up and back, up and back…

Blaaaarrrr!

Halftime horn.

Hattiesburg 43, Bay St. Lucy 29.

The McNulty girls have four fouls apiece.

They are on the bench as the second half begins.

Weave weave weave Samantha for three:

SWISH!

Next time down…

Weave weave weave Alyssha drives the middle!

Lay-up.

Nobody there to stop them.

"Infantry, infantry," whispers Nina. "Hancock's middle softening up."

FAST BREAK BAY ST. LUCY!

TWO!

45 to 31.

BLAAAAH DE BLAAAAAH DE BLAAAAH!

Rest rest

BLAAAAH DE BLAAAH DE BLAAAHH!

Alyssha all alone inside.

Lay-up.

41 to 33.

Time out.

"Okay Coach. What are you going to do? Put them both back in? Or just one?"

Both McNulty girls back in the game.

And the Bay St. Lucy bench staring at them.

Nina to her team:

"I see you stand like greyhounds in the slip! Once more into the breach, dear subs!"

Blaaarr!

Horn sounds.

"Okay, girls. Go get 'em."

Five minutes into the second half, the first McNulty girl fouls out.

44 to 33.

Patricia, Emily, Maggie, and LaToya are gone.

Two more minutes and Patty drives.

TWEET!

"Number 51, you're..."

REF YOU IDIOT! YOU IDIOT!

Paper cups everywhere.

The second McNulty girl, incensed, shouting, red-faced, stalks to the bench.

Both McNulty girls are gone.

And Nina, always standing in one place, turns her head, stares straight into the Hattiesburg bench, and whispers:

"Now how tough are you?"

"Father said clocks slay time."
—William Faulkner, *The Sound and the Fury*

Eleven minutes to go.

Nina is now moving from cone to cone, shouting at the top of her lungs:

"Front her, Sonya! No, closer! Atta girl! Move in behind, Alyssha! NO! NO! MOVE AMANDA! That's right; that's...Now...now get into the press *now*_DOUBLE TEAM DOUBLE TEAM DOUBLE TEAM...

"GAME CHANGE!"

"THAT'S RIGHT TAKE IT FROM HER TAKE IT FROM HER TAKE IT FROM HER! YES YES YES YES ...TWO! TWO! TWO! TWO!"

On you Mare ners On you Mare ners

FAT FAT FAT FAT FAAAAAT!

"Get back get back double down double down on her KEEP PRESSINGKEEPPRESSING...

"GAME CHANGE!"

"WATCH THAT BASELINE DO *NOT* LET HER TAKE YOU DEEP HAYLEY STAY IN FRONT OF HER!"

"MOVE HER DOWN MOVE HER DOWN WATCH THE PICK WATCH THE PICK OK OK NICE PASS NOW SCREEN AND ROLL SCREEN AND ROLL SHOT SHOT SHOT! TWO TWO TWO ATTAGIRL ATTAGIRL!

Cheer cheer for St. Luuucy Hiiiigh!
Bring on the whiskey bring on the rye!
Ever loyal to those mare ners

Fighting for victory!

Six and a half minutes to go.

54 to 48.

Baddadadadadda…

"NO DON'T LET HER SLIP BACK DOOR ON YOU BABY FRONT HER POST HER UP POST HER…OH!"

"GAME CHANGE! GAME CHANGE!"

"YES! YES, WAY TO PICK IT UP YOU MARINERS! NOW THREE QUARTER WATCH CENTER COURT WATCH THE SNOWBIRD WATCH THE SNOWBIRD THAT'S GOOD ALYSSHA HAWK HER HAWK HER PRESS PRESS PRESS PRESS…"

"GAME CHANGE!"

Foul.

Haley at the line.

Swish.

Swish.

"ATTAGIRL NOW STAY AGGRESSIVE STAY AGGRESSIVE! MAN DEFENSE NOW SLIP INTO NUMBER TWO ATTACK NUMBER TWO WAY TO MOVE SONIA TAKE IT TAKE IT TAKE IT YES YES YES NOW…"

"GAME CHANGE!"

"GREAT STEAL SHE'S OPEN DOWN COURT HIT HER HIT HER NICE PASS LAYUP YES!"

"GAME CHANGE"

"NOW DOUBLE DOWN POST HER UP POST HER UP POST HER UP!…"

Three and a half minutes left.

58 to 54.

"Front her, Sonya! No, closer! Atta girl! Move in behind, Alyssha!

NO! NO! MOVE AMANDA! That's right that's…. Now…now get into the press *now* DOUBLE TEAM DOUBLE TEAM DOUBLE TEAM…

"GAME CHANGE!"

"THAT'S RIGHT TAKE IT FROM HER TAKE IT FROM HER TAKE IT FROM HER! YES YES YES YES …TWO! TWO! TWO! TWO!"

"GAME CHANGE!"

Two minutes left.

One minute left.

Thirty seconds.

60 to 58.

Foul.

Alyssha at the line.

Swish.

Clang.

60 to 59.

Hattiesburg ball.

Time out, Bay St. Lucy.

The players come to the bench.

Nina kneels in the circle and looks up at them:

"Twenty eight seconds left. The shot clock is off. They have a one point lead. All they have to do is hold onto the ball. If we foul them, they get two shots. They make those and we're down by three. We could tie with a three. *Or we could just go take the ball away from them*! What do you want to do?'

Ten faces staring down at her.

All of them grinning as one.

And all shouting:

"PICKETT'S CHARGE!"

And Nina responding:

"OKAY! GO TAKE THAT WALL!"

Hattiesburg inbounds.

"Front her, Sonya! No, closer! Atta girl! Move in behind, Alyssha! NO! NO!

Clock winding down.

Twenty seconds.

Fourteen seconds.

Eight seconds.

"MOVE AMANDA! That's right that's.... Now...now get into the press *now* DOUBLE TEAM DOUBLE TEAM DOUBLE TEAM...

And the ball is knocked away at the free throw line on the Hattiesburg end of the court.

Four players fighting for it.

Slap and the ball rolling toward mid-court.

Four seconds, three…

Alyssha Bennett running fast as she can scoops up the ball dribbles once dribbles again crosses half court…

One second…

SHOOT!

…and the ball arches upward, soaring toward the rafters, Alyssha falling and sliding forward as the horn sounds.

The ball is flying.

Time stops.

"For every southerner there is the instant when it's still not yet two o'clock on that July afternoon in 1863, the brigades are in position behind the rail fence, the guns are laid and ready in the woods and the furled flags are already loosened to break out... and that moment we all think This time. Maybe this time with all this much to lose and all this much to gain... to crown with desperate and unbelievable victory the desperate gamble, the cast made so many years ago...."

—Faulkner, *Intruder in the Dust*

SWISH.

An instant's pause.

Then:

OHMYGODOHBYGODOHMYGOD!

And the gym is chaos.

Nina could remember taking two steps out on the court, remember the clacking of her high heels, remember the people flooding beside her, all moving in the same direction; then she was caught up in it, and for some reason the stream came to mind, the kayak, the rush of it all and the impossible mixture of sounds.

WE'RE GOING TO STATE WE'RE GOING TO STATE WE'RE GOING TO STATE!

OHMYGODOHMYGODOHMYGOD

Now she was off the ground.

Going up, going up, carried, flat on her back, the thick, light blue, diamond-shaped rafters of the gym ceiling above her.

The whole huge yellow hot-dogged pulsing quivering shouting irrational one-being crowd was chanting:

NINA! NINA! NINA! NINA!

And:

ALYSSHA! ALYSSHA! ALYSSHA!

They were carrying her.

The town was carrying her!

But players all over the court were being carried!

Sonya, screaming deliriously as she, also flat on her back and floating in the waves that were people's arms, piston-pumped her fists YEAH YEAH YEAH heavenward…

…as if heaven were anywhere other than here right now…

NINA! NINA! NINA!

ALYSSHA! ALLYSHA! ALYSSHA!

SONIA! SONIA! SONIA!

HAYLEY! HAYLEY! HALEY!

AMANDA! AMANDA! AMANDA!

It swirled around and around and around and around and the band blared…

BLAAAAH DE BLAAAH DE BLAAAAH!

Rest rest

BLAAAHH DE BLAAAH DE BLAAAH!

And the people blared:

WE'RE GOING TO STATE WE'RE GOING TO STATE WE'RE…

And the sea looked in from out where it was and laughed.

And the moon looked down from up where it was and laughed.

And the universe looked everywhere from the everywhere it was and laughed.

And things were right in Bay St. Lucy.

The crowd poured out of the gym and onto the streets, finding that everyone else was there also. It was Mardi Gras in Mississippi. Players, coaches, parents, grandparents, loved ones, neighbors, stray dogs, raccoons, and novelists careened through the town, which, being a seaside resort, lived its existence continually in a kind of mild buzz but seldom if ever got completely drunk.

This all changed on the night of the Hattiesburg victory.

Everyone loved one another. Everyone grouped together in little caramel-clusters of humanity and careened from street to street, forming streams of jubilation and singing and hugging and yelling out cheers to other groups of people, who were going in the opposite directions.

"Everyone's meeting on the town square!"

"Come on come on come on come on!"

Nina Bannister was ultimately put down but she was never exactly let go.

Mobs of people continued to embrace her; the players cried in her arms, and she soon found that her voice, which had been screaming something or other for an indeterminate amount of time, had gone from Lauren Bacall to Woody Woodpecker.

Somewhere—she had lost track of the streets—she found herself encircled by reporters, flash bulbs exploding no more than a foot or so in front of her.

"Coach Bannister!"

"Yes!"

"Tell us about the last play!"

She took a deep breath:

"We work on it all the time!"

"Really?"

"No, that was a joke. We work on it all the time, but usually we like for Alyssha to wear a cast on her shooting hand. That makes it more challenging."

"Really?"

"No, that…"

She shook her head.

Her voice had now moved from Woody Woodpecker to Minnie Mouse.

"Forget what I said before. The last shot was a miracle. The whole game was a miracle. God must have wanted us to win!"

She moved on down the street or up the street she did not know or care which, cheerfully oblivious to the theological implications of the notion that the supreme deity might take sides in a high school basketball game, and quite content simply to be carried along by a wildly swirling and cascading torrent of Bay St. Lucyans, moving inexorably toward a makeshift platform that had been thrown together just in front of the county courthouse.

"Speech! Speech!"

Alyssha Bennett was being herded up onto the platform.

She was waving now, as a microphone was placed before her.

"We thought we could win this game by giving two hundred percent. But it wasn't enough! We had to give two hundred and fifty percent!"

"How did you hit that last shot?"

"I don't know. I just threw it up and prayed!"

There it was. Theology again.

"I just want to thank…oh, there she is! Coach! Coach Bannister!"

And the chant began again:

"NINA! NINA! NINA! NINA!"

She was escorted to the stand. She had no idea what she was going to say.

Here was Jackson Bennett, leaning down and yelling in her ear:

"Incredible game, Nina!"

"Thank you, Jackson!"

And here was Edie Towler:

"Great game, Nina!"

"Thank you, Edie!"

And here was Tom Broussard:

"Unbelievable, Nina!"

"Thank you, Tom!"

And here was Moon Rivard:

"You better come with me, Ms. Nina. We just found out who killed April van Osdale."

CHAPTER 23: THE WOLFMAN

"We shall not kill and maybe next time we even won't."
—William Faulkner, *Intruder in the Dust*

Within a minute she'd found herself in the back seat of a squad car.

The crowd was pounding on windshields and windows.

Moon Rivard had slid in beside her, after gesturing to the young, black-haired patrolman who was driving the squad car.

"Just go nice and easy, son. Don't want to run into any of these folks."

"Moon, what are you talking about?"

"April van Osdale is dead."

"Oh God."

"Yeah, I know."

"And you know who killed her?"

"Looks like it."

"Who?"

He ran a gnarled hand through his iron gray hair and breathed deeply:

"That English teacher of yours who we had to lock up."

"What?"

The car was moving away from the worst of the crowd now, and they picked up speed as they entered Breakwaters Boulevard.

"Yeah, that guy who got drunk with Tom Broussard."

"Max? Max Lirpa?"

"That's the one."

"But that's who's crazy. He's down at the docks right now. He got himself out onto one of the big yachts. *The Sea Beagle."*

"That's the senator's yacht!"

"Yeah, that's the one. Anyway, he's up on one of the masts, yelling that he's gonna throw himself off."

"Moon, he's probably just drunk!"

"Maybe. But it looks like he did the murder, all the same."

"He couldn't have!"

"There's evidence."

"What evidence?"

They were on the main road now, coastline to their left, heading west.

The patrolman turned on the siren.

Behind them, Bay St. Lucy glowed like a Christmas tree.

"The state men found it, going over that house on Fairway Drive one last time."

"State troopers?"

"Yeah. As it happened, one the men assigned to go through all the drawers and stuff was the same one who was there when they had to escort that lady from the school."

"Meg?"

"Yeah. You remember how bad that was."

"I do, but how…"

"Well, this Lirpa guy made a fool of himself then, too."

"Yeah. He yelled at the troopers."

"He insulted them, apparently."

"Oh, not really, Moon. He just called them Nazis."

"Yeah. Well, some of them boys is overly sensitive."

"People just can't take criticism anymore."

"No, ma'am. But when this patrolmen was going through one of the clothes drawers at Dr. van Osdale's place, he found this silver jewelry-like thing. Something you would wear around your neck."

Nina whispered:

"A werewolf pendant."

"I guess that's what you'd call it. Something crazy like this idiot would wear. Anyway, this patrolman remembered that Lirpa was wearing the same pendant that day at school."

She continued to whisper as the dashboard glowed green, the moon sparkled on the waves, and the siren droned on:

"He was wearing it the first day I saw him. I won't forget it."

"No, ma'am; I guess you wouldn't. The patrolman got to wondering why that piece of silver would come to be in Dr. van Osdale's bedroom."

"I wonder that, too."

"So he went over to Broussard's house. That's where this guy's been living."

"What happened?"

"Found him. Showed him the damned pendant and Lirpa just kind of went crazy. I don't know what happened, but I read the report. In fact, I got the report right here. Let's see…"

Moon reached up and switched on the car's overhead light; then he squinted down at a sheaf of official looking documents that lay on his lap.

"They asked him this and they asked him that, and he was getting more and more upset—and finally they asked him, 'Did you kill this woman?' And he laughed and answered: 'Yes but that was in another country. And besides, the wench is dead.'"

"Marlowe."

"What?"

Nina nodded.

"It's a famous line of literature, Moon. Christopher Marlow. *The Jew of Malta.*"

"This Lirpa is a Jew?"

"Don't worry about it. It just means he might have been quoting something. He's crazy that way."

"He's crazy in a lot of ways. Main thing is, he broke free from the two patrolmen as they was taking him out to the car. Don't know how he did it. But you know that place of Broussard's out there. Not much more than a jungle anyway."

"Yes. I've been there."

"It was dark. This happened a couple of hours ago. And he got free. Then, no more than half an hour ago, one of the yacht owners called in. Seems he's out there on *The Sea Beagle*, up on the mast, yelling."

"Anybody else on *The Sea Beagle*?"

"No. It's been moored up for the week and deserted. Nobody can figure out how he got onto it. But anyway, he's yelling that he wants to see you."

"Me?"

"Yeah."

"Why me?"

"Don't know. We was wondering if you could tell us."

"I can't begin to tell you," Nina answered.

But she also began to think.

A man in my life.

He first came into my life years ago, when I was first at university.

Ice and fire.

Ice and fire.

Could this man have been Max Lirpa?

That was absurd!

Why the two were like…

…like ice and fire.

My God.

Could Max Lirpa have killed April van Osdale?

"Moon, could I see that report?"

"Yes, ma'am. Here it is."

She took it, not knowing what she was looking at.

The words jumped off the page at her.

CONFIDENTIAL REPORT ON MAX LIRPA.

She stared at it.

MAX LIRPA.

LIRPA.

LIRPA.

Then she saw.

"Oh, my God," she whispered.

"What is it, Ms. Nina?"

"Oh, my God."

They were pulling into the main wharf area; she could see the tall masts standing like bare pines in the moonlight.

"That can't be. That just can't be."

"Do you see something in the report?"

"Yes. No. Yes."

"That don't make no sense."

"No. Yes. No."

The car stopped.

It all did begin to make sense.

Piece by piece by piece by piece.

"I was conceived and raised in Oxford."

"She's a classic schizophrenic paranoid."

"He has been in my life since university days."

"But that was in another country. And besides, the wench is dead."

The wench is dead. The wench is dead.

"You ready, Ms. Nina?"

"Yes," she whispered, "I'm ready."

And she was.

Because, finally, she realized what had happened to April van Osdale.

"A man will talk about how he'd like to escape from living folks, but it's the dead folks that do him the damage. It's the dead ones that lay quiet in one place and don't try to hold him, that he can't escape from"

—William Faulkner, *Light in August*

"What matters is at the end of life, when you're about to pass into oblivion, that you've at least scratched 'Kilroy was here,' on the last wall of the universe."

—William Faulkner, *Lion in the Garden: Interviews with William Faulkner, 1926-1962*

The scene at the gangway leading out to *The Sea Beagle* was not the tangle of mass confusion one might have expected, the main reason being that a large majority of Bay St. Lucy was still in the center of town, reveling in Basketball Bacchanal. Here there were four police vehicles, an ambulance, and a cordon of gray uniformed officers, peering out at the yacht, where a searchlight was casting its sun-white circle of phosphorescence.

In this center of this spotlight, his shirtless body impaled against the mainmast, was Max Lirpa.

His hair was wild, his eyes were wild, his clothes—those he was still wearing—were wild and his eyes were alternately wolf-like and maniacal.

A bit of each quality intensified in them when he saw Nina making her way along the wharf.

"My headmistress!"

She continued to walk.

The officers closed in around her, and she could hear one of them ask:

"Are you Ms. Bannister?"

Why were people always asking her that?"

And why did she always find herself replying:

"Yes."

Shouldn't there have been an alternative?

Why wasn't 'no' a possibility?

Because then she could go home!

"Yes. I'm Nina Bannister."

"You know this man?"

"He teaches for me. At the high school."

"Did Officer Rivard fill you in on what's happened here?"

"Yes."

"You know we have reason to believe he may have some involvement in the disappearance of Dr. April van Osdale?"

She spoke quietly as she walked, always keeping an eye on the gaunt, ancient mariner figure that was Max Lirpa.

"He has more involvement than you know."

"Ma'am?"

"Sorry."

Why was no one getting her jokes these days?

Perhaps because nothing seemed very funny these days.

"He seems to want to talk to you."

"So I understand."

"Do you know why that would be?"

"Well. We work together. I suppose I've been supportive of his teaching methods."

"Has he seemed…well, erratic in the past days?"

"He's seemed erratic ever since I met him."

"Do you think he's capable of committing an act of violence? Of killing someone?"

She paused, then said:

"I don't think he's capable of committing an act of violence; I do think he's capable of killing someone."

Silence for an instant.

Then:

"Ma'am?"

"I know. It's confusing."

"I'm not sure I understand."

"That's all right. I'm just beginning to myself."

They were at the edge of the gangplank now.

Max Lirpa shouted at her:

"Mistress Mine, with Eyes a-Shining!"

She answered:

"Max! You need to come away from the boat!"

He shook his head"

"Oh, but I can't, dear lady! You see I must go down to the sea in ships! I told you, you remember, how very Masefield-like it all was! Very much like Cornwell!"

"Yes. I remember."

"So you understand why I can't give it up."

"You wouldn't have to give it up."

"Oh, but I must disagree with you there! You see they want to pen me up!"

"No one wants to pen you up."

"You're wrong, Headmistress. They pen up people who do murder. Or they guillotine them. Or they hang them. I think I'd sooner drown. More poetic, don't you think?"

"You didn't do murder, Max."

"Really? Then what would you call it?"

"I don't know. But I just know you're…"

"Sick? That's the very word, isn't it?"

"No. That's not the word."

He was silent for a time. Then he said:

"You understand what's happened? What's been happening, all along?"

She nodded:

"I think I understand."

"When? When did you know?"

"Not until a few minutes ago."

"And what, as the students are so fond of saying now, was your first clue?"

She paused, then said:

"Your name. I never really looked at it before. Then when I remember the things that April said. The things that you said…"

"I might have known. I suspected that, if anyone would figure it out, it would be the indomitable Ms. Bannister. The lady pitched from the pitch. And so, by the way, how did the match go tonight?"

"We won."

"Capital!"

"Max, I want to come aboard," she heard herself saying, "and talk with you."

Now why would she say a thing like that?

Fifty-three voices buzzed around her:

"You can't do that, ma'am!"

"We don't even know if he's got a weapon!"

"We would have no way of protecting you!"

"There's no way we can authorize that!"

And that was only four, leaving forty-nine, all stating persuasive reasons why she could not go on board and talk with Max Lirpa.

Then she turned to Moon:

"He's going to jump if I don't go out to that yacht."

"Yes, ma'am, but…"

"I know what's happened. I know what happened to April van Osdale."

"All right then, Ms. Nina…what did happen to her? Where is she?"

"Nowhere. She isn't anywhere at all."

"You mean she's dead?"

"In a way. Just…in a way."

"You're not making any sense."

"A lot of things in life don't make sense. There are things that can't be measured. Things that aren't on the test."

"Ms. Bannister, I don't know what test…"

"Skip it. Please, Moon, I have to go out there. I think I can talk with him. He just needs to know that someone understands what is happening."

"I'm just not certain…"

"He's not dangerous."

"But if he's killed somebody…"

"It's not what you're thinking."

And after pleading her case, and pleading her case, she was finally allowed to say:

"Max!"

"Yes, my dear?"

"I want to come aboard. The patrolmen, and Moon Rivard, have told me that I can do that. They insist on coming too."

"Oh, it will be a splendid party!"

"You're not armed, are you?"

"Definitely not! I'm as disarming as one can be!"

"You won't kill me?"

"No, no, not a chance of it! I've done all the killing I care to for a time!"

"You realize these people don't understand your humor."

"But you do, don't you?"

"I understand a lot, Max."

He began climbing down from the mast.

"I'm sure you do, fair lady. I'm sure you do."

And with that it was decided.

Moon Rivard, two patrolmen, and Nina, headed up the gangplank and onto *The Sea Beagle*.

"It takes two people to make you, and one people to die. That's how the world is going to end."
—William Faulkner, *As I Lay Dying*

"Sometimes I ain't sho who's got ere a right to say when a man is crazy and when he ain't."
—William Faulkner, *As I Lay Dying*

The scene in the small stateroom of the yacht was far cozier than one could have expected, given the presence of three armed police officers in the room, standing against the walls staring outward, their hands resting upon glistening revolvers.

Max Lirpa, still bare-chested, appeared not to notice them.

He'd found a bottle of port.

She wondered how he could have been so familiar with *The Sea Beagle*.

But, of course, she knew, once she thought of it.

He was familiar with *The Sea Beagle* because he'd been on it.

Had probably, in fact, been given a key to it.

Because he'd been a friend of the senator's.

Even though the senator had not known it.

She forced herself to take a sip of the glass of port Lirpa had given her and said, quietly:

"I can't claim that I've figured it out, Max. Not all of it. Not the inner workings of it."

"Ah, but who *could* make such a claim? The inner workings of the human mind…no, who *could* make such a claim?"

The wind was freshening; they could hear it begin to sing around the corners of the yacht.

"I was in the police car. Moon showed me the report. It had the name LIRPA typed in large letters on top of it. I just kept staring at it. Finally things began to make sense."

"I'm glad they did. It would have been difficult to explain. Difficult to put into words. At least, the words we commonly use."

"*April* backwards is *Lirpa*. That was the only name you could have given yourself; you were her mirror opposite."

"Yes. No choice about the name. Max Lirpa. Maximum InsideoutApril!"

"And that day when you told me you were 'conceived in Oxford,' I didn't really understand."

"Nor would I have expected you to."

"When April said she had 'come to know you during university days,' she meant The University of Mississippi. Oxford, Mississippi."

"Yes, I…I came into being there."

"April's alter-ego."

"I suppose the doctors might call it that. 'But that was in another country; and besides, the wench is dead.'"

"You killed her."

He shook his head.

"No. I willed her out of being. Two entities in one body. It could not have lasted forever. And I proved the stronger."

Silence for a time.

"Like *Psycho*," said Nina.

He frowned.

"I hate that film. Completely unbelievable. And so much blood. So much violence."

Then he said quietly:

"The most difficult battles are not fought with knives."

Nina knew nothing to say to that. She thought for a time and finally whispered, more to herself than to the figure sitting opposite her:

"I was so crazy. I was worrying about what would happen when April van Osdale might come into the building and run into this wild Max Lirpa. But that was never going to happen, was it?"

"No. At least not in the way that you had imagined. In another way, of course, it was happening all the time. Right under your nose."

"Right under all our noses. And the reason I could never seem to call April in her Hattiesburg office was not that she was in high-level meetings; it was simply that she—being you—was in Room 102. Everybody around southwest Mississippi thought that she was somewhere else. Which I guess was true."

"I suppose when one thinks about it, it's not too uncommon. There's a bit of the April/Max conflict in all human beings. The measurer and the romantic. She's a very dangerous kind of person, you know. She would rob the world of its mystery. And ultimately of its beauty."

"Goldmann Bristow said that April was deeply disturbed. Classic paranoid/schizophrenic."

He chuckled.

"Poor April. She suffered a great deal. She wanted everything to be perfect. And that striving...well, it called me forth, so to speak. I am the mirror opposite of schizophrenic paranoia; I am hemophilic/adenoia. And, by the way, I remember quite clearly working with you at the university."

"You already existed at that time?"

"Yes. In not quite so tangible a form. But yes."

"Why didn't April remember me?"

"Because of who you are. Your love of true literature. Of true poetry. You represented everything she detested. And so she shut out the very memory of you."

"You kept that memory."

"Yes, but for obvious reasons I couldn't tell you about it."

"No, I suppose not. But...I still have to ask you..."

"Yes, yes, dear lady, ask away!"

"Why the games? The test? The trip out to the island?"

"Isn't it an enchanting place? Tom Broussard took me out there fishing some weeks ago. I knew at that time, of course, that I was going to win. I decided it would be the perfect place to have April's 'burial.'"

"But why me and Penn?"

"Simply because you are the two most formidable ladies that I know. And because ceremonies require witnesses. Did I not hear, did not the talk around the school make clear, that you are going in some months to a gothic romantic settlement to commemorate the nuptials of your best friend?"

"Yes. To Candles. I'm to be Margot's Best Woman."

"Exactly! Weddings, funerals...they are society's way of measuring passages, changes."

He poured another glass of port, drank from it, and said quietly:

"This is only another...well, I think you would call it a GAME CHANGE. Only another movement from one stage of being to another."

"And the standardized tests?"

He brightened:

"Wasn't that a splendid notion on my part? I was in and out of the office all the time, of course, and so had no problem dropping them into your mail box. They were life and death to her. So it was only appropriate that they would play a final role in announcing her life and death."

Somewhere out in the ocean a tanker brayed.

"Do you think she will come back?"

"No. She's gone. I can't tell you how I know that. But I do."

Silence for a time, or as near to silence as the ocean offers.

The moon had risen; the water sparkled.

"Max," she said, "you know what needs to happen now."

He nodded.

"I think so."

"And it's not suicide. You don't need to jump into the ocean."

"I suppose not. But it was such an inviting thought."

"We can't lose you. The world can't lose you."

"I'm not absolutely certain that the world has ever had me."

"You suffered from multiple identities. I'm not even a psychiatrist, and I know that much."

"It is a bit easier to know of such things than to suffer from them."

"I'm sure it is. But you can be…"

"Cured?"

"Yes."

"Oh, God how I hate that thought! What a terrible fate, to be 'cured.' It sounds like a ham."

She looked at the officers ringing the room.

None of them were smiling.

Just not a good night, she found herself thinking, for humor.

"Do you want me," she asked, "to go with you into town?"

He brightened.

"I would like that. It would mean a great deal to me."

"Then I'll do it. It's all right isn't it, Moon?"

She looked at him; he nodded.

"I'm sure it will be fine, Ms. Bannister."

"You understand don't you, Moon, that Mr. Lirpa has not actually harmed anyone?"

"If you know it, ma'am, then I believe it. You always seem to be two steps ahead of the rest of us. Even with Eve Ivory and the Reddington fellow…"

She shook her head:

"Those were different. Very different."

And not, she found herself thinking, *so very different.*

Two bad beings, two threats to the community, had been eliminated.

Someone innocent had been accused, believed guilty, and ultimately would be exonerated.

The community was saved.

Had not that happened here?

Yes, but with one exception.

There had not been another Eve Ivory in Bay St. Lucy, nor another Reddington.

But there would be more April van Osdales.

Others who did not understand the Grand Mystery of Things, and who wanted to tell people…the artists and seafarers of Bay St. Lucy, of all beings!—how to chart and diagram and measure all humanity.

Even the sea itself could not keep them out.

Well. That was for tomorrow.

"Are you ready, Max? Once we get into town I'll call Margot and Goldmann. He's a leading psychologist. I'm sure he can be here by tomorrow morning."

"And do you trust him, Dear Lady?"

"I trust both of them. And you will too, I promise."

"Then so be it. Let us go."

And they did.

Three hours later, at four a.m., she'd finished walking on the beach and was returning to her shack, still deep in conversation. She had conversed about the new job that Margot had offered her, and whether she should remain a principal, and how improbable and remarkable her victory

Friday night had been, and how utterly exhilarating the kayak trip had been, and how fine and beautiful the trip to The Candles would be…

…and he had remarked about the incomprehensible case of April van Osdale.

To which she had remarked, that it was not incomprehensible at all.

"Why not, Nina?"

"Because she had two people living inside her, Frank. And so do I."

Then she said good night, waved at his image as it faded beyond the moon, turned, and went to bed.

EPILOGUE

"The past is never dead. In fact, it isn't even past."
—William Faulkner

Looking back upon her memories of the dreamlike days in early May—which Nina Bannister was to do often in the weeks and months to come—the most striking thing about her initial impressions of The Candles Plantation was that they did not concern the building itself. They did not concern the deep, blue-board walkways that surrounded it and offered the inhabitants of each room a place to sit, and rock, and sip, and experience life in what had once been the headquarters of a thriving agricultural enterprise and had since become a mausoleum. They did not concern the great shambling polar bear that masqueraded as a dog, wagging its tail slowly and dutifully, as though eschewing the purpose of all other tail wagging and accepting the daily responsibility of driving flies away from the doors and windows of the downstairs residents.

Rather, they all centered on a rain-stained wooden table in the front yard, shaded by massive oaks that masked a fast disappearing evening sun, and rocking ever so gently on the soft turf of the lawn each time one of the three or four wedding guests seated around it happened to lift or replace a glass of champagne, or a snifter of cognac.

But the building was always there, in background if not center, always acting as a base for everything else.

This building smiled. Every part of it. The color of its exterior walls—a soft and mellow off-peach which was the precise color of slanted sunlight on a late Sunday afternoon—this color smiled. The broad porch smiled at the white and motionless rocking chairs which sat upon it, while they smiled, in turn, at the dilapidated outbuildings, which smiled at the rusted farm machinery and antiquated carriages that sat within them. And from the well in the middle of the back yard, its wooden frame apparently on the point of disintegrating with age and dropping into water far beneath ground level, the bucket which hung gleaming in the dying light. From the very moss-covered stones rising above this well, there emanated a kind of benevolence, as though coming out of the deep earth itself, seeping over the lawns and fall gardens, and settling quietly at dusk into the not very recently mown grass.

She was to think of these things often as she remembered Margot's wedding.

And she was to remember the wedding guests, all in formal wear, all milling about the grounds, all mixing with the ghosts that haunted Candles.

They were of all ages, but they might as well have been of all centuries, wearing well-pressed and pale gray Civil War uniforms instead of coal black tuxedoes and wedding gowns.

"For the past is not a diminishing road but, instead, a huge meadow which no winter ever quite reaches, divided from us now by the narrow bottleneck of the most recent decade of years."

She was to remember the conversations on the grounds, just before the wedding itself.

Conversations with Meg and Jenny:

"You didn't quite win state, Nina. But you got there."

"We won Pickett's Charge. But the North of Mississippi was ten points too much for us. You'll get them next year!"

For Meg had, of course, been hired back as coach.

And Nina had resigned two weeks ago as principal.

She would, beginning in June, run Elementals.

She remembered the conversation with Bristow concerning his most storied patient, Max Lirpa:

"He's doing fine. He suffered a great mental trauma. But he feels it was a victory. He pulled away from a part of himself that he hated, and formed a new self. It can happen. We heal."

And she would remember the ceremony itself.

Margot so resplendent as a bride.

The five of them: Bristow's best friend and Best Man; she herself as Maid of Honor; Margot, Goldmann…

…and the minister, asking:

"And do you, Margot, take this man to be your wedded husband?"

Margot smiling at Nina, who nodded and said, quietly:

"Game Change."

"I do."

"Then I now pronounce you man and wife."

Those were then the things that she would remember.

For the rest of her life.

THE END

ABOUT THE AUTHORS

Pam Britton (T'Gracie) Reese is an Assistant Professor in the Communication Science and Disorders Department at Indiana-Purdue University Fort Wayne. Previously, she worked as a speech pathologist in schools in private practice. She was also a supervisor in communication disorders at Ohio University. She likes nothing better, professionally, than helping small, silent two year old boys start talking. She has also published books about autism with LinguiSystems for the last 15 years. *The Circle of Autism* was previously published on-line at ken*again e-magazine

Joe Reese is a novelist, playwright, storyteller, and college teacher. He has published four novels, several plays, and a number of stories and articles. When he is not teaching (English and German), he enjoys visiting elementary schools, where he tells stories from his Katie Dee novels and talks to students about writing. He and his wife Pam have three children: Kate, Matthew, and Sam.

www.ingramcontent.com/pod-product-compliance
Lightning Source LLC
Chambersburg PA
CBHW050400260626
47156CB00003B/811

* 9 7 8 1 9 3 9 8 1 6 4 2 9 *